THE CORNISH COTTAGE BY THE SEA

KIM NASH

Boldwood

First published in Great Britain in 2025 by Boldwood Books Ltd.

Copyright © Kim Nash, 2025

Cover Design by Alexandra Allden

Cover Images: Shutterstock

The moral right of Kim Nash to be identified as the author of this work has been asserted in accordance with the Copyright, Designs and Patents Act 1988.

All rights reserved. No part of this book may be reproduced in any form or by any electronic or mechanical means, including information storage and retrieval systems, without written permission from the author, except for the use of brief quotations in a book review. This book is a work of fiction and, except in the case of historical fact, any resemblance to actual persons, living or dead, is purely coincidental.

Every effort has been made to obtain the necessary permissions with reference to copyright material, both illustrative and quoted. We apologise for any omissions in this respect and will be pleased to make the appropriate acknowledgements in any future edition.

A CIP catalogue record for this book is available from the British Library.

Paperback ISBN 978-1-83561-380-1

Large Print ISBN 978-1-83561-379-5

Hardback ISBN 978-1-83561-378-8

Ebook ISBN 978-1-83561-381-8

Kindle ISBN 978-1-83561-382-5

Audio CD ISBN 978-1-83561-373-3

MP3 CD ISBN 978-1-83561-374-0

Digital audio download ISBN 978-1-83561-375-7

This book is printed on certified sustainable paper. Boldwood Books is dedicated to putting sustainability at the heart of our business. For more information please visit https://www.boldwoodbooks.com/about-us/sustainability/

Boldwood Books Ltd, 23 Bowerdean Street, London, SW6 3TN

www.boldwoodbooks.com

John

April 1967 – June 2024

Our very good friend and one of the best people I know.
Thank you for the love, kindness, patience, friendship and support you gave to me and Ollie over the years since we first met you. Thank you for being part of our lives.

There are so many things to thank you for. The wonderful memories we made with you, Lynne and the boys, and the fun and laughter we had along the way.

Thank you for helping me (when I say helping me, I mean you doing it and me standing watching) when I got a box of something that was flat-packed, unpacked the box and then rang you to come and do it for me. Thank you for running down the road in your pyjamas at night to rescue mice from my loft. Thank you for escorting us through the German market every Christmas. For rallying the whole street with your outdoor singing and guitar playing during lockdown. For being the unofficial neighbourhood watch and looking after our community.

For letting the dog out for me so I could go out for a day. For tiling, fencing, painting, mending and so much more in our house. For the big things like these and the small things too. The film nights, the football matches, the meals we shared, the days out, walks over the Chase, the times you were singing and playing the guitar and never minding when I used to ask, 'Have you got any Take That?'

I wish my last text message to you was more than 'Did you know your driver's side brake light isn't working?' If I'd known it was the last one, I'd have said something more meaningful. Told you how much you meant to your friends and neighbours. How we'd miss you if you weren't here. What a legend you were.
You will always be remembered as 'our John' and we will always keep you alive in our hearts. Much loved and never forgotten.
A shining light.

PROLOGUE

'How can people ever think of leaving here? This is just glorious! I don't think I've ever loved a place more.'

I couldn't drag my eyes away from the window, which overlooked the golden sandy beach of Sandpiper Shore, where the sea shimmered in the midday sun. We had been watching Aunty June's next-door neighbour move out that morning.

'Oh, trust me, Jo. This place always looks better when the sun shines. Remember you've only ever been here for a holiday. When you live here permanently and it's chucking it down non-stop for the third week on the trot, you'll probably be glad to leave here too.'

Not even a little bit possible, I thought to myself. Even torrential rain of biblical proportions for six months solid wouldn't make me fall out of love with this fabulous cottage in this stunning village by the sea. People who didn't appreciate it fully didn't deserve to live in a place like this.

'Well, Aunty June, if you ever think about selling, make sure you let me know. I'd snap your hand off!'

Little did I know how a flip comment like that would be so very life-changing.

A huge turning point in my life occurred a good few years later one grey, miserable, drizzly afternoon. Putting the bins out was the job I hated more than anything else. It was always Michael's job when we were married and probably one of the only things he did around the house. Feeling incredibly sorry for myself and having a little tear at the realisation that this was now my life, cursing the fact that now I was a divorcee and lived alone I had to do everything myself, I was quite startled when my home phone rang. The fact that someone hadn't called my mobile should have set alarm bells ringing straight away.

'Hello, is that Joanna Jenkins?'

I knew I recognised an accent but couldn't quite put my finger on where from. Also, no one called me Joanna unless it was someone official, which threw me right off.

'It is. Who is this, please?' I hoped it wasn't another marketing call. They were happening more and more these days.

'Hello, Joanna, my name is Rebecca Farringdon, from Farringdon and Sons solicitors in Sandpiper Shore in Cornwall. I'm calling with two bits of news regarding a Mrs June Cooper. I believe she was the aunt of your husband.'

I sighed loudly.

'Yes, that's right. June is Michael's aunt.' Quite quickly, a penny dropped. 'Oh! You said *was*?'

'Yes. I'm so sorry to be the one to inform you of the death of Mrs Cooper, Joanna. She passed away a few weeks ago after a short spell in hospital.'

'Oh, poor Aunty June. How sad! I didn't even know she'd been poorly. As you know, she is, well, was, my husband's aunt.' I could feel myself wittering on but couldn't seem to stop myself. 'She never had children of her own, and I think I was the only one she ever got on with and because of that, the only one who ever bothered with her really. We kind of lost touch over the last few years. Fiercely independent and wouldn't accept any help. Cut herself off from us all. Didn't want to be a burden to anyone in her old age apparently.'

I sat down on the stairs where I'd picked the phone up, feeling quite sad. I had really like Aunty June and felt like we had a special connection.

'I'm sorry for your loss, Joanna. Mrs Cooper left instructions for me to contact you should anything happen to her, and talk to you about the property.'

'Do you not mean Michael?'

'No, definitely you.'

'Oh, OK, but in what way?' I couldn't even begin to imagine why she was contacting me about this and it was scrambling my brain a little.

'Mrs Cooper said in her letter that you'd always been very fond of her little cottage?'

'Err... Yes, I was, although it's not so much of a little cottage. A blooming huge one with loads of outbuildings more like. I used to wonder how she got on rattling around in that big old place.'

Aunty June's home was absolutely glorious and in such a stunning location. I'd always loved Sandpiper Shore. When Michael and I were first married we couldn't afford a honeymoon, so she let us come and stay with her. Then, when we had children, we never had much money so we used to go for our family holidays. Sometimes just me and my girls when Michael was busy working. Our time there was always so much fun and she made us feel so welcome. We last visited five or so years ago, Michael and me. It was our anniversary and June was going on holiday and had asked us to look after the house for her. Over the years she'd had extensive work done and she'd started converting one of the outbuildings into a holiday let and had ambitious plans to do so much more with the rest of the property, despite her age. I frowned, still wondering what on earth this had to do with me.

The solicitor continued.

'As instructed by Mrs Cooper, the property has been valued and she wanted you to have it.'

Confused, as Rebecca's words started to sink in, there were lots of things instantly whirring around in my head.

'What do you mean have it? I can't afford to buy a house of that size. At the moment, I can barely afford to live in the rented flat I own. She obviously hadn't heard of how, well... how my circumstances have changed since I last saw her.'

'Ah, sorry, Joanna, I clearly didn't explain myself very well. She has willed the cottage to you on the strict condition that you move in.'

'*What*? To me? Oh, God. Now why on earth would she do something like that? And I have to move in?'

Much as I'd always said I wanted to live by the coast, it had always been a pipe dream. Something that I could dream about. The reality was very different.

'I can't possibly do that. I live miles away. I can't just drop everything and move to the seaside.' I ran my hands through my hair, catching sight of myself in the mirror opposite. Some days I didn't even recognise myself. Talk about a hot mess. Tear-marked, mascara-stained cheeks were not my greatest look. 'I don't know what to say, to be honest. Everything has changed since we last went to visit. It's my husband, you see. He...' Despite trying to keep it down, I could feel a crescendo of upset overtake me and I promptly burst into tears, not able to form the words to explain what had happened, though I did still try to apologise through the sobs.

'Look, Joanna, I've clearly called at a bad time for you. I have an email address here which Mrs Cooper had written down.' She read it aloud. 'Is it still the same one?'

I nodded, then realised that I was on the phone and she couldn't see me. Some days, I was quite ridiculous. Since I'd hit middle age, I seemed to have lost the ability to get my brain to work properly. Mental fog was real. I spluttered my affirmation instead.

'Yes, the same one I've had for years.'

'Right, then I suggest you take some time to compose yourself and maybe have a little think. I'm well aware that this will have come totally out of the blue for you too. I'll confirm everything in an email, along with the conditions Mrs Cooper stipulated. Please do read it carefully. She was very specific. June did say that she knew how fond of her home you were when you visited and that she would love to think of it going to someone who would give it back what it deserves. I'll ring you on Monday and see if you've had a chance to give it some consideration. No pressure at all, honestly, but I just wanted to let you know before the weekend.'

Then she was gone.

I stared at the phone in my hand, not quite believing what was happening. As soon as I laid eyes on Aunty June's cottage, I had fallen totally and utterly in love with it. From the minute I walked on the shiny black and white tiles up the steps to the black glossed front door, with its stunning stained glass, encased under a brick arched porch, I'd felt a shiver run up my spine. Deceiving from the front, once inside, it went back and back, and the land outside was vast with many large outbuildings. When I saw the amazing views from the French doors and the wide sandy path that went straight onto the beach, I gave a huge sigh of envy. From its elevated position looking down onto the dunes and out to sea, the house had captured a very special place in my heart.

On our last visit, I had even commented that it had felt more like home than our own, much to my husband's disapproval. He couldn't understand that I loved this, in his words, 'rickety old cottage' more than the modern home he'd spent so much money on. In a strop, he declared that Aunty June's place was a complete shithole and he wouldn't live there if someone paid him. His mood didn't improve when he had to drive back home and the M5 was full of stop-start traffic nearly all the way and when he realised that it had taken us nine and a half hours, he was furious. Happy anniversary to us!

A ping came from the phone to signify that I'd got an email and, sure enough, the solicitor had sent through the details. Luckily my phone was connected to the printer, one thing that my daughters did sort out when they last visited, and I printed out the letter and put it on the breakfast bar. Whilst putting a load of washing in the machine, my mind was all over the place.

'Right, my lovely. Let's feed you some lovely clothes, shall we?'

I shook my head at myself. Chattering away to the inanimate appliances and objects I shared my house with was a habit I'd acquired since I'd lived alone and went for whole days not talking to another human. Some days seemed to last for forty-eight hours. Sadly not in a 'I've-got-so-much-to-do' way but in a 'oh-God-is-that-all-the-time-is' way. I'd even resorted to buying and doing jigsaws, to pass the time of day when I didn't feel like reading.

While preparing dinner, I realised that I hadn't told the solicitor the full story about Michael. My middle-aged memory was shocking these days. June was Michael's aunt, not mine, and when the solicitor knew that we weren't married any more everything would change.

Maybe I wasn't destined to live anywhere but this little village in rural Staffordshire. I turned my thoughts back to what to have for dinner, trying to dismiss the idea of that beautiful cottage overlooking the dunes of Sandpiper Shore from my mind.

1

They say that when you can't sleep, it's because you're awake in someone else's dream, yet I couldn't think of one person at all in the whole world who would be dreaming about me. Since my divorce, I had never felt more alone in my life. When I couldn't sleep, everything that was swirling around in my mind came back to keep me awake. Normally my middle-of-the-night thoughts were about how I'd managed to let my marriage stagnate to the point that my husband left me, and how I'd missed all the signs. I must have been so stupid. The girls were also constantly on my mind, even though they were both living their best lives.

I couldn't get the image of that gorgeous cottage with its big windows and view over the sand dunes out to sea out of my head. As I lay in bed, I couldn't help thinking that if I lived in Sandpiper Shore I'd get up and walk along the beach even if it was chucking it down with rain.

Eventually, at 5 a.m., I decided to get up and make myself a cup of tea. It was a clear spring morning and the birds were getting on my nerves, having the audacity to be singing loudly. I wasn't a great sleeper at the best of times these days. The bed felt like a huge space for one and I missed the body heat from my husband, although at my time of life, it was my body heat that he'd always complain about. I was taking my mum to a routine doctor's appointment at 9 a.m. anyway, so may as well get a head start on the day. However, sitting in my lounge window looking up the street and contemplating life wasn't really inspiring me to do anything particularly exciting. Sometimes I felt like my life had completely stopped and that I didn't know how to live it any more. While some people weren't even waking up, and didn't have the option to live their life, I felt guilty that I felt like I was constantly bored and just missing something, not quite able to put my finger on what.

Since Michael had gone and the girls had built their own lives, I had no purpose. It was nice that Mum had asked me to take her to her appointment. It felt as if someone still needed me from time to time. As I grabbed my handbag and my car keys from the hook on which they were hanging in the hall, I wondered if Mum felt the same when I left home and whether she'd felt lonely too.

Mum was ready and waiting on her porch when I pulled up and I noticed that she'd got some lovely pots of vibrantly colourful plants outside the front door which really brightened up her driveway. She'd been quite chatty since I'd picked her up but my mind was all over the place. The waiting room was full and we were squished into the remaining two chairs.

'Come on then. Out with it.' My mother gave me a look that only mothers can give.

'With what?'

'What's on your mind?'

'I'm fine, Mum, it's nothing. Just didn't sleep very well.'

'Again? Is that because you've got something on your mind?'

'I'm fine, honestly.'

'Well, tell your face that then. You look like a wet weekend in Wales!' We both laughed, remembering a childhood holiday in Rhyl when it rained constantly for two whole weeks. We'd always refer to it when something was making us miserable.

'Joanna Riddle Martin. I'm your mother and you know I know you better than anyone. What's up?'

I knew I was in trouble when she added my very unusual middle name into the mix. I'd never forgive her for blessing me with that. I constantly had the mickey taken out of me at school. But she was right. She did know when something was troubling me.

'Do you remember Michael's Aunty June?'

'Wasn't she that cantankerous old biddy that Michael couldn't stand?'

'Yes, but I never could understand why he said that about her. He really didn't like her. I got on with her like a house on fire.'

Mum raised an eyebrow.

'Probably because she was someone that he couldn't manipulate. Anyway, what about her?'

'She died.'

'Oh, that's a shame. Didn't she stop you all having anything to do with her?'

'Strangely, yes. She said she wanted us to remember her how she was and not as a little old lady incapable of looking after herself.'

Aunty June had been amazing. When we last saw her, she'd been booking herself on a Caribbean cruise.

'She must have been quite an age?'

'She never would tell us her real age. Said she wanted to

remain an enigma. Do you remember me telling you about her cottage, Mum?'

'The one you fell in love with. The one by the dunes?'

'That's the one.'

'What about it?'

'She's left it to me.'

Mum's mouth dropped open. I continued.

'She has stipulated, though, that I have to live in it.'

'Oh, that's wonderful news, Jo. I know how much you've always wanted to live by the sea.'

I was still trying to work out why this was happening, still sure that at some point, the solicitor would realise that the situation with Michael meant that things had changed.

'I had a call from a solicitor saying she'd willed it to me. You know how I always told her that I'd love her home? Well, she clearly didn't forget. I couldn't move there, could I? It's just so far away. I have you and the girls to think about too.'

'Why are you even thinking about the girls? They never come back anyway. I never did know why you didn't rent a smaller place with fewer rooms.'

'It's so they could come and stay if they wanted to.'

'And have they been back at all since you moved in two years ago?'

'Well, only once, but...'

'They've got their own lives now, darling. And, to be honest, so have I. If you seriously want to move, you shouldn't let anyone else stop you. I might be seventy-five but there's a lot of life in this old dog yet and life is too short to live it because of other people. If you did move, I could come and stay. That would be lovely! And just imagine living by the sea. You've always wanted to do that, Jo. You should do it before it's too late.'

This time it was my turn to frown.

'I'm not being maudlin, but it's true. Life is too bloody short to not do the things you want to do. What's the worst thing that could happen? If you don't like it, you could sell up and come back.'

'Or there might be another way,' I mumbled.

'Which is?' My mother turned her head to me sharply.

'You could come with me.' I thought I'd put that idea out there. My mother threw back her head and laughed.

'Darling, once children become adults, they should never live with their parents. There's a reason why children leave home, you know.' We both laughed at this point. I had always had a fabulous relationship with my mum, which had grown even stronger over the years and recently she'd been my absolute rock through the toughest of times. The breakdown of my marriage had been the hugest of surprises to me and a massive wake-up call. I'd never felt so low and without her I wasn't sure how I would have coped.

The fact that I was adopted had never been hidden from me, and Mum had always tucked me in at night, said she loved me to the moon and back and said that I was more special than a birth child, because she'd chosen me. I never thought of her as anything but Mum and had decided at a very early age that no good would ever come of seeking out my birth parents. No one could have been a better mum than mine.

I berated myself now for ever thinking of leaving her behind but my mother was making me question myself. 'You should seriously do it, Jo. Without being rude, you're not getting any younger and surely the last couple of years of your life since Michael left have taught you that you never know what is just around the corner.'

'I get that, Mum, but I don't even know what state the house is in. The solicitor said it would need modernising and I just don't have any spare cash. Maybe the universe is telling me that this is not my time.'

'Well, you never know. Maybe the very clever universe has a plan for you that you're not aware of. Life can be full of surprises when you're not expecting them. On that note, there was something I wanted to talk to you about too. You know Barry from my crib club. Well, it's like this...'

2

I had dithered so much before making my final decision. Most of the very small number of friends I did have thought I was mad to sell up and move to the seaside; they said that just because my life had changed so drastically lately, from being a busy parent of two and wife of one, and now there was only me to consider, rash decisions still shouldn't be made. My two girls were completely and utterly horrified that I was even considering moving from the village they'd been brought up in. The place where they said all their memories of their family life together were made. The place that they'd both visited just once in the last two years because they were too busy with their own lives to fit in a visit.

But Mum was right, they did have their own lives. Melissa had not long qualified as a doctor in a city hospital in Manchester and worked all hours and Lucy had become a vet in a country practice in Derbyshire, recently engaged and in the throes of planning the wedding of the year. Even though neither were far away in miles, they were never around and I'd found recent times really hard and had honestly never felt so alone and so adrift in my life. But those days were over. I was fed up of wallowing.

It was in fact time for me to grab life with both hands and move on. The fact that this was where all our memories were made was exactly the reason why I had to move away. After all, memories were in your heart, not within the walls of a building. It was time for me to grab life by the short and curlies and have an adventure of my own. Time to make new memories that no one could taint.

And after Mum had declared that she was, in her own words, going to be shacking up with Bazza from the crib club, it felt like the final sign that I should make a move.

'Close your mouth, darling,' she'd said as I sat there, stunned. 'I have a right to a life too, you know.'

'I'm happy for you, Mum, I'm just surprised, that's all.'

'Well, the fact that I've moved in with Bazza means that I'll be selling my house too, and I'd like to gift you fifteen thousand pounds of your future inheritance. So you can put it towards creating a new life for yourself.'

Mum was making an amazing gesture. I'd been forking out money on the forthcoming wedding like it was going out of fashion. Whilst fifteen thousand pounds would come in incredibly handy, this was an offer that I wasn't comfortable accepting.

'I can't take your money, Mum, that's yours. You should be spending it while you can.'

'I'm not *asking* you to take it, Joanna. I'm *telling* you that you are taking it. I have a little set aside for the girls but I'd rather you have it while I'm here so I can see you enjoying it and living your dream. You deserve this, darling. I am doing it anyway, so it can either sit in your bank, or it can go towards your house by the sea.'

I wasn't sure whether her telling me about the money was to throw me off the story about Barry. But the more I thought about it, the more she was right. Life was short and maybe we did all deserve a second chance at life. She was pretty inspirational turning her own life around after my father had died years ago.

'Are you sure, Mum? This seems awfully generous.'

'You are my one and only daughter. I've never been surer of anything in my life.'

'Well, in that case, thank you.' I threw my arms around her as tears rolled down my cheeks. I'd longed for a house by the sea for years. I'd been within touching distance of a holiday home that Michael and I had found, before it was all snatched away. Now finally, my dreams came first and were coming true. While it was a good thing, a great thing even, I felt totally and utterly overwhelmed.

When Rebecca Farringdon phoned me back as promised, I said that I would love to take her up on her offer. I'd never done anything so spontaneous and at the same time as being exciting it absolutely scared the living daylights out of me.

And that was how I ended up in Cornwall, in the cottage that I'd always adored.

The memories that flooded back to me were quite mind-blowing. The years we'd spent there with the children when they were growing up. Our picnics on the beach in all weathers, determined to enjoy our holidays. Our last time there had been for our twentieth wedding anniversary. Getting Michael away from the business was a trial in itself. He worked longer hours at that point than he ever had, telling me that I didn't understand that in this day and age it was needed to keep up with the competition. In return, I had told him that if he didn't try and get some time away now, he'd be dead before our long-planned twenty-fifth wedding anniversary trip-of-a-lifetime holiday to the Maldives that we'd been saving for. The one that never happened.

3

As I stood on the slimy algae-covered decking at the side of Aunty June's cottage, I realised how ridiculously stupid I'd been not to have visited before packing up my worldly possessions and moving here for good. I had never thought that in the five years since we visited last, a place could be so very different. Long gone were the beautiful sparkling clean windows that looked out over the beach. In their place were damaged windowpanes, with condensation that had somehow crept between the double glazing and frames that were literally falling out. The mouldy patch on probably very dangerously damaged floorboards and the wallpaper hanging down, along with the bin that was half full of murky, stinky water, signified that there was a leak somewhere in the flat roof above the dining room window. Those were just a couple of the minor issues that I'd discovered when I got hold of the keys to my 'dream home' that morning. Knowing the house as well as I did, I hadn't felt the need to visit before I signed all the paperwork. The irony that Michael would have been horrified at what I'd done didn't escape me. There was now an overwhelmingly gigantic list of things that needed doing that were starting to form in my mind and some I reckoned were way bigger than a leak.

The one major thing that I had forgotten was the vastness of the buildings and land. It was way larger than I ever remembered and we'd only really stayed in a few of the rooms, though I did remember there being a lot of paraphernalia. We'd both commented to each other at the time that June seemed to be a bit of a hoarder but since the previous time I'd been there, it would appear that she'd taken it on as an Olympic sport. I'd seriously never seen so much stuff in my life. It needed a hell of a clear-out as well as a lot of doing up. I was finding so many doors leading to more rooms and cupboards that I thought it'd be weeks before I discovered them all. The rooms were all huge, with high ceilings and cornicing around the tops of them, which were also in dire need of attention.

Looking up at the cottage from the decking now, I noticed that the gutters on the outside of the property were sprouting things, they didn't look like they'd been cleared out for a long time.

Poor Aunty June had clearly been struggling for a while and, after all, she had been a grand old age when she died. How on earth could an old woman keep on top of a house the size of this? The solicitor had said that she'd been very healthy up until those final weeks and didn't bear any malice towards anyone that she was alone. She was widowed when she was a young woman and never did marry again. She swore that she'd already lost the love of her life and wouldn't ever meet anyone like her Alfie so she wouldn't even bother trying to. I berated myself now for not making an effort to keep in touch more. It was so sad to think she died alone. My life had been busy looking after Michael and the girls and I was incredibly sorry to think that I'd neglected her. On paper, I wasn't really her family anyway. She was Michael's aunt and his side of the family had never bothered with her.

All I knew in that moment was that I wanted to do her beautiful home justice and bring it back to life. I knew I was up for a challenge in this new life of mine, but certainly hadn't realised quite how much of a task it was going to be.

A fuzzy little feeling in my stomach, I grabbed a notebook and pen from my handbag, and started to make a list of what needed doing. It was going to be a *very* long list.

The shrill tone of my phone ringing made me jump and my heart sank when I saw the name on the screen. Trouble was, if I ignored his call, he'd just keep on calling, knowing how annoying he could be and how I'd eventually answer. I may as well answer it the first time and get it over and done with.

'Michael?'

'Hello, darling, how are you?'

How my ex-husband had the gall to still call me darling after everything that had happened never ceased to amaze me.

'OK, thanks, how are you?' I could have kicked myself as soon as the words left my mouth. I really wished that instinct and politeness, even after everything that had happened, hadn't taken over because I knew just how much detail he'd go into. I should have just left it at OK, thanks.

'I'm fabulous, thank you. The sun is shining here in the Costa Del Sol and we're just sitting around the pool having lunchtime drinkypoos. We're off out for a meal this afternoon to that lovely place up in the mountains. You know, the one where they do the paella that you raved over. You'd love it here.'

Yeah, I would have done. Because I bloody chose it! My 'darling' husband was talking about the house just outside of Marbella that we'd very lovingly chosen and fitted out together. However, instead of me being the co-owner of our gorgeous holiday home in the sun, he had moved there with Claudia, his personal assistant, who had clearly been giving him more than just secretarial support for longer than I cared to know. Not only that, but she'd also been my very best friend in the whole wide world. How insensitive could an ex-husband be?

'The weather is glorious, the pool is a fabulous temperature and we're having a lovely time, thank you. Claudia sends her regards.' Clearly, more insensitive than I originally thought. Tosser. How can you be in love with someone one minute and then hate their guts within a very short space of time? Sometimes life seems so mad when you think about how quickly love turns to hate. And at a time when most women would have turned to their best friend to confide in, I couldn't do that because the person he'd gone off with was her. So I'd lost two of the most significant people in my life, not just one.

'What do you want, Michael? I'm busy.'

'Oh, sorry, darling. I wondered if you could tell me what the password is for the Wi-Fi. I know it was on a little card somewhere by the router, but I can't bloody find it for the life of me and the world will come to a standstill if I can't get on the internet, as you know. A smart house is only smart if it has Wi-Fi. We had to sit in the dark last night because I couldn't operate the lights.' I tried not to snigger at this.

'Oh, that's a shame. I'm so sorry, though, Michael. I don't know. And if that's all, I have to go. I'm in the middle of something quite important. Bye.'

I disconnected the call and smiled to myself, safe in the knowledge that in a fit of rage one day I'd changed the Wi-Fi password online so even if they found the card with the code on, it wouldn't work. I flicked the TV back on, tucking my legs underneath me. It would be ages before they discovered what a calculating cow I could actually be when I wanted to. And how much they deserved it.

4

Now that I was down here, I was determined that I would walk along the seafront at every opportunity, even if it wasn't the best of weather; I would never take it for granted. No point being by the sea and not making the most of it, especially when it was dry. There was so much to do at June's, and I had no idea where to start, so instead, as the sun was starting to peek out from behind the grey clouds, I grabbed my gilet and decided that I'd take myself for a walk.

Half of me wanted to curl up and acclimatise myself to my new surroundings before I put myself out there. The other half thought I wasn't going to meet new people and make new friends if I didn't leave the house.

As I walked along the promenade which led along the beach front, I took a deep breath in. There weren't many people around so it was perfect to have a good nose around. Familiar with the streets from my last visit, I noticed that in just a few years things had changed quite significantly. Old businesses had closed down and new ones had opened up. There was a small supermarket on the junction of the roundabout opposite the lifeboat station and I decided that was a good place to visit. I could pop in, have a mooch about and see how the land lay, see if anyone spoke to me, so I headed in that direction.

The shop was reasonably quiet when I arrived. Meandering around the aisles, I threw some chocolate in the basket, which I cancelled out with a prepared bowl of salad. I then thought I'd treat myself to a bottle of bubbly to celebrate my dream coming true. It was extravagant but it wasn't every day you started a new adventure like this one. As I approached the counter to pay, I noticed a basket at the front with some marked-down items and right on the top were a couple of Cornish pasties and some manky-looking turnips and carrots. They wouldn't have them there if there was something wrong with them, I thought to myself. They were probably just odd-looking because I wasn't used to farm shop quality. I even thought of getting a couple and putting them in the freezer.

A cough to the left signified that I was no longer alone and as I turned, I was approached by a little old woman. As our eyes connected, I felt a shiver run down my spine. How odd.

'You planning to buy them?' she asked. I dithered. I didn't want to take these from a pensioner who might not be able to afford to pay full price when I'd got a bottle of expensive champagne in my basket.

'I was but I'm very happy for you to have them. I'm sure I can find something else for my tea instead.' I smiled at her and received a stare that Paddington Bear would have been proud of.

'But they're for the pegs,' the woman exclaimed.

'The pegs?' I repeated.

'Yes, dear. The pegs.' The woman looked at me like I'd gone mad.

'Oh, right. The pegs.' Still totally unsure of what the woman was telling me, I thought it better to just agree. Maybe I'd managed to connect with the only mad old woman in the village. Just my luck.

All of a sudden, the woman started running over to the till area of the shop, snorting as she moved. With what I could feel was a horrified expression on my face, I looked over at the shopkeeper who had now appeared behind the counter. Judging by the grin on her face, she was clearly finding this all quite amusing.

'Pegs. The pegs! Oink oink! You don't want to eat that old food, m'darling. It's on the counter for the pegs! It's the stuff that's way out of date and the shop can't sell. You don't want to be eating it, lovely. You'll have the shits for weeks. Everyone around here knows that.'

The penny finally dropped.

'Ah, you mean pigs?'

'Yes, pegs. That's what I said, didn't I?' She grabbed the pasties from my hand and put them into her own basket, handing it to the shopkeeper.

'Tessa, where are your manners? We have a newbie in town. Wait your turn.'

'No, it's fine, honestly. I'm happy to wait.'

When the shopkeeper had bagged up the out-of-date items into a couple of carrier bags that the old woman had handed over, after staring at me for an uncomfortable period of time, she grunted, shook her head and shuffled out of the shop. Only then did my heart rate start to return to normal.

'You must be the new lady that's moved into Coop's old house.'

I smiled. 'That's me.'

I offered the shopkeeper my hand to shake but it was refused and she told me to 'bear with' as she walked away from the counter towards the back of the shop. While waiting, I clocked the noticeboard by the counter and saw that there were a lot of local businesses advertising their trades. That might come in handy sooner than later. I also noticed an advert for a craft club in a café on the high street. I grabbed my phone out of my back pocket and snapped a couple of photos. Maybe a craft club would be a good place to meet some of the locals. They had a website so I'd have a mooch at it when I got some free time.

A minute or two later, the shopkeeper was back, wiping her hands on her jeans to dry them and reached out to me with a firm handshake.

'Let's start again. So, I'm Mary. Born and bred in town. And this shop has been in our family for years. You've obviously met Tessa. Otherwise known as Dame Tessa. Yes. Believe it or not, she's a dame. Story goes that she was given a medal to thank her for some sort of hush-hush work she did in the early seventies, but she never speaks about it. She's as mad as a box of frogs but completely harmless. Her heart is in the right place and she'd do anything for anyone if they needed her to. She lives at the big old farmhouse at the top of the cliff and keeps herself to herself most of the time. She has a smallholding, hence the err... pegs.'

We both laughed. 'I honestly don't know how she does it all but she refuses the help that we in the village offer her and always says she's fine. She and June were as thick as thieves and always helped each other out. Never would have put the two of them together but they were the best of friends for many years. She must be lost without her.'

'Aw, that's so sad. But how lovely to have lifelong friends like that.'

This made me think about the very small number of friends I did have and none in this area. Maybe Mary could be a friend in time and even introduce me to other locals.

'Nice to meet you, Mary. I'm Jo. Jo Jenkins.'

'Welcome to our lovely little town. You've certainly got your work cut out in that old house, haven't you? Are your family here with you?'

I had forgotten how intrusive small communities could be, but decided in for a penny, in for a pound. People would get to know that I was here on my own after a short while, so while I still found it difficult to say out loud, I decided to get it over and done with.

'No, it's just me. Newly divorced and ready to start a new chapter of my life.' I smiled.

'Blimey, that's a big old house for one.'

'It is.'

'It'll surely keep you busy, my dear. It was such a lovely old place, such a shame that June let it deteriorate over the last couple of years.'

'Yeah, I didn't quite realise that had happened when I agreed to live here. The first time I ever saw the cottage, years and years ago, I fell head over heels in love with it. So I didn't even bother to come and see it before I moved here. God, I sound like such an idiot. But all the reports came back to say it was structurally sound.'

'Ah, yes, structurally sound and liveable are two very different things I expect. But there's lots of builders around that should be able to help you. I'm sure you'll have it looking fabulous again in no time. Houses are like husbands. When you know you've met the right one, you just know.'

I smiled, not wanting to tell her how topical I thought her sentence was. I thought Michael and I would be together forever. I hoped I would have more luck with this house.

'It's a pleasure to have you, m'dear. I hope you'll be very happy here.'

As I walked away from the shop, clutching my handbag to me,

The Cornish Cottage by the Sea

the shopping bag swinging by my side, I could hear the sound of the bottle of champagne clanking away against the rest of my shopping. I approached the cottage and sighed. Long gone was that chocolate-box image of a gorgeous seaside abode and in its place was a tatty, run-down ruin, in desperate need of a lot more than a jet-wash and a lick of paint, but even more than that, some love and attention. After the few months that I had recently had, I realised that the cottage wasn't the only one in need of those things.

5

Before I walked back to the house, I decided to cross the road and sit on the beach wall and just take in my new surroundings. Still quite overwhelmed by the fact that this was my new life, I hadn't noticed that there was a man sitting just a little further up the wall. When he raised his travel mug at me, he caught my eye.

'Afternoon.'

My first thought was that no one left you alone here. Everyone spoke to you. But I couldn't complain because back at home I went for days without seeing a soul. It would take some adjusting to, but I needed to embrace it and make as many new contacts as possible along the way. Mum had given me a pep talk before I moved here, saying that every new person you encounter could either be or know just the person that you need to meet.

'Good afternoon,' I replied. 'Lovely day it's turned out to be.'

'It has. It's a funny old place where you get all seasons in one day. Not seen you around Sandpiper Shore before. You here on holiday?'

I had forgotten that in a small place where everyone knew

everyone else a stranger in town was probably one of the most interesting things to happen.

'I've just moved here actually. Literally. This morning.'

'Ah, then you must be the lady that's moved into Coop's old house.'

I smiled. Seemed like everyone knew June.

'That's right.'

'Blimey! You've got a job and a half on your hands.'

'I do, but I've always loved a challenge,' I answered.

'Hope your husband is good with his hands.'

'I beg your pardon?'

'Hope your husband is good at repairing stuff. You are going to need a lot of work doing up there.'

I sighed. People still assumed that if you were a certain age then you were in a couple.

'Is your wife good at cooking?' I replied, feeling quite prickly.

'No. She's dead.'

'Oh, Christ! I'm so sorry.'

'No need. She was a right old cow.' I smiled and my eyes met the man's as he winked at me. 'Sorry, love. Didn't mean anything by talking about your husband.'

'Ah, that's OK. I'm just feeling a little bit oversensitive today. I'm here alone actually.' I sighed. 'Just me.' It had taken me a while to get used to saying that. For nearly twenty-five years, I had been part of a couple, and a family. The structure and dynamics of the family had changed significantly to something I didn't even recognise and I was still adapting.

'Gorgeous, isn't it?' He nodded to the view. I looked out towards the horizon and took in the cloudless blue sky, the twinkly sea, and the golden sand, and once more, the feeling of peace in my heart suddenly felt quite overwhelming. I turned my face to the sun, feeling the warmth on my face, and sighed loudly.

'It really is.'

A comfortable silence fell.

'Do *you* live here?' I asked after a while, finding myself intrigued by this friendly stranger.

'I do. Been here for more years than I wish to count. I was an engineer all my working life. Hated it. But my old dad used to say that if you had a job that you could do for forty-odd years or more, you could eventually retire and live the life you want. When my wife died, I knew I couldn't face the ten years I had left until my retirement day doing the same thing day after day. And being alone.'

He took a deep breath and stared out to sea. I looked to see what he was looking at but there was nothing there apart from maybe his memories. After the long pause, he continued.

'I'd always loved nature and, as a boy, used to mess around in the woods. Bloody loved it, I did. I felt an unexplainable pull to do something different and knew that I wanted, or probably needed, to be immersed in nature. So, I did all that I could to come to Cornwall and be by the sea. So I bought a ramshackle old bungalow that my son helped me do up and now I have my own forest next to my house and a view of the sea from my lounge and my bedroom window. What more can a man ask for? If I die tomorrow, I'll know that I've lived my best life.'

That was exactly how I was feeling now. That it was time for me to be doing the same.

The man shuffled over. I wasn't sure of his age. His craggy weather-beaten face could have put him at a bad sixty or a good eighty. It was hard to tell.

'Bill Shaffernakker. Nice to meet you.'

An unusual name which I recognised because I'd seen it before on one of the cards that was up in the shop. Not the type of name you forget.

'Jo. Jo Jenkins. Good to meet you too.'

'I'm down here most days. Grab myself a coffee from over there.' He nodded to the café on the corner. 'Maybe one day you'll join me.'

'I might just do that, Bill, thank you.'

'You're welcome, m'darlin. And if you need any advice on the house, let me know. My son is an electrician, and knows a lot of people in the trade. He might be a useful contact for you.'

'Thanks, Bill, I'll bear that in mind.'

'Welcome to Sandpiper Shore, I hope you'll be very happy here.'

I hoped so too.

I didn't realise what a rabbit hole I could go down when I began to unpack. It was as if every time I opened the lid of a box, memories came floating out and hit me like a ton of bricks. Sitting on the floor and sorting through photographs was probably not the best use of time. Not only was it nostalgic, it wasn't making me happy and when I had made a decision to move to the seaside, Mum had made me promise that if things didn't make me happy I wouldn't do them. I'd only got through two boxes in as many hours, when I knew that I needed to get up and stretch my shoulders and back.

As I stood, stretched, and looked around, I decided to make several separate lists. These days, thoughts popped out of my head as quickly as they popped in so I knew the only way to unclog my brain and remember the important things was to put them on a list. Part of the reason that so many things felt overwhelming, I'd recently realised, was because you hadn't yet made a decision. Once a decision has been made, that overwhelm goes away. The new Jo Jenkins was going to be much more decisive.

The first thing on my list of things I needed to buy were noticeboards. A very good friend of mine, an incredibly inspirational lady, was a life coach and a master of vision boards. She always said that if you are looking at things regularly, they're far more likely to happen than if they're tucked away and only spotted occasionally. It made sense and I thought that it could only help. Now that I lived alone, I could do what I liked without someone constantly asking questions or ridiculing my ideas. She had also told me to look through some magazines and when something caught my eye, cut it out and pin it on the board. Part of the vision board process for some people was to visualise the things that they wanted. I wished now that I'd thought to buy some magazines while at the shop. I added that to the list of things to do.

The little resort of Sandpiper Shore didn't have many big shops, and the nearest town was about a fifteen-minute drive away; there was still time to get there before the bigger shops shut. There was a large supermarket there near a small retail park, which I was sure I would come back to when I needed to do a big shop. The car park was busy, but it didn't take me long to find a parking space with people constantly going in and out of spaces. I found it quite liberating to be shopping and, finally, only to be considering my own tastes. This house was going to be all about me and my wants and desires. It reminded me of another conversation I'd had with my mum when I was dithering about the decision to move to the seaside.

'Darling, your job as a mother and a wife is now over. You're not being selfish to want your own life back. The time has come. By now, you'll probably have totally forgotten what you even like. You've been putting everyone else's needs and wants before your own and it's time to take your life back now and live it.'

'Is that what you've been doing, Mum? You make it sound like you hated that part of your life, you know.'

'Oh, Jo darling. You couldn't be further from the truth. I have loved every single second of being your mother. It honestly has been my favourite thing that I've ever done. However, you get to an age where you need to spread your wings and it's a mother's job to let your babies go out into the world and fend for themselves. I spent years putting you and your father first. And that was absolutely my choice. But, until someone once asked me who was putting me first, I hadn't realised how much of myself I'd lost along the way. This time of your life is all about you now. You should cherish and savour every moment. Throw caution to the wind. Join clubs. Learn about what you like and don't like. Try foods you've never tried before. Visit countries you've always wanted to go to. Make new friends. Sleep with strangers if that's what you want to do.'

'Mum!'

'That's just a suggestion, darling.'

One that horrified me. I'd only ever slept with Michael. Only ever kissed Michael. We'd been together since we met at school and I couldn't ever imagine taking my clothes off in front of anyone else, let alone doing anything far more intimate. I shuddered at the thought. Although maybe I'd never have to shave my legs again unless I wanted to. However lonely I felt, I always tried to find something to be grateful for. Maybe there were benefits to being on your own after all!

The make new friends option was an interesting one. I'd never found it particularly easy to do that. I was quiet and inoffensive and found that because I'd never worked, I didn't really have a lot to talk about to people. That was one thing that had scared me about moving to a new place, but like Mum had advised me, I was going to have to put myself out there. Here, as the new Jo, I could be anyone or anything that I wanted to be.

In that moment, I realised that I was actually looking forward to discovering the me I was these days as well as finding out about local clubs and meeting new folk. Hopefully, not all of them would tell me off for taking food away from the 'pegs'.

6

I was in one of the large superstores which sold everything from ladies' clothes to soft furnishings and even small pieces of furniture, and I was enjoying meandering around.

'Oh, are you a toucher too?' A lady smiled and I realised that I'd been wandering around fondling fabrics between my fingers.

I laughed. 'My husband always used to tell me off for that,' I explained, and bizarrely my eyes filled up with tears as once again it hit me how much my life had changed. I wasn't sure if it was relief or sadness that Michael wasn't in control, telling me what I could and couldn't do or buy, or ridicule me for my little quirks that made me me.

'Oh, I'm sorry. I didn't mean to upset you. Is he...?'

'A twat?' I laughed. 'Yes, he is.'

The other lady joined in with my laughter. 'Most of them are. I suppose that's better than dead. Although...'

We smiled at each other, realising that we clearly had something in common.

'Ex,' I amended. 'Not husband.' The little stab to my heart I felt every time I said this little word seemed to be getting less powerful as time passed. Maybe time is a healer after all. Perhaps Sandpiper Shore was working its magic on me already and making me stronger.

'You do realise that ex-husbands are exes for a reason, don't you?'

'Excellent point,' I said, and with our kind little chat over, we both went off in different directions.

I chose a pair of lovely ready-made Orla Kiely curtains with matching bed linen and then went to eye up the four contrasting cushions. Michael hated cushions on a bed. In an act of defiance, I grabbed them and as I handed over my payment card to the lady on the till, I grinned to myself. The knowledge of knowing that I could decorate and furnish my new home exactly the way I wanted to felt rather liberating, although with the moving costs and even more wedding costs eating into the money that Mum had given me, I'd have to start to watch my spending soon, although I thought my new home deserved a treat today.

As I put the shopping in the boot of the car, I glanced over the road and noticed a little bistro. If I went in there and had something to eat now, and a drink, I wouldn't need to worry about food when I got home. Whilst treating myself to a meal out felt like an extravagance I couldn't afford, I remembered that Mum said I deserved to spoil myself now that I didn't have anyone to spoil me. Not that Michael had spoilt me in any way in recent years. Yes, I would definitely go and have food.

The bistro was heaving. It was lovely to see that it was clearly thriving. There was just one table left which the waitress led me over to. How lucky I felt to get that last spot.

While drinking a cup of tea and waiting for the food, I grabbed my Kindle from my bag. I never went anywhere without it. An avid reader since being a child, I always made sure I had something to read at all times, especially since I'd been on my own. I felt a bit of a 'Billy No Mates' when eating out but no one ever thought any wrong of anyone who was reading.

When I heard the bell over the door go, I noticed that the lady who I'd been joking with in the store had also come in. The waitress looked around for a table, shook her head and then looked at her watch as if she was telling her that there would be a wait. It seemed a shame for her to be sent away again when there was space at my table.

I took a deep breath, embraced the moment and the knowledge that I needed to make new friends and raised my arm to catch her eye before beckoning her over.

'As long as you don't mind sharing, you can come and sit with me,' I said.

'Are you sure? I'd hate to intrude.'

'Oh, God. Not at all. I've read this page about ten times already. I just can't seem to connect with the main character, to be honest.'

'Hate it when that happens and honestly, it's so kind of you. Thank you very much.'

As she took a seat opposite me at the table, and placed her handbag over the back of her chair, I realised how nice it was to have company for a change.

'You're most welcome. I'm Jo, by the way.'

'Michelle. Nice to meet you. Are you local?'

'No, I'm...' I stopped myself, realising that this wasn't the case any more.

'Yes, actually. Yes, I am.'

'Are you sure about that?' Michelle had a lovely tinkly laugh and she seemed to have a happy smiling expression on her face all the time.

'I've just moved to a village close by. Sandpiper Shore it's called. I'd almost forgotten the name then!'

'You've just moved? That's exciting. I want to hear all about it.'

Once Michelle had placed her order, and we'd told the waitress to hold back with my food and bring the two plates together, I told her briefly about how I'd ended up moving to my new home by the sea.

'God, you're so brave. I really admire you, Jo. Doing something like that, at... well, I hope you don't mind me saying because you're clearly younger than me, but at our age I was going to say.'

I was a little bit flabbergasted. I didn't feel like I'd done much in my life that had been admired before. What a nice lady she was. I could feel my spirit lift even further. It's amazing how a compliment can boost someone's self-esteem.

'Gosh, I'm sorry. I hope I didn't insult you then?'

'Not at all. The fact that you said you admired me way overshadowed the age reference.'

She smiled. 'It's courageous and it's awesome. Honestly, I wish I was brave enough to do something like that. So come on then.' She giggled. 'How old are you?'

'I'm fifty-two.'

'Snap!'

'August 18th.'

'September 10th.'

'Ah, not much in it at all then. We're almost twins.' I grinned at her, realising just how far from the truth that was. She was so lovely. Beautifully made up, blonde bob swinging from side to side, signifying a blooming good hairdresser, confident, attractive; while if I managed to swipe a slick of lip gloss on before leaving the house I considered it a good day.

'Gosh, sorry, obviously you are much more glamorous than me. Look at the state of me today, my hair looks wild and I'm about to stuff my face with fish and chips when you've just ordered a Caesar salad.'

'Ah, Jo. As women, we never like ourselves, do we? I'm always trying to eat healthily to keep this trim figure because I have to really bloody work hard at it. Everyone thinks it's easy and that I'm naturally like this, but not a chance. Every day at 6 a.m. I spend half an hour on a running machine before traipsing into the office in London, getting in before my male colleagues rock up. And with a full face of make-up to ensure they take me seriously! As the only female director on our leadership board, I feel like I have to work twice as hard as them to be seen as equal. It's bloody exhausting and I'm sick and tired of it. God, I'd do anything to be able to do what you've done. Wow! Why have I just told you my life story?'

We both laughed.

'I love learning about other people,' I said. 'So I take it you don't live around these parts then? What brings you to this part of the world?'

There was a huge sigh and I thought I could spot sadness behind those beautiful blue eyes.

'I had an appointment down this way with a client last night, so I thought I'd give myself a day off and make a long weekend of it. Breathe in some beautiful sea air. Walk along the beach. Recharge my batteries. You know how it is.'

'I do. After running around after my husband and our two girls for years, I thought it was just me who felt like that, but a recent trip to my doctor made me feel like I'm not on my own at all. Two months ago I started on HRT patches and I feel like a different woman.'

'Maybe I need to go and do the same. I could do with feeling like a different woman. I'm not sure I like the one I feel like right now.'

We both stared out the window, lost in our separate thoughts, before turning back to face each other. When our eyes met, we both started laughing again. I loved how much this woman made me smile. Although she seemed sad, she had a really nice energy and I had a good feeling about her.

'So what are you doing while you're here?'

'Christ knows. I don't know anything about this area at all. Got any recommendations?'

'Ha. You're asking the wrong person. I literally moved in *today*. I know nothing.'

'So you moved to a place that you've never been to before?'

'Not quite.' I explained our history with Sandpiper Shore and how I'd now ended up living there.

'You're honestly my hero, Jo.'

I could feel myself blushing. This woman had been kinder to me in the last half an hour than my husband had been to me for the last few years.

'I don't feel very heroic,' I replied. 'Tomorrow would have been my silver wedding anniversary. Instead of us being on a holiday in the Maldives, my husband will be in our Spanish villa with his fiancée, who is also my ex-best friend and I'll be spending it a sad single divorcee alone in my ramshackle cottage with a big bottle of wine, probably drinking it from the bottle because I'm too tired to be arsed to get a glass. A cottage which appears to be not quite the glorious cottage by the sea that I remember from years ago but a crumbling old wreck. That will probably be confirmed by the builder who's coming round tomorrow to take a look.'

A tear plopped onto my plate.

'Gosh, sorry. I'm not sure where that came from.'

'Don't apologise. You think you're a bad case. If it makes you feel any better, I'm a sad single spinster. When I finally retire from work, I'll adopt lots of cats and push them around in a pram and the local kids will all laugh at me. At least you had a husband and a family that loves you.' Michelle laughed. 'We're a right pair, aren't we?'

Her eyes were sparkling and as she grinned I could tell that an idea was ruminating. She drummed her fingers on her chin and chewed the inside of her cheek before she spoke again.

'How's this for an idea? How do you feel about going out for dinner with me tomorrow night, Jo? We could find somewhere fancy and dress up and go and drink wine. From, like, proper glasses.'

The old Jo wouldn't have dreamt of going out with a stranger. She was stuck in her ways, constantly being told that she was no fun, sensible and frumpy. But the new Jo was spontaneous, ready for adventure and planning to say yes to anything that was offered to her. What's the worst that could happen? I thought. We might not get on, and there might be some awkward silences, but I didn't think so. I had a really good feeling about this lady and despite only meeting her less than an hour ago, I felt like I'd known her for years. I'd opened up to her so much in that short time. We'd shared more than I'd shared with anyone for a very long time. What did I have to lose?

'Why the hell not!'

'Ah, it was the glasses part that sold it to you, wasn't it?'

'It's a lovely idea, Michelle. I'd bloody love to. I accept your kind and fabulous invitation.'

'OK, leave it to me. I'll find us somewhere and let you know. Here, pass me your phone.'

I did as she requested and she tapped her number in then pressed the call button.

'Perfect, we have each other's numbers now. I'll text you tomorrow and let you know what time.'

As I headed towards my car, I could feel myself smiling and something in my heart lifted a little. Michelle had said that, while she always found it difficult to make good friends and couldn't say why, she felt that she'd just clicked with me. I felt exactly the same and grinned as I slammed the car door. Maybe making friends later in my life wasn't going to be too hard after all.

7

Exhilarated by my day of meeting folk, but exhausted by peopling all day, I walked back through my new front door and looked around with fresh eyes. Instead of seeing all the things that needed doing, I saw opportunities. The chance for me to prove myself, not to anyone else but only to me. My back felt straighter. My shoulders felt lighter. I was holding my head higher. I could do this, and I absolutely would do this. I would prove to Michael and Claudia that I didn't need either of them in my life.

One of the things I had loved so much when I first visited this exquisite cottage were the floor-to-ceiling whitewashed shutters on every floor. Beyond them the matching-coloured decking opened onto the grassed lawn, which clearly needed a good tidy up, and the sand dunes beyond, leading to the turquoise sea which was glinting in the early-evening sunshine. I grabbed my phone and took a photo but when I went to send it to the girls, I realised that the phone didn't capture the beauty and depth of the layers of natural habitat, so didn't bother.

As I walked over to the shutters and ran my hands along the

grain of the wood, chunks of age-old paint came off in my hand and dropped onto the floor. The wood seemed solid enough, but it'd need a good sanding down and a re-paint. Despite always fancying the idea of getting my hands dirty, I'd never really been one for DIY, Michael claiming it as his area of expertise, but I knew that would need to change. I wanted to do things myself. I wanted to make myself proud. I would show them all. Something told me that this house was going to be a money pit so once I'd got a builder's professional opinion I would have more of an idea of what I could pay someone to do and what I'd have to do myself.

Back at home in Staffordshire, I knew quite a few people that I could call on to help, but here I knew no one. Maybe I would go and grab a cuppa with Bill down at the beach one of these days and find out more about the sort of projects his son had worked on. You never knew when you'd need certain skills in the future, even if you didn't need them right then. And people like that normally had a plethora of tradesmen contacts of their own.

Venturing out onto the decking, I trod carefully. A few of the panels were quite squishy in places and would need repairing or probably replacing. How hard could it be?

'Hi there.' I turned in surprise to where the voice was coming from. 'You must be Jo. If there's anything I can help you with, just give me a yell.'

On the adjacent decking, which looked a sight safer than mine, a woman was sitting on a swinging bench with a book in her lap. She gave a little wave.

How lovely it would be if I could have some nice garden furniture on my own decking in time. Or even a cocoon chair. I'd always wanted one of those but Michael never fancied one.

The neighbour coughed and I realised that I'd drifted away for a moment. My family always did call me a daydreamer, although back then it was because I was trying to think of twenty-five different things all at the same time. And that was quite a task for a woman of a certain age!

'I was just saying, if you need anything, let me know.'

'Thanks, that's really kind of you.'

'No problem at all. There are only these three buildings up here in this part of the resort, so we'll need to stick together. Also, I'm a boutique bed and breakfast so if you have any visitors that you don't like enough that you want them to stay in your home, maybe you can point them in my direction.' Her tinkling little laugh was a pleasure to hear. 'I'm just grabbing half an hour before the next lot of guests arrive. I've been running round like a woman possessed today getting all the linen changed after the last people. Honestly, why us guest house and hotel owners think white towels are a good idea is beyond me. I mean, I know it's because people can see how clean they are but believe me, when you've had a hen party of twenty-year-olds staying for a weekend and they've all wiped their fake tans on my gorgeous white bamboo bath towels and Egyptian cotton sheets, I'm thinking that white is the worst colour. I'll need to boil them for weeks to get the stains out. Filthy madams!'

I made a face to show her I understood, remembering a time when one of the girls had used fake tan and I'd had the same issue. I'd ended up throwing her sheets away because I couldn't get the stains out and made her promise never to use fake tan again until they left home. Strangely, the girls never used it when they were the ones who'd have to wash the towels.

'The new people the other side of you should be moving in soon too. Rumour has it he's an ex-footballer and she's one of those influencer types. I've not met them yet but I hope you'll all settle in wonderfully. I won't bother you, but feel free to bother me if you need anything.'

I moved nearer to next door and the woman so I could chat better.

'Thank you. It's a bit daunting being somewhere new. Especially when I'm on my own. But I'll get there in time. There's no rush.'

'Well, good luck to you. I'm sure you'll be fine. We're a welcoming bunch here. I'm Kate, by the way.'

I turned and grinned.

'Nice to meet you, Kate. I'm Jo.'

'When you're settled, maybe we can have a glass of wine together to celebrate your arrival.'

'That would be lovely. Thank you.' I couldn't believe how friendly everyone had been so far today. There were days at home, old home now, when I never spoke to a soul. Everyone was busy getting on with their own lives. Maybe everyone was so chatty here because they lived in a lovely place and were doing things they wanted to in life.

Kate picked up her book, signifying that the conversation was over. She looked so relaxed and at peace, her chair swinging gently in the breeze, and I hoped that it wouldn't be too long before I started to find my own peace. I thought back to the old garden in our family home. It was so very different to this one. A real family garden. We'd gone from having a huge Wendy house and swings and slides when the girls were little, to having it landscaped beautifully with rows of flowerbeds on each side. In more recent years the garden had been pristine, with artificial grass rather than real turf and plants in pots. Not something I particularly liked but again had agreed to because it was what Michael had wanted. He'd loved the idea of plants in pots, whereas if I'd had free rein, I would have had colourful wildflowers filling the flowerbeds.

I realised how much I'd missed having a garden. Even the

place I'd moved into recently had only a small, grassed area and it had never really felt like home so I didn't do much with it. The thought of the small plot of land I had here filled my heart with joy and my brain was working overtime, thinking about how much work it would take to get it into some order. Aunty June had obviously had someone helping her to keep it neat and tidy, but there were so many things I would do differently.

It was only recently that I'd begun realising how much I had forgone a lot of things that I liked to please Michael and the girls. Now I only had myself to please. It felt exciting yet so unfamiliar and very daunting at the same time. I just needed to break the habit of thinking about Michael and what he would think all the time. As I looked around me now, I realised how a beautiful garden full of multi-coloured poppies like Mum used to have would look stunning against the backdrop of the sand dunes and grassy verges and the sea beyond. I grabbed the small notebook and pen that I'd tucked into the back pocket of my jeans and wrote down 'ask Jill about poppy heads'. Jill, one of the ladies in the WI group I'd been a member of, had a beautiful garden and offered poppy heads to all the members each year. Some now would come in very useful. In fact, maybe when the house was a bit more habitable, I thought to myself, I could invite Jill to come and stay. She would definitely be a great help with gardening advice and I missed our friendship.

My phone rang and I glanced at the screen to see that it was my daughter Lucy. I also realised it was nearly 8 p.m.

'Hi, Mum,' she said.

'Hi, darling. How are you?'

'Busy as always. It's just a quick call to check in. Have you spoken to Melissa today?'

'Not yet, no.'

'She's probably busy too. I know she had a week of back-to-back surgeries. Hold on a mo.'

I could hear her talking to someone in the background; she was telling them that she'd only be a few seconds.

'I'm really sorry, Mum, but I have to go. It sounds like one of the heifers at the farm up the road has got a calf on the way and it's got stuck in the birth canal. One second.'

Sadly, this was a common occurrence whenever Lucy phoned. She was such a busy person.

'Just get me a new pack of those long rubber gloves from my office, please. Sorry, Mum, that wasn't meant for you.'

I laughed. 'Thank goodness for that. Although I could do with some of those for cleaning this place.'

'Sorry, Mum. Got to go. Speak soon.'

And then she was gone. I'd had many conversations like this recently – with both of my daughters. Both over-achievers with huge jobs and not much time for long conversations. I was so proud of all that they had accomplished. I mean, there weren't many parents who could say that one of their children was a vet and another a doctor. But sometimes it did make me feel sad that they gave so little thought to me, though it also made me more resolute about doing something for myself.

Like Mum said, there comes a time when you realise that it's your time. Your time to take back your life and live it to the best of your ability. Life really is too short to be sitting around waiting for people to come to you. I realised that last Christmas Day when I thought that because of the situation with Michael and I being apart, the girls might come and stay, but both of them were on call. I'd spent the day on my own. Mum had invited me round to her friend's house where a big group of them were getting together as they did every year but I was in such a funk, I hadn't wanted to go. I wanted to spend my first Christmas on my own reflecting on how the hell I had got there.

Laughing to myself and realising how far I'd come since those very early dark days, I removed the new bedding I'd bought from its packet. I would normally have put them in the washing machine and ironed them so they looked pristine before putting them on the bed but again there didn't seem much point when it was only me.

After fluffing up the pillows, I walked over to take another look at the view from the window. There wasn't much to see at that time of night apart from a few twinkling lights across the bay, but in the distance it looked like someone had lit a fire on the beach, and there was a group of figures huddled around it.

As I looked out, I felt my shoulders relax and I sighed, realising just how much I was looking forward to getting stuck in. I'd be breathing life into this cottage and doing the same for myself too. We deserved it.

8

I didn't think I'd slept as well in years. After it initially took me a while to go off, probably because I had the creaks and groans of a new house to get used to. I only woke up, around three thirty because there was a clanking noise coming from the hall. Tentatively, I'd tiptoed down the stairs, with an umbrella in my hand poised for smacking someone over the head if needed. My relief was amazing when I realised that it was one of the radiators clanging into life when the heating had kicked in. Funny, after all this time of living in only one place for so many years, there was so much more to learn about a new house. I got back into bed and put my earplugs back in.

Glancing at the clock, I smiled as I saw that it was seven thirty. I stretched my arms above my head and stretched my neck, rolling my head from side to side. Not wanting to waste this glorious spring morning, I slid my feet into my slippers and pulled my fleecy dressing gown around my shoulders before walking towards that window again, the view drawing me in. I could see that the sun was just starting to peek out from above the mountains and I couldn't think of a more beautiful way to start the day. The sky was a myriad of colours ranging from yellow to gold and speckled with pink.

Throwing open the windows lifted my spirits. Despite the gorgeous sky, the temperature was still cool as the breeze hit me, but felt refreshing. Exhilarating even. I pulled my gown closer and tied it tighter. The sound of cawing seagulls was a joy to hear. I couldn't believe I'd be getting up to that sound every morning.

Tea. That's what I needed right now. As I headed downstairs and took in my surroundings in the cold light of day, I could feel a grin spread across my face again. I flicked on the kettle and while it was boiling, the clanking of the letter box jolted my attention. I bent down to pick up a pink envelope with my name and my new address on, which I tore open and grinned wider still. Lisa had sent me a gorgeous 'New Home' card with her warm wishes to enjoy my new adventure. It was so nice of her to do that.

Bang. Bang. Bang. A hammering at my door made me spill hot water all over the work surface and I cursed as I mopped it up, yelling, 'Hang on!' to whoever it was.

Bang bang bang again.

'All right, I'm coming…'

I flung open the door to the rear view of what appeared to be a tall man in combat shorts, boots and a hoody, the hood part pulled over the back of his head. My heart started to pound. Who on earth was this person at my door this early? I was almost scared of him turning round, but when he did, he was grinning.

'Hello. Jo Jenkins?'

'That's right. And you are?'

'Seamus, Seamus Shaffernakker. My dad Bill sent me.'

'Oh, right.' I glanced at my watch. 'You do realise that it's only just after seven thirty in the morning, don't you?'

'Yeah, I'm an early bird. Sorry about that, but I was taking an early-morning walk along the beach with this one.' He reached down and ruffled the ears of the scruffy-looking soggy dog next to him, who looked up at me with beautiful big brown eyes. 'I'll go and stick him in the van as he's just come out of the sea and is filthy but I hoped you didn't mind me popping by to introduce myself.' He removed his hood, looking so much less intimidating now. Men shouldn't be allowed to put the hoods up on hoodies, I thought to myself. I mean, I know that's what they're for, but I don't think they realise just how scary it can be.

'It's fine, he can come in. It's not a problem at all.'

'Are you sure? He'll be no trouble but he might just walk sand everywhere, he went in the sea and then had a good roll in it. Filthy animal.' He tickled him behind the ears and the dog looked up at him. They clearly adored each other.

'He'll be fine. I can sweep any sand up afterwards. The beauty of a wooden floor. What's his name?'

'Theodorus Lunablue Shaffernakker the Third.'

'Crikey!'

'Don't say a word. I know. That's obviously his pedigree name. But you can call him Theo.'

'Thank you, that's definitely less of a mouthful at this time in the morning.' I turned down to the dog, who was looking up at me expectantly. 'Come on, Theo, do you want some water?'

'Gosh, you'll never get rid of him if you're nice to him.'

'He's lovely.'

Despite Theo being a total sweetheart, I pulled a bit of a face when he dribbled water all over my kitchen floor and headed over to the French doors where the net curtains I'd hung yesterday were blowing gently in the breeze. He turned round three times, plonked himself down in a patch of sunshine and sighed really loudly before placing his head on his paws and closing his eyes.

'Dad said you'd bought this place from Mrs Cooper and might

welcome some advice before the builders called in today. I didn't know what time they were coming, so as I saw the shutters opening while I was walking, I knew you were up. Sorry, do you want me to call back another time?'

I could hardly say yes, when the man was doing me a favour. Well, I hoped it was a favour.

'Do you charge for this advice, Mr Shaffernakker?'

'Please call me Seamus. It's such a mouthful and I've had the mickey taken out of me for years. Trust me to get a German dad and an Irish mum, hey?' He winked at me and when I saw his eyes crinkle I realised just how much he looked like his father – from the little that I'd seen of him. 'And no, I don't charge for a little friendly advice for a pal of my dad's.'

'I've just put the kettle on, Seamus. Can I get you a drink?'

'Coffee, big splash of milk, four sugars, please.'

My eyes widened.

'Yeah, I know,' he replied. 'Stopped smoking two years ago and started a sugar addiction instead.' He started scanning around the hallway. He was actually rather handsome now I got the chance to look at him.

I handed him a mug and excused myself for two minutes for not being dressed yet, while I threw some clothes on, telling him to feel free to wander around. I grabbed the jeans and jumper that I'd had on the day before which would do for now and, after walking past the mirror and seeing how my hair was sticking up all over the place, tried to smooth it down. I'd literally put the clothes back on, on top of the pants I'd had on all night. Good job I wasn't considering spontaneous sex with a stranger today. Though why on earth was I even thinking of having spontaneous sex with a man I'd only just met?

Gently shaking my head at myself, I walked back downstairs, fanning myself with my hand, sure that I was probably looking flushed. Seamus turned and asked if I was OK. I felt quite flustered.

'Always wanted to have a look around this old place, you know. It's a gorgeous building. One of the loveliest spots in the resort too. Lots of people around here have been waiting for these two places to come up for sale for ages.' He pointed to the vacant house next door. 'And this one didn't even seem to go on the market. How did you swing that?'

Once I told him a little of my history with the cottage, he nodded approvingly.

'Nice work, Jo Jenkins. I like your style.' He winked as he wandered back into the lounge and looked out towards the beach. 'I mean, I don't think you'd get a better view than that in heaven, would you?'

We both stood and watched the long grasses swaying in the gentle breeze and the sea beyond twinkling in the early-morning sunlight.

'Are you local, Seamus?'

'Yeah, just further down the resort. One of the houses on the high street. It's nice enough but you can only see the sea if you stand on the bed and stretch your neck to look out of the skylight. I'd kill for a view like this.'

'Ah, well, hopefully, you won't have to be murdering anyone. You could just pop round for a cuppa on my decking instead. Less messy too. No blood to clear up on the whitewashed wood.'

He threw back his head and laughed.

'I like you, Jo Jenkins. You're funny.'

9

I stood and stared at this big man who was now walking around my home. I didn't think anyone had ever said I was funny before. Certainly not my family anyway, although Lisa and I did have a good laugh whenever we got together.

Seamus walked back into the hallway and as I followed him, I couldn't take my eyes off his broad shoulders and slim waist and his rather pert, firm backside. His big strong hand grabbed the handrail at the bottom of the banister.

'May I?' He tilted his head in what I felt was quite a suggestive manner but then realised that I must be just having a middle-aged moment having improper thoughts about this man. It was those utility trousers he was wearing. I always was a sucker for a tradesman in those. I think it was because Michael went to work in a suit and tie and wasn't the least bit good with his hands – which I reckoned Seamus was. Because he was an electrician, of course.

I scooted into my bedroom and straightened the duvet and made sure the lid was on the laundry basket. There's something very intimate about someone being close to your dirty pants.

When we went into the second-largest bedroom, I was glad that I had thought to make the bed up in there too. It looked so much better since the bed was dressed. Although the suitcase that I'd discovered under the bed, that I'd kept stubbing my toe on, was still poking out and wouldn't fit properly. I didn't want to act like a helpless female but I decided to ask Seamus to help me with something while he was here.

'You couldn't just pop that suitcase on top of the wardrobe, would you, please? I tried to lift it but it's really heavy and I couldn't manage that and balance on a chair at the same time.'

'No problem.' He lifted it above his head with no effort at all, all six feet of his height helpful, and placed it above the wardrobe. 'If you need any help getting it down again, just let me know. I can soon pop round.'

'Thanks, that's very kind of you. I think it's more of Aunty June's paperwork to go through by the look of it when I took a quick peek in the top of it the other day. I'm not sure she'd ever thrown anything away in her life. It's not an urgent task in the great scheme of things, but I will get round to it at some point.'

My phone rang and I grabbed it to see that it was Michael. I bounced the call but he immediately called back so I answered, knowing he wouldn't stop calling until he spoke to me.

'Michael!'

'Jo darling. Good morning. How are you? Settled into your new home, have you?'

I supposed at least he'd remembered.

'I have, thanks. It's...'

'I still can't find that bloody Wi-Fi code, you know. Are you sure you don't know what it is? I even rang the provider yesterday but they didn't even bloody speak English. Couldn't understand a word.'

Of course that's why he'd called. Because he wanted something. I suppose I shouldn't really expect anything different, but after twenty-five years of marriage surely he must still have some sort of feelings of responsibility for me. If I was still getting used to him not being around, maybe it was the same for him.

It was at that moment that Seamus came wandering into my room.

'Good lord, look at the size of those,' he exclaimed and I couldn't help but laugh at the gasp that came from the phone. What Michael couldn't see was that he was staring out the window at two huge seagulls which were perched on the top of the balcony railing. He whispered sorry as he realised that I was on the phone.

'Jo! Is someone there with you?' It felt like I was being grilled.

'I'm sorry, Michael, but I'm going to have to go.'

'Jo, have you got a man there? It's not even eight. Did someone stay over? You certainly didn't waste much time, did you?'

'Goodbye, Michael. I have to go now, I have things to do.'

'I bet you do,' he accused.

The cheek of him. After all he'd done, the fact he thought I'd be moving on as quickly as he had.

'If I remember where the Wi-Fi code is, I'll text you. Bye.' I pressed the red button on my phone as hard as I could.

'I'm so sorry, Jo. Did I get you into trouble?'

'Not at all. It was just my ex-husband, who was horrified at the thought that his ex-wife might be entertaining at this time of the morning. Cheeky git.'

'I'd take it as a compliment if I were you. A gorgeous woman like you will be beating them off with a shitty stick when the local single men find out there's a single woman in town.' He winked again as he walked out of the room and wandered up to the third floor.

The only part of that sentence I'd heard was the fact that he'd called me a gorgeous woman. He was clearly a bit of a player. Charming the pants off his potential clients just so he got the work. But then again, I realised that I wasn't actually paying him for anything so he didn't need to do that with me. He was just clearly a smooth talker. And a right winker. And the fact that he kept doing that was not making my heart flutter a tiny bit. Not at all.

'So, Seamus. What's your verdict?' I felt like it was time to get back to business. 'Have you seen everything you'd like to see?' His eyes lingered on me longer than was totally necessary and he smiled.

'How about you make me another cup of coffee and I'll tell you everything I'm thinking while you show me your decking.'

'I bet you say that to all the girls, Seamus Shaffernakker.'

He threw back his head and roared with laughter. At me. Maybe I was funny after all.

When I went outside, Seamus was sitting on the edge of the decking looking out to sea.

'Thanks, lovely.' He took the mug from me and our hands brushed while our eyes connected. He eventually looked away. 'It's my favourite place in the world, you know.'

'It is lovely.' I breathed in. 'I can't believe it's mine.'

'You're a lucky lady, Jo Jenkins.'

I should probably correct the way he called me that, but there was something about the way my full name seemed to roll off his tongue. It sounded so sensual. Gosh, I was at it again.

'So hit me with it. Is this house going to be a total money pit, and I'm wasting my time and money?'

'I wouldn't say that exactly, but I would say that you've got yourself a right job on your hands. I don't want to belittle you in any way at all and pull the sexist card, but do you have any building skills at all?'

'Yes, I trained as a carpenter at college and have spent the last twenty-five years working in a joinery. I'm very handy with a screwdriver and drill and have my own workbench in the garage,' I responded as Seamus took a sip from his mug.

Which he then spluttered out, covering up with a cough.

'Oh, well, in that case...'

I burst out laughing. 'I have no skills at all, Seamus. I'm pulling your leg. I reckon I could learn though. I've watched a few impressive women builder types on TikTok videos though. Looks dead easy.'

He joined in with my laughter and I noticed that his eyes crinkled up and then he took me by surprise as he flattered me again.

'Honestly, Jo Jenkins. You are hilarious. You should try stand-up comedy. You'd be wonderful. We have an open mic night down at the local pub. I'm going to sign you up.'

'You'll do no such thing, thank you. I won't have time for shenanigans like that. I'll be building my fabulous dream home.'

'Mmmm, now, about that...'

'That sounds ominous.' I could feel myself frowning.

'Why don't I go away and put some thought behind the ideas that are going around in my head right now? You've got a builder coming in later today anyway?'

I nodded.

'Maybe you could make me another early-morning cuppa one of these days,' he said, 'and we can discuss what the builder from today says and compare notes.'

'That sounds perfect,' I replied. 'I'm an early bird. I did have a bit of lie-in today which is very unlike me.'

'Maybe it was the excitement of moving in yesterday.'

I sighed.

'Something like that.'

'Or maybe you just feel really settled already?'

That was an interesting thought. I did feel safe and secure here. Maybe I was finally feeling as if here was going to be my happy place. This cottage did seem to have magical healing properties.

Seamus grabbed his car keys from where he'd left them on the dresser in the hallway.

'Come on, Theo, time to go.' Theo raised his head, did a big stretch and was soon by his master's side. 'Thanks for the drinks.'

'A pleasure.'

'No, Jo Jenkins. I can assure you, the pleasure was all mine.' His big blue eyes lingered on me and a little shiver ran down my spine as he gave a mock salute and the door closed behind Seamus and Theo. There must be a breeze coming in through that open window, I decided.

It was only then that I remembered that today was my wedding anniversary.

10

The honk of a car horn, followed by the knocking on my front door, let me know that Michelle had arrived right on time. As I opened the door to her, the taxi reversed away from my house and the driver shouted, 'I'll pick you up at ten thirty,' through his window.

Michelle kissed both of my cheeks as she openly gawped in amazement.

'Oh my God, Jo, this is absolutely stunning.'

'Would you like to...'

'Yes! I! Bloody! Would!' she laughed as she walked into the hall. 'If you knew me better you'd know that my favourite programmes are where you get to have a nose around people's houses. Oh, Jo, the potential here is just limitless. Look at these flagstones on the hall floor, they're exquisite.'

I was so pleased that she'd come in. I was feeling particularly shaky about the whole move here after the builder had been this afternoon. He and his brother seemed like a proper Bodge It and Scarper company who spent most of their time shaking their heads and sucking air in through their teeth as they walked around, mixed with the odd very loud tut and blowing out hefty puffs of air too.

Michelle's oohs and ahhs were restoring my faith in humanity. When I told her my thoughts so far and my vision of what the place could look like, she looked at me in wonder.

'It's going to be fantastic, Jo. You've got this. And it's a huge deal, you know. This place is enormous inside, considering it looks like a cosy little cottage from the outside.'

As we headed up to the third floor, she gasped as she looked out of the side window.

'What are those buildings?'

'I'll show you properly another time but that one at the back, believe it or not, is a smallish, converted barn which has been kind of converted into a little holiday let.'

'Wow. I'd love to have a nosy around at some point. And that other one?'

'That one is a massive freestanding garage with huge space above. The solicitor said it has all the planning permission to make that into a living space too. Although I can barely afford the renovations in the main cottage, according to the builders that came and looked around, let alone the other buildings.'

'Yeah, but they probably suggested selling it on, didn't they?'

'They did and told me to let them know if I was planning on doing that.'

'I bet they bloody did too. The businesswoman in me is wondering why the hell you don't do the rooms up as apartments and rent them out to long-term people. I'd rent one of them from you. The location is absolutely lush!'

While that was a great idea, I couldn't afford to do anything so extravagant, and I didn't think I had the energy to do anything like that. I also didn't know how I felt about sharing my home with others. It was never meant to be that, so it would mean totally changing my mindset too. However, these were all things for me to think about at another time. Right now, I was thinking about my stomach which had just started to rumble loudly. Michelle clearly heard because she made a funny face at me, and we both laughed.

'So I've booked us a table at the local pub if that's OK.'

Her sentence stopped me in my tracks. There was only one pub in town, and it was the place that Michael and I visited each night when we were here last.

'I knew you'd be horrified at first, Jo, but I've done my research and it's been totally refurbished since the last time you were there and under new ownership too, so it won't even feel the same to you.'

'Gosh, are you in my head or something, Michelle?'

'I just tried to think about how I would feel, to be honest. And hoped you would be the same.'

'Well, you are really thoughtful and even if it hadn't been refurbished, at some point you have to stop looking back and look forward instead, don't you?'

'You're so brave, Jo. I admire you so much. I'm so glad we met.'

Today had been a bit of a shit sandwich, each side so full of lovely people and compliments, with a dollop of the builders Bodge It and Scarper in the middle.

My phone rang. It seemed to ring at all the worst moments lately. It was Melissa this time. I would answer and tell her I couldn't speak.

I held my finger up to Michelle, signifying that I'd be one minute. We both headed downstairs as I answered.

'Hi, Mel, how are you?'

'Mum, I've just come off shift and Dad has left me a message saying that I have to call you because you are clearly having a mid-life crisis and clearly had a man staying overnight. What is going on? What's got into you?'

This was just too much. I didn't like the tone of her voice, nor the fact that she was so obviously siding with her father before even finding out what was going on. I was a grown woman and would not be spoken to in this way by either of my daughters or my ex-husband.

'Melissa darling, it's really nice of you to worry about me but I can assure you that if, and it's a huge if, I'm ready to have a man stay overnight, I do not need either yours, your sister's or your father's approval. Your father, who left me for my best friend, if you'd forgotten.'

I could hear her begin to protest; however, I was on a mission and drowned out her words with mine.

'I'm going out now, darling, with a friend, female for your information, to celebrate moving into my new house, which you have failed to even ask about. So, I don't think that qualifies you to have an opinion on anything I do today. Let's speak soon. Sending you lots of love, darling. Take care.'

My hands were shaking as I disconnected the call. I could imagine Melissa would be staring at the phone, wondering what was going on. I had never in all of my years spoken to her like that. I'd had my fill of this family taking me for granted.

This was the start of my new life, a new me, and it felt particularly good.

'Come on, let's go, Michelle. I think I need a stiff gin or three.'

11

The pub was absolutely gorgeous. Much more upmarket than it was before with a more varied menu, handed to us by a young lady who guided us to our table, which overlooked the sea.

'Gosh, Michelle, this must be one of the best tables in the place. How on earth did you get this at such short notice?'

'Well, you might have to act surprised when they congratulate us on our wedding anniversary.'

I laughed.

'No, really. They told me that they only allow people to book it for special occasions so the first thing that came into my head was that it was our anniversary.'

'Oh my God, that's hilarious.'

'You might not think that when you're getting approached to join all of the local LGBGT groups.'

When the waitress approached our table again and took an order for drinks, she winked at us as she was joined by someone who introduced herself as the manager.

'Don't worry. We know you're not a gay couple. We're not daft, you know.'

'How do you know that?' Michelle asked.

'Our gaydars would have been going off by now and we just saw you checking out the backside of the man in shorts at the bar, madam.'

Michelle laughed. 'God, I'm so obvious.' The three of us joined in with her laughter and because we were causing quite a commotion in the quiet pub, it alerted the attention of the aforementioned man with the perfect bottom at the bar.

He turned and gave me a mock salute. 'Good evening, Jo Jenkins.' His eyes travelled from my head down to my toes and I thought that if he ever looked at me that way again, my clothes would literally fall off on the spot. I gave a little shiver.

I raised my hand and grinned. 'Hello, Seamus. Fancy seeing you here.'

'You looked beautiful first thing this morning. Now you look, well... stunning.'

When Mum had called earlier and I told her I was going out, she said that she hoped I was going to make an effort and dress up. When I said that there was no one I was trying to impress, she told me that I should be doing it for myself, not for anyone else. I hadn't realised that I'd let myself go until I thought more about it and as time was something I had in abundance, I'd taken the time to curl my hair and apply more make-up than I normally would. Mum was right. It had felt nice. And while I was doing it for myself, it was lovely to get a compliment, my cheeks were definitely becoming quite flushed.

As he turned back again, Michelle mouthed, 'Phwoar. Who the hell is that?' at me, and grinned.

The manager returned with a bottle of house Prosecco which we'd decided to order as we were celebrating, after all, and as she was pouring, Michelle asked, 'So are you going to tell me how you've been here for less than a week and you seem to have already met the most gorgeous man in town? You're a right dark horse, aren't you?'

I relayed the story of meeting Bill on my first day here and how Seamus had popped by that morning.

'Honestly, Jo, that cottage is colossal in itself. How many bedrooms does it have again?'

'Err... only three but five if you count the holiday let.'

'Seriously, you'll never use them all. You should definitely convert the garage into an apartment too. Believe me, you can't get a decent property round here. They just don't come up for sale at all. You inspired me to have a look around and see if I could afford to relocate my life. I've been into every estate agent in town today and they're all saying the same. Cornish properties are being snapped up left, right and centre, the majority of which are literally on the market for a couple of days. It's a seller's market right now. With two buildings to rent out long term, and keeping the main house to yourself, it would still be huge. You'd never need all that space, surely.'

'Well, I'll be having visitors come and stay, obviously.'

'And there's a stunning B&B next door, I saw. Couldn't your visitors stay there? It would save a whole load of washing and cleaning up after people.'

'Yeah but when my mum and her partner come to stay and my daughters maybe, I'll need lots of bedrooms and those extra spaces would come in really handy so that they can have their own place in the garden.'

'But how often will that happen realistically? Will they all visit at the same time?'

I thought back to the last time we were all in the family home together. I had to work it out on my fingers and was totally shocked when I realised that it was Christmas five years ago. And it was a complete disaster. Michael and Mum had got under each other's feet; she was trying to help me, but he saw it as interfering, which led to her trying to tell us both what to do in our own home. The girls had ended up arguing with each other because they had to share a room now because Michael had turned one of theirs into an office. They reverted back to their childhood selves, which was bizarre to see. Mum had gone home a day earlier than planned, telling us that her friend needed some help with something, but was very vague over what it was.

I'd been looking forward to us having the perfect family Christmas and even if everyone hadn't been getting on everyone else's nerves, I still wouldn't have got to spend much time with the family together. Because it was actually me in the kitchen doing all the work, Michael not accepting help from anyone else, but insisting on supervising what I was doing rather than helping me himself, and at the end of dinner, I was completely knackered after running around after everyone. At one point, Mum told him that if he didn't stop telling me what to do and when, she'd ram the garlic baguette that he was insisting on going in the oven at a precise time somewhere that the sun doesn't shine. He did wince and seemed to calm down a little after that but ever since then, I had insisted that we go out for dinner, and it was normally with one or the other of the girls as their busy jobs needed people to work on Christmas Day.

'Hello...' Michelle waved her hand in front of my face.

'Gosh, sorry! My mind had gone on a little wander then.'

'Yeah, so I gathered.' She laughed at me, indicating to the bar where Seamus was chatting to another man.

'So, Michelle,' I said, changing the subject, 'tell me more about your property search. I know you touched on it yesterday a little bit.'

'Yeah, well, as I said, I'd got an appointment down this way so thought I'd make a long weekend of it because I've always wanted to buy a property down here. If I didn't like you so much, I'd be right jealous of you.' She laughed. 'In fact, I've rung my boss today and taken next week off at late notice, I thought I'd use the time to look around more.'

'So are you looking for a weekend place?'

'To be honest, I think I was, but now you've inspired me to maybe even move full time, Jo. You're a proper legend for doing what you've done.'

'Gosh, me?'

'Yeah, you. You're a proper badass bird. Look at you. You've got life sussed.'

I scoffed loudly.

'Ha! You think? My husband of twenty-five years ran off with his secretary, and yes, I'm aware of what a cliché that is, who is many years younger than me and also my best friend. They now live in the luxury villa *we* chose together in Spain. He thinks he can still demand my time and attention when it suits him and I agree to keep the peace. My girls think I'm a complete lunatic because I've moved to Cornwall, yet they don't really think that badly of him and what he's done. I've got no money, a house that appears to be falling apart around me – according to the builders that came in today – and for the first time in my life I might have to get myself a job and support myself. So, I'm not really feeling very badass at the moment, Michelle. Not at all.'

'Oh, Jo, but look at all the endless opportunities that are open to you right now.'

I dipped my head to one side, and raised my eyebrows, inviting her to elaborate. It was certainly an interesting way to look at things.

'So, you just say no to your ex-husband. That's the easiest of all. Change your number if necessary. If he needs to contact you, he can contact you through the girls.'

'Oh, but I can't do that.'

'Because...?'

'Because, well, there might be something serious he needs me for.'

'Now listen, love. He made his choice. Without wishing to be harsh here, he is no longer your responsibility. How old are your girls?'

'Melissa is thirty and Lucy is twenty-eight.'

'Well, they're not kids any more, are they?'

'I suppose not.'

'You've got an exciting new life in front of you. That's a huge, exciting opportunity in itself.'

'But I don't know anyone here. I've got no friends.'

Michelle took a slow sip from her glass and placed it back on the table.

'Jo, you've been here no time and you've already been hit on by the local fit bloke and you are out in the local pub on a Saturday night with me, your fabulous new friend.' She flicked her long hair behind her and preened.

'Well, when you say it like that...'

'And job wise, if you need to get a job, then that's something to look forward to as well. Have a think about the things that you've always wanted to do. Before you met Michael, before you had a family. What did you want to do? What ignited your passion? What were your hopes and dreams? Is there anything there that might still float your boat, so to speak? I mean a metaphorical boat, rather than a real one, although we are in the right place if that was your thing.'

How did this woman, who I'd only just met, manage to inspire me? Manage to make me think that I could do anything that I wanted to do? She was the badass, not me.

'OK, Michelle, enough about me. Stop trying to steer the subject away from you. What's your plan?'

'Oh, look, here's our food.'

We didn't get to chat much about the personal stuff during dinner, we just oohed and aahed a lot at how fabulous the food was. I'd chosen salmon and new potatoes with fresh spring vegetables, and Michelle had chosen steak and ale pie, chips and peas. As always, I wished I'd had what she'd ordered now, as it looked delicious, especially as the dark brown gravy oozed out as she cut into the pie and she declared how divine it was.

Despite us both only agreeing to look at the dessert menu to pacify the waitress as we were full, we both chose sticky toffee pudding and clotted cream and managed every bit.

When she came back from the ladies' room, and sat back down, I rested my chin on my hands and looked directly at her. There was no escape for her now.

'So, you can't avoid telling me about you all night, you know.'

She took a deep sigh and rubbed at something on her arm, and I could see that she was considering whether she could open up. I could tell that this made her uncomfortable.

'I rarely share anything personal about myself with anyone.' She chewed the inside of her cheek and I knew she was contemplating whether she could trust me or not. We'd not known each other very long but I hoped that she would open up to me. We all needed someone to be open with. If you try to keep it all in, that's where things manifest and become huge, and end up affecting you more than you could ever imagine.

'It's hardly like I know anyone that you know, so even if I did tell anyone, then it's never going to get back anyway. Also, I'm not a blabbermouth. I have two daughters. I have more secrets inside me than Boris Johnson's private secretary.'

She laughed and took a deep breath before she uttered her next words, which came as a big surprise.

'On the outside I have the perfect job, the perfect life even. But the truth is... I'm utterly and painfully lonely, Jo.'

12

Only a person who has felt sheer loneliness can know how hard it is to say those words.

Lonely can mean something different to everyone.

It reminded me of a conversation I had with the girls when I told them that I was having to move out of the family home and into the flat. Even after all that their father had done to me, I hadn't the heart to tell them that his business had gone bankrupt and that our home had to be sold to pay off his debts.

Melissa was the first one to be brave enough to say what she'd been thinking.

'But, Mum, can't you see how ridiculous you are being?'

'Ridiculous how, Melissa?'

'That's our family home, Mum. That's where all our happy family memories were made.'

'You think I don't know that, darling? It's the place where I made my babies.'

'Ew, Mum!' Lucy mock heaved.

'Well, it's true. Not only that, but also the place that I brought my babies back to. That was honestly the happiest time of my life.

When you came home, Lucy, you completed our family. It was the four of us against the world. But then it was the three of us because your dad was never around, always at work. He thought more of that bloody business than he did of his family.' I did think it was important to tell them about some of my frustrations with him, if not all of them.

'Oh, Mum, that's unfair. You didn't work. He had to work hard.'

'No, *that's* unfair, Lucy. I would have loved to go out to work. I was stuck at home with you two.'

'Thanks a lot.'

'Let me finish, Melissa. I was stuck at home with you two but I loved it, I was going to say before you so rudely interrupted me.' I smiled. 'I adored you both. You were my world, but my world had shrunk to the three of us. It was more trouble than it was worth to go out because it was bloody hard work on my own. When you started at school, Melissa, it was a little easier but then everything was about watching the clock. Before we knew it after we'd dropped you off, it was time to pick you back up again.'

Melissa went to speak again but I raised my hand.

'Please let me finish. It's bloody hard work bringing up two kids on your own and yes, I didn't work, but I wish I did. Other friends of mine had their kids and still went to work. They had childminders or their children went to nursery but your dad didn't want that. I should have put my foot down then because when I didn't, I lost a lot of myself along the way.'

'I'm sorry you felt like that, Mum,' Lucy said. 'I didn't realise. And it's not that we want to spoil your fun now, you know. Me and Melissa, we just want you to be happy and your friends are all around here. This is our home to come back to.'

'But you don't come back, darling. You both have your own lives. And suddenly, with you both gone and your father gone, and your grandma shacked up with Bazza...' we all grinned at that, before I turned sad again. 'What do I have left really? I've lost touch with a lot of my friends over the years, especially since your dad and I parted.'

'We'll try to come home more, Mum.'

'You have your own lives to live, darlings.' I took my daughters' hands in mine and looked from one of them to the other. 'This isn't a decision I've made lightly, you know. I've thought about nothing else for months.'

That was bad enough, but when I told them that I was moving to Cornwall, they were positively outraged, even though their promises to come home more often hadn't materialised. I couldn't hang around for them in the hope that they might occasionally drop around. It was time for me to make a new life for myself.

'But won't you be lonely stuck down there in Cornwall, Mum?'

'I *am* already incredibly lonely, girls. And maybe I'd be better being lonely in my dream cottage by the sea than lonely in the village where I'm surrounded by ghosts and memories that are no longer happy but mixed with sad ones. I've made up my mind and there's nothing more to be said. I'm going and that's that.'

I turned back to Michelle now.

'Tell me more.'

'I'm not bigging myself up, well, maybe a little, but I'm a hugely successful businesswoman, Jo. I've worked my arse off to get to where I am today. Harder than any of the men I work with, just to be seen as equal. Not fair but it's just how it is. I have a team of people who love working with me. We go out for drinks after work. I run the company social media profiles and chat to all sorts of people online. I'm dead busy, always on the go. I'm the face of the company and am seen as a leading influencer.' She sighed and I waited, before prompting her to continue.

'But...'

She pulled a face.

'But, when I go home from work at night, particularly after a fun night out, I close the door behind me and I'm sad. I'm lonely. No one really gives a shit about me.'

'Oh, I'm sure they do.'

'Oh, don't get me wrong. They do in the moment. But when I'm out of sight I'm out of mind. I have friends but none that are single. When I need something doing, they say that they'll get their husband or partner to help, but then when I'm not there, they've forgotten about the thing I needed doing and then I have to find someone else. A professional. And when I find someone else, they say that I should have reminded them. That makes me feel like I have to beg for help and I won't beg anyone. I'd rather go without.'

'What about family? Can they help?'

'Mum and Dad are both long gone. Mum died of cancer fifteen years ago now and Dad's heart just stopped a year and a half later. Doctors said it just stopped working properly. A mystery really. One doctor said it happens sometimes. There's a technical word for it but I forgot it. It's basically a broken heart. He couldn't live without her.'

'Oh, Michelle, that's so sad.'

'It really was. At first, when Mum died, I felt like I had a purpose. My brother moved to America years ago. He had a wife and two kids out there so it was all down to me. When Mum was poorly, she needed me. Dad needed me to look after him after she'd died, and then all of a sudden he wasn't here any more and I didn't know what to do with myself. It was like I'd got no purpose in life. I almost felt like he didn't love me enough to stay for me. That must sound ridiculous. I'm pathetic, aren't I?' She took another sip of her drink and a tear fell from her eye. 'No one needs me any more.'

'It doesn't sound ridiculous at all. That's similar to how I felt when Michael left. The girls had left home years ago, first one, then the other to go to their universities and I had a severe case of empty nest syndrome. I honestly didn't know what to do with myself. At that point I should have returned to work, but in truth, I didn't know what I was good at any more. I'd lost any type of skill years ago.'

'That's rubbish. I reckon you could give any mother a job and they'd be able to manage a company blindfolded with their hands behind their backs. Their organisational skills of running a family would be perfect for a PA role. I've always said it. Mums are the ones that make the family work. They make sure everyone is where they need to be at the right time wearing the right clothes with all the right accessories. Most bosses would bumble their way around life if it wasn't for their wife or their secretary.'

'Never thought of it like that to be honest, Michelle. Michael definitely needed his secretary more than he needed me.'

'Probably because she stroked his ego more than you did. Sometimes that's what men need. Most of them are quite pathetic. They just want someone to tell them how fabulous they are.'

'Yeah, well she certainly stroked a lot more than his ego.'

Michelle spat her drink out at that and couldn't stop laughing. It lightened the moment for sure.

'So, is there not a man in your life, Michelle? Or a woman, of course. Mustn't assume.'

'No, and no, I'm straight, although never say never, eh?' She winked at me. 'Seriously though, I've not met anyone for a long time that I wanted to be with. I was with someone when Mum started to get poorly. Steve, I really liked him, but he ran for the hills when things started to get hard. He liked to go out partying and I did it because he enjoyed it but I had to stop all of that so I was around for Mum through her treatment. He ended it. Said I was dragging him down. That I was miserable all the time. After that happened and then I lost Mum and Dad, to be honest with you, I wouldn't let anyone get close to me again. I've been on my own for years now.'

'Oh, Michelle.' I reached for her hand.

'Sometimes I can cope with it. Then other times it hits me hard how alone I am. I went to a friend's house for dinner last Saturday evening with her and her husband. It's unusual to be asked, to be honest. Have you noticed when you're on your own, you don't really get invited to stuff?'

'I have!'

'Well, they did invite me round and it was lovely. The three of us sat in their kitchen and their son was home from university too and he joined us. We had some drinks and we'd got some music on and we danced around their kitchen and we laughed and it made me realise how much I miss having that in my life. Just having someone. Not just for the big stuff, but for the small stuff too. Someone to make me a cuppa after a busy day at work, and ask how my day was. Someone to run me a bath, rub my feet, give me a hug, a little kiss on the forehead. Someone to pour me a glass of wine. Someone who actually cares about me. I'm tired, Jo. Tired of doing every fucking thing on my own or for myself. Does that make me sound really ungrateful for what I have?'

'It makes you sound really honest.'

'What is it about you? I've only just met you and for some bloody unknown reason have told you all my innermost thoughts.'

'I'm flattered!'

'You'll wish you hadn't asked. You're a good listener. Thank you. You should be a counsellor or a psychotherapist.'

'Funnily enough, that was something I always wanted to do after I studied psychology at A Level. But then I never did.'

I thought back to how much I'd really wanted to do this at one point. Was that another opportunity that had passed me by?

'You should think about doing it again. You'd be amazing, you know. God, is that the time? My taxi will be here any minute.'

We noticed that we'd been sitting talking so long that the staff were standing around, waiting for us to go. We didn't want to outstay our welcome so asked for the bill, thanked them profusely for their amazing food and hospitality and told them what a lovely evening we'd had.

We arranged to meet for coffee the next day. I wanted to pop back to the shop we'd met in because there was a gorgeous pair of chairs in there that I couldn't stop thinking about. They would be perfect to place either side of the French doors in the lounge and hopefully I could fit them in the back of my Range Rover, if I put the seats down in the back.

That night, before I went to bed, I flung open the French doors and marvelled at how stunning the sea looked shimmering in the moonlight, while reflecting on the ups and downs of the day. Maybe I'd look into researching what training was needed to become a counsellor. Sometimes, I thought, it was the tiny rays of possibility that offered you that little bit of hope for the future.

13

The next day I set my alarm for seven, thinking it would be less embarrassing if I was up and dressed before Seamus arrived. It was once again pure delight to hear those seagull noises first thing, and once I'd opened the French doors onto the decking, they were an even louder accompaniment to the sound of the sheer voiles fluttering in the gentle breeze. A sure sign you were at the seaside.

I knew it was still only my first few days here, and that maybe at some point I might take it for granted, but it really did fill my heart with joy when I sat on the rickety old wooden bench that Aunty June had left behind, with a blanket over my knees appreciating the view across the dunes and down to the turquoise sea, which was shimmering in the early-morning sunlight.

By the time there was a knock at the door at 8 a.m., I was on my second coffee and was just about to give up on Seamus turning up.

'I thought I'd leave it a bit later today because you'd clearly only just woken up yesterday. Theo and I are probably a bit much first thing in the morning for people who are not used to us.'

This morning Seamus was wearing shorts again and a sweatshirt, with a black beanie hat, and his greying sideburns were just visible beneath them. He must have seen me looking as he removed his hat and said his mum had always told him off if he wore a hat indoors. We both laughed.

'You'll just have to excuse my bed hair, I'm afraid.'

Gosh, my tummy did another of those little flips at that comment. I must be ready for breakfast!

Standing back, I felt that inviting him in was the most natural thing in the world, and Theo bounded across the hall floor, and sat in the same spot he'd sat in the previous day where he stretched and lay down in a little pool of sunshine.

'He's so cheeky. I'm sorry. Are you sure you don't mind him being here with me? He's proper stinky this morning too. Just rolled in a dead fish he found on the beach.'

'Ew, that explains that revolting smell then. At least it's him. I thought it might be you.'

I grinned and walked towards Seamus, needing to pass by to get to the kitchen but not before watching him as he held his hand to his heart.

'Oh, she has such an ability to wound with her words.'

'You're a big boy. I'm sure you can take it.'

He raised an eyebrow and as his eyes locked onto mine, I could feel the heat start to rise around my neck and into my face. Why did this man make me have such thoughts? Thoughts that I didn't think I'd experienced ever before, come to think of it. Maybe Michael was right and I was having a mid-life crisis.

'Tea or coffee?' My question came out more of a high-pitched squeak than my normal voice for some reason. I took a few, what I hoped were, inconspicuous deep breaths before I noticed that he'd spied a plate of pain aux raisins, which made his eyes light up. I offered him the plate.

'Thanks so much. I'm always starving after a run on the beach first thing. And coffee, please.'

'So admirable. I can't do much till I've had two hot drinks and come round. And I'm losing hours to just sitting looking at my view, to be honest.'

I handed him a mug and grabbed mine along with the plate and nodded towards the lounge.

'Shall we?'

The view from the lounge was just as beautiful and we both stood and stared out to sea. I had felt like this since the very first time I visited Sandpiper Shore. That view had captured my heart.

'It's stunning up here in this little corner of the village,' he said. 'It's like two completely different towns and you are definitely in the better end. That's why the properties are so sought after. I'm still super envious that you managed to grab one.'

'Do you think it'll make a difference to people here? You hear stories about how the locals are awful to out-of-towners.'

'You should be fine. If Mrs Cooper wanted you to be here, then I'm sure that's an endorsement in itself.'

'Bless her.' I wish I'd made more of an effort to keep in touch. I know she didn't want us to, but I should have done it anyway. Been there for her in her final years.

'She was a good 'un. Big pals with my dad actually. I did wonder at one point if it was a little more than that, but he's always saying he can't be bothered to be in a relationship again. My mum did give him a hard time while she was alive, to be honest. I think she's put him off for life.' He looked upwards. 'Sorry, Mum.' He stared out to sea again. 'So shall we make a start?'

He got a notebook out of a small man bag that I hadn't noticed he'd got slung across his body.

'Mmmm, yes, please.' I spoke, spraying a little bit of pain au raisin out of my mouth. Seamus either didn't notice, or pretended he didn't notice, thank goodness.

'So, tell me about the builders that came yesterday then. What did they say?'

As I relayed to him what the man had said, referring back to my phone where I'd made a record in the notes section, Seamus's face made several weird movements and his eyebrows lifted and lowered as many times.

'So, I agree with some of the things he said and disagree with some others,' he said, his hand in his hair. He then proceeded to go through his list and every time he moved on to something new I could almost hear the money registering in the till. New wiring throughout, walls needing replastering, repairs to rotten floorboards, roof tiles that needed replacing, a new flat roof where the water was coming through were just a few of the things that he mentioned for starters.

I was starting to feel quite panicky.

'Why was this not picked up on any of the surveys that were done on the house?'

'Well, they probably were, but they're all inside things really, rather than structural. Most of the stuff that surveys pick up are on the building rather than the cosmetics. And most houses these days over a certain age need rewiring.'

'It all sounds really expensive, Seamus. I'm normally someone who has a glass half full but my glass is feeling quite empty right now, I don't mind admitting.'

'It ain't gonna be cheap, Jo Jenkins. I can help with quite a lot and give you mates' rates but there's a lot of stuff that you'll need professionals in to do. I do know a lot of people in the trade and could maybe call in some favours but it's a huge place and there's a lot to be done. I reckon Mrs Cooper would have had a whole lot of problems ahead if she'd still been here. It would have become a giant millstone around her neck.'

A feeling of nausea swept through me and I could feel the blood drain from my face. I ran my fingers through my hair. Had I really been so stupid as to think that I could just move into a cottage that looked really pretty years ago and expect life to just fall into place? Most things that sound or look too good to be true normally are. If Michael knew how daft I'd been, thinking I could pull this off, he'd be laughing his head off. The girls would be right too. They thought I'd been ridiculous deciding to go ahead with this move. I'd have to admit to them all that they were right and I was stupid. My heart felt heavier by the moment.

'Of course, she was much older than you, and you have more options. There is one I'm thinking of but I'm not sure whether you'll like it.'

I could hear Seamus talking, and looked back at him, trying to concentrate again.

'Sorry, can you repeat that, please?'

'Make the other buildings into luxury apartments and rent them out. It would mean a lot of work out there too.' He pointed to the garden. 'I know a cracking electrician that could do the rewiring work for you.' He winked but I was still trying to comprehend what he'd said. 'Something to ponder maybe. I'll leave you this breakdown of estimated costs. Obviously it's very rough but I reckon based on the work we did at Dad's and the similar things that need doing here, it's not too far off the mark.'

He passed across a piece of paper with figures and scribbling on it, but I couldn't focus on it. My eyes were starting to get blurry and I could feel a headache coming on. Bearing in mind that I didn't have a job *or* a fat lot of money in savings any more, I'd probably be ninety years old before I could afford to have the necessities done, let alone do most of the things on my wish list.

'You OK, Jo Jenkins?'

'Huh. Tickety-flipping-boo!'

'Sorry to be the bearer of bad news. I'd hate to make it something that it isn't though. I really do think you need to go into this with your eyes open. I'd hate to tell you it was one price and then you get stung with another fifty grand at the end that you weren't expecting.'

Seamus chewed the inside of his cheek. I could see that he was worrying about whether he'd done the right thing or not.

'Not your fault, Seamus. I should never have thought that I could pull this off. I've just realised how very stupid I am. Maybe I should go straight to the estate agents and put the house on the market. There's no way in the world I can get my hands on more money. I've sold everything I have just to get this far. When my husband's business closed down, I was left with hardly anything and what I did have has gone towards my daughter's wedding.'

'I thought you said he had a house in Spain.' He looked puzzled.

'He does and he very cleverly put it in his partner's name before anyone else got their hands on it. It was untouchable. He consequently didn't have any money to pay for Lucy's wedding so that has all fallen to me too. And, my goodness, I didn't know that I'd brought my daughter up to have such highfalutin ideas.' I felt my whole body go limp with dejection as I flung myself into the armchair.

'He's despicable, Jo. Look, there's always a way. We just need to find it for you.'

I smiled but it didn't even reach my cheeks, let alone my eyes. I stood, the need to be alone totally overwhelming.

Seamus luckily took the hint and started to put his things together.

'Have a think about things and if you want to talk through it all again, here's my number. Come on, Theo, time to go, pal.'

He put his business card down on the table while Theo stretched into the sun and looked at his master as if to say, 'Must we?'

'Come on, pal. Let's leave lovely Jo Jenkins to get on with her day.'

After I closed the door behind them, I leant up against the wall and slid to my feet. The tears that I had been hanging on to began to fall and I bashed my forehead with the heel of my hand, whispering, 'Stupid, stupid, stupid.' I was such an idiot.

14

'Look at you, looking all Sophia Loren in your mysterious dark sunglasses.' Michelle leaned down and kissed my cheek.

I took off my glasses and placed them on the table as she sat down.

'Shit, who died?' she exclaimed.

'Just my dreams,' I replied dramatically. I couldn't help my mood. I felt like my whole insides had been crushed. She ordered herself a coffee then turned her attention to me.

'So come on, you'd better spill. What the hell is going on?' she asked, clearly worried.

After her coffee arrived, I told her about my morning and the extent of the work needed, and she blew out a great big breath of air.

'Fuck!'

'Fuck indeed!'

We both sat in silence and gazed out of the window. I normally loved watching the world go by, but now mine was falling apart.

Michelle broke the silence when she banged the table loudly.

'There's still the solution I mentioned the other day. Convert the other buildings and I'll rent one of them from you and you can find someone else to rent the other. You still have two bedrooms left for visitors in the main building. Have you thought any more about that?'

'You're not the first person who's suggested that, you know. Are you in cahoots with Seamus?'

'Phwoar. I should be so lucky.'

Despite my gloomy mood, the sleazy way she said it made me laugh.

'Seriously, Jo. I'd love you to show me around the holiday let. I can't find anywhere in Cornwall that I'd want to live and the view from the hill is to die for. It's perfect. The more I think about it, the more of a fabulous idea it is. I could relocate down here and if work won't let me do my work from here, then I'll find a new job.'

'I can't ask you to do that. Besides, there's a hell of a lot of work that would need doing in there to make it habitable.'

'You're not asking me to do anything. Just think about it, Jo. It could be a perfect solution. With a monthly income coming in from the rental, and I'm very happy to sign a long-term lease, with a lump sum deposit, then you could afford to maybe have the other stuff done. It could be the answer to everything for you. We could go to an estate agents and find out how much you'd get if you rented it. I'm very happy to pay you the going rate. It could be right for both of us. And it'll give me the kick up the bum that I've needed. I think I've been wandering round looking at properties finding fault in everything because the perfect property doesn't exist. But it could. My perfect property could be your perfect solution.'

'But the fundamental piece of the puzzle that's missing here is that I don't have enough cash to do the house or the buildings up. I just don't have any spare money. What I did have I've given to

Lucy for her wedding. She'd set her heart on this country house hotel which is costing an arm and a leg.'

'Surely her dad can give her some towards that. When is it?'

'I can't think about the wedding. Every time I do, I come out in hives at the thought of us all being in the same place together. I just keep pushing it away. And with regards to the money, he says he doesn't have it. So my settlement and house renovation fund is going to get spent on *one* day. It had better be a good day! So unless you have a spare hundred grand lying around then I'm well and truly stuffed.'

'I wish I did. It's mad, isn't it? Could you get a bank loan?'

'It's a good question and according to the bank when I spoke to them this morning, the answer is no. I don't have a job or a guarantor. When you have no money, that amount is huge and so out of reach. If you had millions, it would be a drop in the ocean and you'd be able to just conjure it up without an issue.'

The pressure in my head was unbearable and I reached down to grab some headache tablets from my bag.

'Sorry, Jo. I don't want to put any pressure on you at all. Maybe you could think about it, though. Could you borrow it from anyone? Michael maybe?'

'I'd never ask him for a penny. I'd rather sell my body on the streets than ask him.' I knew I had a penchant for being dramatic and I tried hard not to smirk at myself now.

'Do you have anything worth selling that could raise any cash at all? You could throw that into the pot. Maybe it's worth looking for work down here too. You could get a job and that would help. I know it's not what you thought living down here would look like but it's an option.'

'It's the only bloody option I have available to me right now.'

'Sorry.' She pulled a face.

'No, I didn't mean it like that. It's just not what I thought would happen. I thought that I'd be living a life of luxury and relaxation by the seaside.'

'Well, life doesn't always go to plan, sweetie. Sometimes obstacles come along to test us and see what we're made of.'

My mind was starting to work overtime.

'I suppose I could get some of the jewellery that Michael has bought me over the years valued to see if there's any cash in it. I never imagined selling them, to be honest, but they're only sitting in my safe. I hardly ever wear them. None of them are really my type of thing anyway. I like simple jewellery, silver particularly. A lot of it is really chunky gold.'

'Well, apparently gold and silver prices are at a high at the moment.'

'That's good to know.'

Michelle studied my face.

'What?' I was as grumpy as hell and needed to know what she was thinking.

'I didn't take you as a quitter.' Her eyebrows lifted.

'I'm not.'

Michelle got her phone out and started tapping at the keys.

'There's a jeweller across the town that does free valuations. I don't want to pressure you, but while we're here, we could pop in. Maybe after you've been back into the store to pick up those bits you wanted.'

I didn't even feel like going back into the store. What was the point of buying furniture and accessories for my dream home when I didn't even know if my dream home was ever going to exist?

I'd been working solidly on the things I could make an impact on. I'd hired a sander and had attacked the floorboards in the lounge, and bought some second-hand rugs to cover up the bits that I couldn't get perfect. I'd taken down every single curtain in the house, which must have been up for years if the amount of dust that fell on me was anything to go by. I'd found some offcuts of material and was rather proud of the curtains I'd made for the spare bedrooms and found some for the lounge that I wanted online which was why I wanted to back to the store to see if they had them in stock. I'd even ordered a gorgeous roll of heavy teal brocade fabric with gold thread running through which kept with the coastal colours that I wanted as a theme and had recovered a couple of Aunty June's old armchairs and a pouffe. Amazing how creative I could be with a staple gun and I'd surprised myself with how much I'd loved doing it. My shoulders ached and I was shattered, but I had loved every minute of it. I was finally starting to feel proud of doing something in my life.

However, it was now hitting home that my money was fast running out and I still hadn't really got a plan.

I was so close yet so far. I wasn't sure where it came from, but an overwhelming feeling of having one last shot at this dream life of mine suddenly whooshed through my body. Nobody called me a quitter.

'Let's go.'

Michelle grinned and grabbed her coat.

After stomping across the town centre, I took a deep breath before opening the door of the jewellery store. It was an old-fashioned shop, all mahogany counters and navy-blue walls. I could imagine a character from a Dickens novel being alerted to our arrival by the jingle of the bell over the door. What I didn't expect was the very attractive, tall, dark-haired lady who greeted us.

'Afternoon, ladies, can I help you?'

'Err, I'm hoping so. Is it right that you do jewellery valuations here?'

'Yes, we do, but sadly not right now. The owner of the business died last year and his brother took over, but he's not here very often and he only does appointments. I can make an appointment for you.'

Gosh, this day was full of ups and downs, I thought. Maybe it was good that he wasn't here right then. It would give me chance to go home and collect everything together and bring it all over. All I had on me today were my diamond engagement, eternity and wedding rings, which I'd moved from my left hand to my right, not wanting to take them off altogether just yet.

'I'd like to make an appointment then in that case, please.'

'Certainly, madam. Can you come along tomorrow afternoon around 2 p.m.?'

'Please call me Jo. Yes. I can definitely do that. Thanks.'

'Great, see you then.' She smiled but it didn't quite reach her eyes and she had an air of sadness about her.

We walked back over to the car park by the café in companionable silence, both lost in our thoughts, knowing that we both still had a little glimmer of hope in our hearts for a future that we both deserved.

As I got in my beloved black Range Rover Sport that Michael bought me for our last Christmas present together, something which I now knew to have been bought from guilt rather than love, I realised that it was something else valuable that I could probably sell. I had loved it initially, but every time I got in it now, I thought about him and that home-wrecker.

They had destroyed my family but I would not allow them to crush the only real thing I had left. My spirit. I would continue with my dream for a new life. And I would not let go of it easily. Not without a bloody good fight.

15

'This is becoming a bit of a habit, you know. I got some right funny looks from Kate next door when I left at 9 a.m. yesterday morning. It'll certainly get the neighbours talking.'

I liked seeing Seamus first thing in the morning. It was a nice way to start the day. He had a really nice energy and I loved being in his company. I wondered, not for the first time, whether he was single. I had already clocked that he wasn't wearing a wedding ring.

'Ah, I only want you for your mind.' I laughed.

'Now that's a shame!' His eyes locked onto mine again. When he looked at me it was as if he could see right through to the very soul of me. Could read my mind.

'Coffee?' I squeaked. 'Croissants?' That came out more normally, thank goodness.

'Anyone would think you were trying to butter me up. Where's Theo?'

Neither of us had noticed him sneak in but Theo was already in his regular spot in the sun. 'Cheeky little bugger.'

Theo lifted an eyelid, knowing we were talking about him, and then closed it again, sighing deeply.

'It's a compliment, really, that he feels like he can come in and relax.'

'Why wouldn't he? I don't know how you've done it, Jo Jenkins, but even without any money behind you, you seem to have created an inviting, cosy, gorgeous, welcoming house that people might never want to leave, you know.'

'Thank you. That's one of the nicest things anyone has ever said and soft furnishings are the easy part. Anyway, while it's nice that you're here blowing smoke up my arse,' he grinned at my choice of phrase, 'I've got a proposal for you.'

'Can this day get any better?'

'Stop it, I'm being serious.'

'Well, so was I, but sorry. This is my I'm-listening-and-serious-face. Better?' He raised an eyebrow and took a sip from his mug.

'Much. Thank you. So what can I get for fifty grand?' Seamus spluttered coffee everywhere.

'Sorry, Jo Jenkins, but after the last time I saw you, I really was not expecting that.'

'Well, you and me both, but I've been doing some thinking and I've got a couple of appointments later and I reckon I could get my hands on about that much money and I was wondering what you could do for me.'

Seamus's face was a picture. 'Hang on, yesterday you hadn't got a penny to your name and today you've got fifty grand. How much do you reckon you can have by tomorrow?'

I smiled at him.

'I'll have you know, there is no end to my talents.'

'I can only imagine,' he muttered.

'Will you have a think and let me know?' I asked. 'I've got a little bit of money left over from what my Mum gave me but when I arrived I had to get the roof emergency repaired and most of it had to go on that. And I know my plan was never to rent out the other buildings but you mentioned it the other day and now Michelle has said that she'll rent one off me...'

'Michelle who?'

'Someone I met the other day. The woman I was in the pub with the other night when you were at the bar.'

'But you've only just met her? How do you know you can trust her?'

My eyes widened.

'I've only just met you. How do I know I can trust *you*?'

I looked into his eyes and felt like I was seeing deep into his soul. My gut told me that I could trust this man with everything I had. But then I'd trusted Michael too. And look what happened there. Can you really trust anyone except for yourself?

'Excellent point but are you sure about her, Jo Jenkins? You have to be careful with people these days, especially when there's money involved.'

'It would all be above board. I just want to know whether we can get the holiday let to a nice, liveable standard, and how much it will cost me. The garage too.'

'Can we go and have a look?'

'Lead the way!' I said enthusiastically as we reached the garage.

'You first.'

I'd forgotten that one of the worst things you can do in life is have someone you don't know well follow you up some stairs, or you following them. It's mortifying either way because there is literally nowhere else to look. And you know that they're looking right at your backside. When we reached the top of the rickety staircase, Seamus was smirking and I was bright red in the face.

'Right, so let's look at it all realistically.'

I looked around me at the shell of the building that was stuffed full to the brim of boxes with goodness knows what inside of them.

'You'd need the floor strengthening, plumbing in, and electrics, of course. The downstairs could be the lounge and kitchen area and this floor could be one really large bedroom and bathroom, or you could go for two smaller rooms, both with en suites. Any thoughts?'

I tried so hard to picture it but the solid breeze block walls and no windows were putting me off.

I was frantically scribbling down in my notepad as he was talking, making sure I was getting all the points down so I could refer back to them.

He did lots of walking around, rocking on the floor, clicking his tongue quite a few times and chewing his lip before he finally said, 'You could have a couple of skylights which would let plenty of light in on the top floor and, to be honest, one big window to overlook the sea would be amazing. Some plastering, heating, a wallop over with some paint, the staircase sanding back and either varnishing or painting again. It would be a shame not to make the most of that gorgeous wood.' He ran his hands along the banister and I couldn't help but look at how big and manly they were. 'The downstairs would make a great open-plan kitchen-cum-lounge-cum-dining room, making the most of a big window. God, Jo, this is such a waste. I had no idea this was even up here and I walk past here every day. Look at that view. You'd get premium rent for this if it was done, you know.'

'I think the thing that's worrying me the most is that there's no separate garden though. I don't know how that would work.'

'I hear you. I need to have a think about that. You could always let them share your garden for the time being.'

'Sounds expensive.'

'Yep, sadly it could be. But we can get some proper prices and work it all out. Maybe you could have a communal garden for the two letting properties. Let's keep thinking though. You never know what might pop up in this tiny brain of mine. I'll do a bit of research too, asking around.'

'If I, that's the royal I, by the way, could get at least one of the properties ready, I could start renting out the flat. And then the money from that could pay for some of the other stuff that needs doing.'

'Are you sure about this, Jo Jenkins?'

It wasn't how I had imagined living in this cottage of Aunty June's but maybe this was the only way I could make life happen for me down here in Cornwall.

'Sadly, Seamus, it would seem that my dream house is more of a nightmare house, so instead of me losing my dream entirely, this gives me the next best option. I don't need all these buildings for just me. It's kind of daft anyway. If someone could give me six months' rent upfront, then that's a big chunk to get some more jobs done.'

Seamus looked at his watch.

'I need to go to drop Theo off at home before going out to quote for a job. Let me mull it all over.'

We headed back to the cottage where Theo was still snoring away in the morning sunshine.

'He's no spring chicken any more,' Seamus said, by way of explanation, 'and an hour's run in the morning wears him out these days.' He called his name but Theo was dead to the world. 'He also has selective hearing. I bet if you rustled some biscuit wrappers, he'd soon hear that!'

We both laughed yet still Theo didn't budge. An idea formed in my mind.

'How long will you be, Seamus?'

'A couple of hours.'

'You could always leave him here. He'd be lovely company for me.'

'Are you sure? He'd love that, poor thing normally has to stop home all day long because I'm out working. When I first had him, I had this romantic idea of us spending our days together, him sitting peacefully while I was getting on with my work, but lots of the people I go to don't want a dog in their house and I don't suppose I can blame them. He'd love a bit of company too, I'm sure. I'll be as quick as I can.'

Just having Theo in the house with me lifted my mood. Who couldn't love it when someone looks that excited to see you just when you speak to them? Dogs are meant to be therapeutic and I truly believe this to be the case.

'Don't rush. As long as I've got time to get into the main town for an appointment at 2 p.m., that's fine by me. Leave me his lead too and we might go for a little potter around the resort. Do you think he'll be OK with that?'

'He'd love it. He's so good on lead. Just don't let him off unless you're on the beach and are prepared to go in the sea when he refuses to come out.'

'Ha. I'll leave that to you. We'll just do a lead walk today while we're getting used to each other.'

Theo was still snoring and didn't even look up when Seamus shouted, 'See you later,' and slammed the door behind him. I realised that I'd missed and liked the thought of someone coming back to me and my home.

While I knew I was still getting used to myself, knowing what I did and didn't like without having to be told, I would always miss being part of something. I hated the thought of no one really caring about me. The girls cared about me, of course they did, but they were so busy with their lives and jobs that they barely had time during the day to go to the loo, let alone speak to their mum. But it was that very reason that I had to do this for myself. Start living my life for me instead of for everyone else. I couldn't sit around waiting for life to happen. I had to get off my arse and *make* life happen.

My phone pinged with a text message, making Theo lift his head lazily and peer at me from one eye.

'Oh, God, Theo. Michael. What now?'

> Jo. Have you found that WIFI code yet? This is getting beyond a joke. Claudia is giving me hell because she's using up all her data.

I deleted the message, muttering, 'Oh, fuck off.'

Another ping.

'Oh, Theo, what does he want now?'

I couldn't resist opening the message. Years of being available to my family at all times was a habit that I was going to have to work on, but this time it wasn't my ex-husband, and the person who was texting brought a smile to my face.

> Don't get lunch. I'll bring something back for us. My treat for you having Theo and it'll save you getting anything before you go out. Text me if there's anything you don't like or are allergic to. Also I may have an offer for you that you might not be able to turn down.

Smiling to myself, I grabbed my laptop and started googling 'how to find a job when you can't do anything'. It was time I started to look around, the money I did have wasn't going to last forever. Strangely there was nothing jumping out, but something would crop up, I was sure of it.

16

'A receptionist? Anyone can answer a phone. And you can look after a diary too, so take bookings. Anyway, darling, don't say you have no skills. You used to run your family calendar, it's the same thing.'

'True.' Mum always believed in me. It was a good idea to call her.

Maybe there was a hotel around that might need some help.

'You could work in a café. Cooking, clearing up and the like. You've been skivvying after that family of yours for years without any help. Lazy buggers.'

'Mum. They're not lazy, they just liked things done a certain way.'

'Darling, there's no way that any other children I knew could put their dirty washing in the laundry and have it hanging back in the wardrobe by the time they got up the next day. Maybe you should run a launderette.'

'Ha. Yes, I did teach them that, didn't I?'

'You did. I don't know why, darling. I never taught you to do it.'

'I just liked that they needed me, Mum.'

'You're a pushover, more like. Anyway, why do you want a job?'

I knew that if I rang Mum and asked her, she'd be full of bright ideas, but then I forgot that I'd have to tell her the reason why.

'Ah, now there's a story!'

Guilt was weighing heavy on my heart when I explained that despite the money I'd managed to save, I still needed more.

'I'm sorry, darling, but I'm not even able to get access to anything more that's not tied up for years. Can't that tosser of an ex-husband loan you anything from his new business?'

Deciding that I wouldn't ask Michael if he were the last person on earth did make me wonder whether I was cutting off my nose to spite my face, but I wanted to show him that I could do this without him. He'd laughed when I told him my plans and said that it would never work out. To go cap in hand, begging for help, wasn't going to do anything for my self-esteem.

'Actually, I take that back. Don't ask him for anything. Let me have a think, darling, about what you'd be best at. Although I'm sure there's nothing you can't turn your hand to.'

'Sadly, I don't think putting that on a CV would stand for much. Maybe I could go and do some cleaning for people?'

'Would you really want to do that though, darling? Cleaning up after your own family is one thing. Cleaning up after someone else you don't know is a whole different matter. Just imagine the things that you might have to deal with if you did that?'

'To be honest, Mum, I don't think I can afford to be choosy. And judging on the cleaners I've had in the past, I'm sure I could do a far better job than some of them. I used to spend my time after they'd gone redoing the things that they hadn't done to my liking. The last one I had clattered and banged around a lot, but

I'm not sure what she did because the house wasn't ever any cleaner after she'd gone and she used to sneak off half an hour early if I wasn't in. I came home unexpectedly one day when she was just leaving.'

Mum laughed. 'Your house was always spotless anyway. Not sure why you even had a cleaner.'

'It was Michael. He liked to tell people he was spoiling his wife by giving her a cleaner. A status thing, I suppose.'

'Idiot. Never did like him.'

'Yes, I think you did mention that once or twice.' We both laughed.

'Will you be OK, darling? I hate to think of you stuck there not knowing anyone in a house that isn't quite what you thought it would be. If you wanted me to, I could see if I could move some of the investments I have around.'

'Mum, you've been amazing and generous enough. I'll be fine once I find a way. Just keep thinking and if you know of anything I can do, let me know.'

'Will do. I need to fly now anyway as Barry has just shouted down that he needs some help in the bedroom and, without wishing to be vulgar, the last time he did that, he'd...'

'That's enough already, Mum, thanks. Speak soon. Love you.'

It was the utter silence in my old house that bothered me, but since I'd lived here, I'd tune into a local radio station which played a selection of music from across the years. Now that I could listen entirely to the music of my choice, I found that I was singing and dancing along to the songs and it lifted my mood tremendously. I'd started to put the music on when I woke in the mornings and left it on most of the day. I even left it on when I went out because it was nicer to come back to something other than sheer silence. This tiny little thing made such a difference to my day and put a spring in my step.

'Fancy a little walk, Theo?' His ears pricked up at the sound of the W word, so I grabbed his lead and we headed out of the French doors, through the dunes to the beach. I walked past a couple who appeared to be a similar age to me, who were walking along, each holding the hand of a little girl. I know these days you shouldn't really presume anything but at a guess, I'd say they were her grandparents. It made me sad to think that the future I'd thought I was going to have one day was going to be very different. Where I thought that Michael and I would be like that couple. If ever one of our daughters got round to blessing us with grandchildren, I would now be doing that alone. And whilst I knew it was fine to be alone, that no one should really need another person to make them happy, I did like the idea of having someone to do it all with me. It gave me purpose and that's what I felt to be lacking in life. Taking a walk would maybe give me some perspective, I decided, and give me time to think away from the mess of the house.

17

Kicking off my trainers seemed like the natural thing to do as Theo and I paddled in the shallow waves that lapped at the shore. When we saw a figure walking towards us, wrapped up in a big coat, it took me a while to realise that it was the old lady who I'd met in the shop. The one who owned the smallholding on the hill. I smiled as she approached with four different-coloured Labradors. They looked like they were a bit of a handful, and the leads were all wrapped around each other.

'Good morning.'

'Hello there.' We stood and faced each other, neither of us knowing really what to say next but because we'd both stopped, I felt like I had to fill the void. I hated awkward silences and the strange staring expression in her eyes was making me feel a little uncomfortable. What was it about this woman that made me feel this way?

'Lovely day again.'

'It is that.'

'I'm Jo. We met in the store a few days ago.'

'We did.' Gosh, she was hard work. There was a little bit of me that wondered whether I should even bother, but then it popped into my head how loneliness could be awful – that I knew for myself – so I made the extra effort and knowing that she'd recently lost her best friend made me feel sorry for her. I realised that I didn't know a great deal about the area beyond my new home and every day is a school day, as my mum always says. As Tessa was also Aunty June's best friend, I wanted to do justice to both her and the area.

Still, her piercing blue eyes never left my face.

Another awkward silence and I was desperately trying to think of something interesting to say. For some reason I wanted her to like me and approve of me being in Aunty June's house.

I went to speak but this time she interrupted me, garbling her next words.

'I didn't want to let these four off the lead. There are skylarks and meadow pipets nesting in the dunes, so we don't want badly behaved dogs like these four disturbing their habitat. Us doggers can all help the wildlife, you know.'

'How so?' I asked, trying not to laugh. I hoped she had no idea what the word 'dogger' could be misconstrued as.

'So many people leave their dog mess behind,' she continued, 'despite the huge signs we put up, but it fertilises the land, meaning that brambles and nettles are encouraged to grow. These are not the things that we want growing in the dunes. We want to keep all our glorious species like carline thistles, ragwort and the beautiful pyramidal orchids. The dunes are an absolutely teeming with these things if you know what you're looking for. Have you seen this sea holly, for instance?' She pointed out a plant just to my right.

I wanted to keep her talking now we seemed to have a bit of a rapport going and she seemed to trust me enough to finally want to chat.

'Oh, that? I thought that was a common thistle, to be honest.'

'Looks similar, but if you look closely, they're very different. They have really waxy leaves and have some amazing health benefits too. They were used in the old days for chronic coughs and consumption. Nowadays, as well as being good for the lungs, they're known to be a good diuretic, good for period pains and helpful for conditions like sweating.'

I rolled my eyes. 'Now God knows this middle-aged woman knows about that!' We both laughed. It knocked ten years off her.

'Listen to me wittering on. Sorry. I must be boring you. I'm part of the local wildlife conservation society so I find it all fascinating and sometimes forget that others don't.' Tessa looked down at the sand.

'Not a problem to me at all. I'd love to learn more about it all. I love to garden but don't know much about wild habitats. Maybe we could walk together one day and you could teach me more.'

'Only if you mean it, obviously, and are not just being polite.'

I smiled at this funny old lady who was nothing but direct.

'I do.'

'Can't stand people who say they're going to do something and then it never happens. Especially if it's just because you feel sorry for me because I'm old.'

I reached out and touched her arm.

'I *do* mean it.'

For a minute, time stood still and I thought she was going to brush my hand away. Her brow furrowed and I thought I saw a flash of anger as her eyes went to my hand and then lingered on my face. Maybe I shouldn't have put my hands on her. Not everyone was as touchy-feely as me. It never occurred to me that some people might not like it.

Tessa nodded.

'Then in that case, that might be nice.' Despite the earlier conversation, she seemed to have gone back to being awkward. Her dogs had calmed down somewhat though, and were quietly getting acquainted with Theo by some hearty bum sniffing.

'I'm a quick learner. Despite my menopause brain.'

She tutted incredibly loudly. 'This menopause malarkey?'

'Yes,' I answered as it dawned on me that somehow, she'd managed to make those three words a whole sentence.

'We just got on with it in my day. Never heard the Queen moaning about hot flushes and the like, did you? What was it she used to say now? Never explain. Never complain. People could learn a lot if they thought about that every time they opened their mouth.'

Her statement made me realise what a difference there was between generations. Tessa nodded up at the house.

'So this is all yours now then. You settling in?'

'I think I'm getting there.' We both looked up at it.

'It was such a beautiful place!'

'Hopefully it will be again at some point,' I said. 'I've been working hard. You must come over one of these days and see the progress I'm making. Well, when I say must, I don't mean must, obviously.' I knew I was fumbling my words. 'Only if you'd like to. You don't have to. I just thought... well... you must miss her. June, I mean.'

'I do.' She nodded and she turned her head towards the sea. 'Friends for life.'

'Well, the offer is there. The kettle is always on. Do feel free to pop in. You'd be welcome anytime.'

'Thank you kindly. Good day to you, Joanna.' Tessa nodded and walked away.

What an interesting lady. As I watched her walk along the beach, I wondered what her story was. When I first met her, Mary in the shop said that she was made a dame in the seventies but that she never talked about it. Sometimes people had the most unlikely lives. Maybe she'd open up a bit to me if she did come and see me. Any friend of Aunty June's was a friend of mine. I always considered her to be a good judge of character and she didn't stand for any nonsense.

As I headed further down the dunes, counting my blessings that I was lucky enough to head out of my back door and literally be on the beach, it struck me that I'd never told her my name was Joanna. Since I'd been here, I'd only ever introduced myself as Jo. How odd. I didn't give it a second thought though as, at that moment, a small wave washed over my bare feet. As Theo barked with joy, I hoped that I would never take how lucky I was to live in such a beautiful place as this for granted.

I raised my head upwards and my words were whispered into the wind.

'Thank you, Aunty June.'

18

Lunch was hurried but nice. Seamus had brought some lovely bread rolls filled with turkey and salad, and we both blushed when he said, 'Nice baps,' and, without thinking, I said, 'Thank you.' He wouldn't let me pay him back; insisted on treating me for looking after Theo. It had honestly been my pleasure, he was not a scrap of trouble.

I told him briefly about my morning: meeting Dame Tessa, and her knowledge about the local habitat. Seamus told me her full name was Tessa Wylie and I thought I might have a little google about her later. Although I doubted very much that there would be anything to find. The medal thing might just be gossip. Seamus also told me that his dad was a member of the same local conservation society and that they met in the village hall once a month. He suggested either chatting to his dad or going along to the meeting. I could probably do both – for some reason I wanted to make a good impression to Tessa.

When Seamus left, I went to the notepad that was hanging up on the side of the fridge and wrote down 'first Thursday of month' so that I wouldn't forget. If I could pluck up the courage to drag myself there on my own, that would keep me busy for another evening. When I'd arrived here in Sandpiper Shore, I'd wondered what I might fill my time with, but it seemed that there was plenty to keep me occupied. I also wrote down 'library' as I'd spotted one in the town but it was closed when I drove past. They might have some books on coastal habitats and hopefully if I did some research first I wouldn't be such an ignoramus when I turned up.

I gathered up my jewellery roll, which contained most of the jewellery that Michael had ever given me, and placing it at the bottom of my handbag, I headed out to the jewellers in town. I wondered whether I'd miss the car after it was collected tomorrow but actually, when it came to it, didn't think I would. Everything I needed was within walking distance and if I wanted to go further afield, there was a small pretty train station that would take me straight to St Ives. Worst case, if I missed it that much, I could buy myself a little old banger to get me from A to B. In fact, that thought made me smile. I could imagine how horrified Michael would be if he knew I was driving around in something without a Range Rover or Jaguar badge on the front. Maybe I should do that just to wind him up, I thought.

'Hi. I'm Jo Jenkins. I made an appointment with you yesterday,' I said as I walked into the shop.

'Of course, hope you don't mind having a seat, Jo. My brother-in-law just called to say he's running about fifteen minutes late. Could I make you a drink while you're waiting?' She was beautifully spoken and she exuded glamour from every pore. Her clothes looked expensive and classy and she had an air of calm confidence about her. I can't imagine she'd have any issues with her self-esteem. She also seemed genuinely nice too. A lovely presence to be in.

'That's very kind of you... erm...' I couldn't remember if she'd told me her name when I met her the first time. If she had, it wasn't coming to me now anyway.

'Did I tell you my name? I'm Emma, by the way. Not sure if I told you that. Bloody brain fog makes me forget most things these days.'

'Join the club. If it's not too much trouble, I'd love a coffee.'

'No trouble at all. I was only offering because it was an excuse for me to have one as well. Bloody electric is off in my house again and I've been rushed off my feet this morning and haven't had chance to make one yet. For the third day in a row, the young girl who helps out here has called in sick, so I'm just trying to get through everything we need to do before the auction next week.'

'You do auctions too?'

Emma nodded. 'You name it, we sell it. Furniture, jewellery, household items, in fact anything that people want us to sell on their behalf. We do house clearances too, which is really interesting.'

'Gosh, I bet. If you sell furniture, you should see some of the stuff that has been left in the house that I've just moved into. God knows how the owner got it in, because it's huge. It's beautiful, but not really to my taste. There's also a load of old tat that I've found in the loft too.'

'You know what they say. One man's tat is another man's treasure. Nothing you want to keep?'

'To be honest, I've got enough stuff of my own, although it is a big place.' When I explained where the house was, Emma said that she actually knew it and had been round to give June a quote not that long ago. This made me feel quite guilty that I was considering giving some of her stuff away.

'If you want me to pop round when I'm over that way, I'd be happy to. I'm the furniture expert and Joseph is our jewellery connoisseur. I could go through the list that I drew up for her and see if there's anything that you're interested in getting rid of.'

'That would be amazing. Thank you.'

'A pleasure. We're here to help.'

At that moment, a four-wheel-drive navy-blue BMW pulled up at the front of the shop and Emma smiled at me. 'Here's Joseph now. I'm sure he'll take care of you. Word of warning though. Don't tell him I told you this, but don't accept his first offer for anything.'

When I came out of the shop an hour later nearly £35,000 better off, I felt like a weight had been lifted. At first, Joseph had said they'd be happy to take the jewellery to auction on my behalf and see what the best bids were. The other alternative, which I much preferred, was that they bought it from me upfront. Using Emma's advice and the one useful thing that Michael had taught me – amazing negotiation skills – we agreed on one price for the lot. I was pretty sure Michael would be horrified to know that I'd sold the jewellery he'd bought me, but there was nothing he'd given me that hadn't been tainted by the fact that he'd lied and cheated. I wondered how many other times he'd done it that I didn't know about and whether that jewellery was his attempt to lessen his guilt. I'd never know, of course, but it was a much better idea to put the money to good use – and he'd probably never find out anyway.

There was also the furniture I could get rid of, and I wanted that to happen as soon as possible; I needed as much cash as I could get my hands on. With the money from the jewellery, the money from selling the Range Rover and anything else I could get, maybe project renovation could commence.

An alert on my phone told me that a text had pinged in.

Hope the meeting went well.

> See you in the morning?
>
> Maybe you can tell me how you suddenly got your hands on that cash! Or maybe I don't want to know! LOL

How quickly Seamus and I had fallen into a little morning routine. I liked it. It gave me a reason to get up. Something to look forward to. There were days after Michael had moved out that I didn't get dressed at all. If it wasn't for Mum coming round and finding me in my pyjamas, not showered for five days and greasy hair that needed a 'bloody good scrub', I'm not sure how long I would have stayed that way.

I quickly fired off a text.

> If you're lucky you might get something extra special

The three little dots appeared and then disappeared.

I put my phone down and went to throw open the French doors. Having them closed made me feel cooped up and I wanted the fresh air in my lungs, even if I was pottering in the house.

> Now that's not a text I get every day.
>
> #FeelingLucky

I peered at the message. I really should wear my specs more often. There was a winky face at the end and then, when I reread my own text to Seamus, I laughed to myself. Here was me flirting without intending to. Maybe this new life was bringing about a whole new me after all.

> Hope it doesn't disappoint you that I meant that I'd cook you a bacon sandwich.

> If you pop me a runny egg on the top, you might just be my most favourite person in the world ever

Whilst I could have happily sat texting with Seamus back and forth for much longer, I had a very long list of things to do. But now, due to our flirty banter, I would be doing it with a smile on my face.

19

Just as I'd handed Seamus a bacon and egg sandwich on thick fresh crusty bread that had not long come out of the breadmaker, my phone rang.

'Hi, Jo, it's Emma here. So sorry to bother you so early, but I'm passing through the village this afternoon and I wondered if you might be in. Probably around 4 p.m. No time like the present, hey?'

'That would be perfect. Thanks, Emma. See you later.'

Seamus stood grinning at me.

'What?'

'You make me smile, Jo Jenkins.'

'Because...?'

His smile disappeared and he became way more serious. He sighed and ran his thumb across his bottom lip.

I gulped, his eyes locked onto mine. My heart missed a beat. I wasn't sure I'd ever seen a man who wasn't on my TV screen ever do something that could make me feel this way. I was not normally what you would call a swooner.

I looked away first, feeling my cheeks starting to get a little on the warm side.

'You've hardly been here a week and you're building up a little community of your own. There's your new friend Michelle who you've been to the pub with, Kate next door, who told me she'd met you, Mary at the shop, who asked me how you were getting on when I popped in last night and Dad also seems to be a fan of yours, wanting to know how you're settling in. Now you are chatty with someone else and arranging to meet up later. You're such a people person. I wish I could be more like you. Dad tells me I'm a grumpy so and so and prefer my own company. Said it's no wonder I'm on my own. Also, how do you get warm bread like this first thing in the morning? You're amazing.'

Cooking was my thing and I knew I was good at it, so I very happily took that compliment. It also hadn't gone unnoticed that he'd said he was single. It was nice to know that a bit of flirty banter wasn't out of order, even though I had enough on my plate at the moment without thinking about the possibility of a relationship. I was far from ready from that.

'Well, my breadmaker has a timer setting so I can put the ingredients in the night before and voila. At the push of a button, the next morning, you get fresh warm bread. Also,' I added, 'what your dad says is rubbish. You're lovely to be around.'

'Well, that's very kind of you. Maybe you're opening my eyes and making me realise that people aren't so bad after all.'

We stood staring at each other for what seemed like an eternity until Theo barked, breaking the moment. Seamus put his hand into his pocket and threw a biscuit onto his makeshift bed by the window. He was lying in that patch of sun again and was properly making himself at home each time he came round.

'So which bank did you rob, Jo Jenkins?'

'No banks. I just sold my worldly possessions.'

I explained that I'd managed to sell my jewellery to Emma and he raised an eyebrow.

'Does that not upset you?'

'I thought long and hard about it before I did it, if that's what you're worried about. As money, it's far more valuable to me. They're just things and things that maybe once upon a time meant something to me, but now sit in a safe and never get worn. It's better that I have some additional cash for the house. Once I have the money from selling the car too, then at least it means that I can get things moving in here.'

'Well, it's certainly a good way to get your hands on some cash. But I'd be gutted if I had to sell a Range Rover. It's a gorgeous car.'

'It's way too big for me and I never wanted it in the first place. It's a nightmare to park and I'd much rather have something not as flashy. It was more of a status symbol for my ex-husband. Also, I do wonder, with all of these presents he bought me, whether they were given because he was feeling guilty about something. I just can't seem to get that out of my head.'

'Surely that's not the case.'

'Who knows? Anyway, my mind is made up. It's going today. So we have some money to spend on this place. Just not sure where to start first.'

'Well, it's Saturday tomorrow and I'm not working. How about when I come round in the morning after taking this one out,' he ruffled Theo's ears, clearly very fond of him, 'we put a firm plan together. We can do some measuring up and working out costs. We could even pop into town to have a look round at some materials if we need to.'

'Don't you have anything better to do on a Saturday?'

He laughed. 'Actually, no.'

'You saddo!'

'Oh, that's harsh.' He held his hand to his heart. 'I'm wounded.' He laughed.

'I'm only saying it because I'm the same. I don't have any plans either.'

'Shall we be saddos together then? What do you think? Also, I'm being totally selfish here, you know.'

'Because...'

'Because I love spending someone else's money.'

I swatted him with the tea towel I was holding and he laughed.

'No, seriously, I live in a modern pad that needs literally nothing doing to it. God knows why, but it seemed like a good idea when I bought it. So to be tinkering and messing around in an old beauty like this is really ticking all those joy boxes for me. I'll honestly be as happy as a pig in shit. Or should I say peg in shit.'

I laughed, remembering Dame Tessa and for some unknown reason a little shiver ran up my spine. I brushed it off and it disappeared as quickly as it appeared.

Laughing with Seamus made me feel lighter. I felt like I'd laughed more since I'd lived here than I'd laughed in years. Maybe I'd forgotten how to have fun. Even to be funny. When I was at school, my friends used to say that I was the funniest person they knew. I knew that I was quick-witted and razor-sharp when I was in my teens, but being married seemed to suppress my personality without me realising how much I'd changed. Michael wanted and needed a wife who was demure and well-behaved. Not someone who laughed so much she cried and blew snot bubbles from her nose. That was always my party piece, unlike my childhood best friend Beth, whose pièce de résistance was to do a fanny fart on request.

'Do you really not have anything you'd rather be doing?'

'It will be my pleasure. Unless you don't want my help.'

'Actually, I was thinking that maybe we could help each other out.'

Seamus chewed the inside of his cheek. Something I'd noticed him do on several occasions while he was pondering.

'How so?'

'You said the other day that you struggle to fit everything into your days and feel guilty after getting back from work that you don't want to take Theo out for a walk when you are shattered. Maybe I could help you out and walk him from time to time or you could drop him round here, in exchange for some other favours in return.'

'And what favours might they be, Jo Jenkins?' He tipped his head to one side and those big brown eyes connected with mine again. It was like he could see right through to my soul. God! Sometimes I looked at him and didn't think I'd ever seen a man quite so handsome. As heat began to rise in my body, I had to look away before I embarrassed myself. I could feel a flush coming on and I didn't think this one was down to my age.

'Jobs that I might need doing around the place, I meant.' I turned away so he couldn't see me blush.

'Are you trying to take advantage of me?'

I couldn't bring myself to look at him and so busied myself brushing away imaginary crumbs from the dresser.

'Ha. This fat, frumpy middle-aged woman wouldn't even attempt to do something like that these days.'

'It's a shame you can't see what I can see, Jo Jenkins. When I look at you, it's far from that. And that's not something I say lightly. Dad always says I'm the person who never gives a compliment.'

This time I did swing round to look at him and got lost in those eyes exactly like I knew I would. I gulped.

'Well, in that case, thank you. It's been a long time since I've been paid one. I'll accept it gratefully. After nearly twenty-five years of marriage, I think my ex-husband forgot what a compliment was.' I wondered when I'd stop thinking about Michael all the time and bringing him up in conversation. He'd been such a huge part of my life and I seemed to still talk about him such a lot.

'He's a fool.'

Seamus's eyes locked onto mine again. I felt like I needed to be very careful with this man. I was feeling things that I didn't think I should be. I needed to spend some time discovering myself and what I wanted and needed, not throwing myself at the first good-looking man who happened to be in my life.

This time, he was the first to look away.

'Right, come on, Theo. Time to go. You do realise that you don't live here, don't you, pal?'

The mood had changed in a split second and I wondered whether I'd imagined what he'd said.

Theo reluctantly stood, stretching before he strolled over to Seamus, leaning into him bum first. I opened the door to see them out and could see Kate from next door tending to some flowers in the front grounds.

'Morning, Seamus. Morning, Jo. What a lovely morning.' She grinned widely.

Great, now she was thinking that I was a complete strumpet and that he'd been here all night.

'Morning, Kate.' Seamus raised a hand to wave at her before turning back round to me and leaning across to kiss my cheek. A stray hair had fallen from my scraped-up hair and he reached out and gently tucked it behind my ear. 'See you soon, Jo Jenkins.' When he reached the bottom of the path, he turned round, winked and shouted loudly, 'Thanks for *everything*.'

I headed straight back inside, not sure where my head was. I wasn't ready for a chat with Kate right now. I needed to gather my thoughts because at that very moment, my mind was in complete turmoil, and all I could think about was how I would be feeling if he really had spent the night.

20

'So nice to see you again, Jo. Hope you've not been working too hard today.'

Emma swept into the house that afternoon leaving a cloud of expensive perfume behind her.

'Just trying to create some space and find the right homes for things. Nothing too strenuous. Tea? Coffee? Come through.' I invited her to follow me and flicked the kettle on. As I got two china mugs down from the cupboard above, she walked over to the huge French doors and let out a sigh.

'I do love that view.'

I smiled.

'Lush, isn't it? I pinch myself every day.'

'I bet you do. This is a bit of a surprise, isn't it?' She stood back and looked around the room.

'What, the cottage?'

'Yeah, it looks like a normal size from outside, but it's like a Tardis. It's huge. And gorgeous!'

'Well, hopefully it will be again at some point. I'll take you on a guided tour later. Come and have a look from the decking. You could be anywhere in the world.'

'Oh my God, Jo, you have really hit the jackpot here.' She looked upwards. 'Don't tell me all the rooms have a view of some kind. I will be so jealous.'

I chewed the inside of my mouth and slowly nodded my response.

'You jammy cow!' We both laughed.

'Do you live far from here?'

'Not really but my house is up for sale.'

'On the move, are you?'

'Sadly, yes.' She took a deep breath. 'I still find it really hard to accept. And to say. My husband died last year and I just can't bring myself to live in the house any more.'

'I'm so sorry to hear that. That must have been really hard. And you're so young too.'

I blew out air. What did you say to someone under circumstances like this? There was nothing you could say to make anything better.

'Yeah, so was he. Just had his fiftieth birthday. Heart attack, totally out of the blue. Lucky for him he wouldn't have known a thing. But hard for the rest of us that we never got time to say goodbye.'

'God, Emma.'

This called for something stronger than a cuppa in my opinion.

'Don't suppose you fancy a gin instead?' I offered.

Emma glanced at her watch and I noticed that it was very similar to the Cartier one I used to have. She obviously had excellent taste. She was one of those people who exuded elegance. Her clothes were classy, her hair perfectly cut into a short, blunt, burgundy bob and make-up perfectly done.

She seemed to dither a little in making a decision.

'Oh, bugger it. I'm on call for the shop but there's nothing I'd love more than a G&T right now. I've had a doozy of a day. And I've literally got nothing to go home for.'

'Well, in that case, why don't you have a seat out here and get yourself comfy, I'll go and pour us a drink.'

* * *

The ice and lime segments in the tall tumblers clinked against the side of the glass, making a musical tinkling sound. Emma had her eyes shut and her head facing the late-afternoon sun. I thought she might have fallen asleep, so placed the glasses down quietly on the low table.

'This... is... bliss.' She sighed. 'I also think it's the first time in just over a year that someone has made me a drink at the end of the working day.'

I was struggling to know what to say to her and hesitated.

'Please just treat me normally, Jo. I'm so tired of that look in everyone's eyes. That pitying look when people don't know what to say. Some are scared to ask me how I am. Others are scared to come anywhere near me and cross the road and wave or they walk up another aisle of the supermarket rather than stop to chat. I mean no one really knows what to say to the woman who has a dead husband, do they?'

I felt myself pull a face and then immediately apologised, knowing I was doing exactly what she detested.

'So what *do* you say to the woman with a dead husband? What would help?'

'Buggered if I know!' she laughed. 'I never said I had the answers, now, did I? Sometimes you just want to hear that someone doesn't know what to say. That's all you need, rather than them not mention it.'

'What was he like?' I whispered. 'Would you like to talk about him?'

'Now *that's* a lovely thing to say. It's very rare that anyone asks me that. Most people, even my family, act like he was never in my life in the first place. It's bizarre. And I *love* talking about him. It keeps the memories alive. I'm not sure if they think it'll remind me that he's died and that's the issue. I mean it's not like I'm ever likely to forget, is it?'

She promptly went on to tell me all about Ben and before we knew it we were at the bottom of our glasses and I asked her if she'd like a top-up, to which she agreed, deciding that she'd leave her car here and get a taxi home. I was feeling a bit squiffy myself so put some crisps in a dish to soak up the alcohol and took them out on a tray.

'Jo, I haven't felt this relaxed for months. This house seems to have magical properties. And the fact that you can walk down a path at the bottom of your garden and be on the beach is just so amazing.'

'That's how I felt when I first came here, you know.' I relayed the story of when I first came to visit and how I'd ended up living in Sandpiper Shore.

'It suits you. You seem right at home here, as if you've been here forever.'

'It feels like that too. It's like I've found my soul home, if that doesn't sound like I'm a complete headache.'

'Don't mind me. I talk to my dead husband all the time. I love a lunatic.' We laughed. I felt so comfortable in her company and between us, we didn't stop talking.

'Do you eat pizza, Emma? I'll have to eat something soon and it's just about all I've got in the freezer at the mo.'

She smiled at me.

'You are a godsend, Jo. Did someone send you deliberately to help me?'

A tear slid down her cheek but to ask her if she was OK seemed such a stupid question.

'You're so kind. This is the first time that someone has done something nice for me since Ben died.' She squeezed my hand. 'Thank you.'

Ridiculously, as this was only the third time I'd met her, I felt like I'd known her all my life. She was so easy to chat with and between us, we put the world to rights. From menopause to brain fog, and from family woes to financial worries, I couldn't remember the last time I'd let go like this and I certainly hadn't drunk this much for a good few years. When we had the third drink, I fired up the patio heater as, despite it being the nicest day of the year so far, it had started to get a little nippy. When we had the fourth glass, I brought out throws after Emma had refused to come indoors, saying that the calming sounds of the sea were therapeutic and made her feel better than she'd felt for months. I suggested that might be the gin.

Emma suddenly shot up and gasped.

'How awful am I? I haven't even looked at any of the furniture or belongings that I came here for. You haven't given me the guided tour you promised either.'

'Well, you can say no if you like and it may just be coincidence but I made up the spare room recently. It's not been decorated for years, and is a bit old-fashioned, but it does have a gorgeous view and French doors and if you're awake in time you might even get to see the sun come up.'

'That's one of the loveliest suggestions I think anyone has ever made. I think you are my new favourite person in the whole wide world. OK, let's do it. And then in the morning, I can take a look at everything. As long as you don't think I'm going to burgle you in the middle of the night or anything.'

We both laughed.

'I think I'm more likely to steal that watch than you burgle anything of mine. You've already had most of my worldly possessions. Also, I'm too tired these days to be bothered about much so if someone wanted to burgle me, I'd just let them go ahead without putting up too much of a fight.'

'In that case, and as long as it's not too much trouble, I'd love to stay. Thank you. You're very kind.'

'It's nice to have the company.'

As I sank down onto my pillows that night, I realised that once again, I'd spent a lot of the evening laughing with a new acquaintance and also that I was starting to feel less alone. Like I was making friends and that maybe I was finally belonging somewhere.

21

'Shit! My head hurts! How are you up and looking as bright as a button at this time of the day?' I asked.

Emma was sitting in the chair by the French doors, wrapped in a blanket, with a fully made-up face, looking glorious, the cool, fresh air making her perfect bob sway slightly in the breeze. She was also drinking what smelt like coffee from the biggest mug I have and rarely use.

'Ah, my secret pint of water and paracetamol before bed. And a huge coffee in the morning. Works for me every time.'

'I honestly can't remember the last time I drank that much. You are a bad influence, Emma.'

'Ah, once in a while doesn't hurt. It's been ages since I've had company to drink with. I've spent a while drinking on my own to just make myself feel better. And that's a slippery slope. Have a seat and I'll make you a coffee. I know it's only six thirty but it's such a fabulous time of day and when you wake up somewhere like this, you just have to appreciate the view. I mean, look at that!'

Pulling my dressing gown tighter around me, I stood at the

open window and looked out towards the sea, which was twinkling in the early-morning sunshine, the waves gently lapping at the shoreline. The long grasses on the dunes either side of the wide pathway down to the sand rippled gently in the light wind.

It was hard to describe the feeling I had when I looked at the view. Maybe it was joy; maybe it was disbelief that it was real, but it was as if I got a whoosh of something lovely within me and, quite simply, it made my heart happy. Every time I doubted my decision to move here, which was quite often, especially when I spoke to the girls, looking out of that window put all my negative thoughts to one side and I knew it was right for me.

Emma handed me a mug of steaming coffee and I sat in the opposite chair to where she'd been sitting and I pulled the throw across my knees.

'I'm so sorry, Jo. I should never have just offered you coffee within your own house. That was so rude of me but I honestly feel so comfortable here. Safe too if that doesn't sound too mad. And honestly, if you *are* after another person to rent the holiday let or the garage space, I would seriously consider it, you know.'

It was certainly something to think about. I needed to recoup some costs to make this work for me but could I go with the first two people that had approached me? It was a little too much for my head this morning but as we sat and nattered like old friends, it seemed like the right thing to do. It was a huge decision to make but maybe I had to have a little faith in myself and my ability to get things right. A chat with Mum might be a good idea. I would give her a call and talk it through. She was so great at grounding me.

'Before I forget, I don't know if you know that there's a suitcase on top of the wardrobe in the room I'm staying in. I was trying to find out the name of the manufacturer and as I moved the wardrobe a little, it nearly smashed me on the head as it fell off. Bloody heavy too it was. I didn't like to go mooching in it, but it was so tucked towards the back, I wasn't sure if you knew about it or not.'

'I've been meaning to look at that for ages. I saw it when I first moved in and keep forgetting about it. I did have a quick look inside and put it down to a load more shite for me to get rid of.'

'Ah, well, have a good look through. You never know what little gems you might find. I recently had someone find a similar thing and it was a case full of cash.'

'Gosh, that would come in handy right now, I must admit. And finders keepers. Isn't that what they say?'

'Well, if that's the case, Jo, then maybe it belongs to me.' Emma grinned.

'Ha, you wish. I think what's found in my house belongs to me. It does seem strange saying that this is my house, you know. I wonder if I'll ever get used to that. I'm still totally flummoxed by the fact that Aunty June left it to me and not Michael, who was, after all, her nephew.'

'Who knows. Did the solicitor not throw any light on that situation at all?'

'Only that the will was registered years ago and that the cottage had always been willed to me. She said she knew how much I'd loved it when we visited years ago and when she recently went to the solicitor and was asked if she was still happy with the arrangements she'd made, she said that nothing would make her happier than seeing me in the cottage, loving it as much as she had all these years. All very odd.'

'She obviously wanted you to have it very much.'

'Yeah, maybe.' I shrugged. 'I suppose it's still just such a bloody massive surprise, that's all. Probably even more so for Michael.'

'God, yes, especially if he thought he might inherit it one day.

What a shame for him.' Her pinched smile made me laugh. 'I've actually shoved the case down the side of the bedside table. Hope that's OK but I'm not tall enough to put it back on top of the wardrobe.'

'Perfect, thank you. I'll have a look when I get five minutes.'

I heard a little bark and all of a sudden Theo came tumbling through the French doors, panting and looking very happy with himself. He plonked himself down on the blanket which was on the floor. I laughed, wondering where on earth he'd come from, and smiled when, ten seconds later, Seamus appeared on the beach path jogging towards the house, breathless too.

Emma blew out her cheeks.

'Christ, Jo! I didn't think that view could get any better, but boy oh boy, it just did.'

I laughed. 'Good morning, Seamus. I'd have got dressed if I'd known you'd be this early.'

'Morning, Jo. Don't mind me, you look all lovely sat snuggled up there. I'm so sorry to interrupt. Well, Theo is. Cheeky little bugger. Look at him sitting there all proud of himself.'

Emma reached out to shake his hand.

'Hi, I'm Emma. Charmed, I'm sure.'

When he shook hers, I studied him. He really was so lovely.

'Hi, I'm Seamus. And this is my very cheeky dog who seems to have taken a shine to our Jo here.'

Emma raised her eyebrows. 'Yeah, she's got a special something about her, hasn't she?'

Seamus locked eyes with me. Seconds passed before he spoke.

'She sure has.'

The awkward silence needed breaking, so I offered him a drink and when he said yes, I went to potter around in the kitchen.

Emma came in behind me and put her empty cup on the side.

'You're a dark horse, madam. You've only been here five minutes and seem to have made friends with the most handsome man in the world.'

'Is he? I hadn't noticed.' I scratched at my neck.

'If I wasn't a grieving widow, I'm not sure how responsible I might be around him. You should totally go for it, Jo. It would do you the world of good. If he looks like that with his clothes on, can you just imagine what...'

'Stop right there, madam. It's not like that. We're just friends and he's been giving me some advice about the house. He's in the trade so he's perfect to help me. And I don't know anyone else around here anyway. Come on, let's go back out there. Or he'll think we're talking about him.'

She raised one eyebrow again and I narrowed my eyes at her and laughed as she swept back out. Emma didn't seem to walk anywhere, she definitely swept.

'I was just telling Jo how much I'd love to live here, and she said you're helping her with the cottage. Isn't it gorgeous? I'm totally in love with it.'

The two of them began to talk amongst themselves, chatting easily, with Emma explaining how she'd come over to value some of the pieces of furniture but hadn't actually got round to it. She laughed as she told him it was the plan for last night but we got tiddly on G&Ts on the decking instead.

'Why don't I go and get dressed and then I can give you that tour that I promised.'

It would do me good to get away because now Emma had put the idea of Seamus with no clothes on into my head, I couldn't think of anything else. Maybe it was a cold shower that I needed. This was supposed to be the time of my life where I was discovering myself, not throwing myself at the first handsome man that appeared before me. I'd been tied to a family for so long that I didn't even know who I was any more, but one thing I did know was that being by the sea and having lovely friends in my life was a really good start to finding out.

* * *

'Christ almighty, Jo, you've got some sorting out to do in here,' Emma said as we made our way into a downstairs room which I'd hardly been in yet myself. It was the room that Aunty June always used to call the best room, but rarely used because it didn't have as nice a view as the room she used as the lounge, and it now housed a huge dining table with two carved chairs at each end and four dining chairs on either side. A massive sideboard with shelves and shelves full of cut-glass decanters, vases and what she always used to call her trifle bowls. I had thought about using the table to do a jigsaw when I first moved in, but hadn't got very far as I didn't think it was light enough and wasn't one of my favourite rooms.

'Tell me about it. I've already done loads too.'

I thought back to the time I just stood and tried to work out what to keep and what to throw away. These were someone's memories and that felt like a huge responsibility. There were bottles of spirits with foreign names, most probably brought back from travels. There were mementoes from all sorts of occasions. Trophies on a Welsh dresser that June had clearly won at bowls and years and years of pictures. And then there were the things that I had no clue about. Photographs of people we didn't know. What did you even do with things like that? The worst of it was that, despite being married to Michael for so long, with this being his family too, I had no idea who half the people were. Did I get him involved? But then again, I hardly wanted to speak to him, let alone be talking to him about things like this. He wasn't interested in his own family memories. Not bothered about having photos of our girls when they were little. I wondered whether it was just a fundamental difference between men and women. Did you feel differently when you'd carried a person around inside you for nine months and then had to be entirely responsible once they were born? Did dads feel differently to mums?

'Helloooo!'

'God, sorry, Emma. I went off on a right tangent then.'

'I could see that.'

'Right, let's start this tour then. Lead the way. Are you coming too, Seamus?'

'Why not? I'll never tire of this beautiful old place.'

We all followed each other in a line.

'It's bigger than it looks.'

I could hear Emma sniggering behind me and it made me grin. She was so childish but hilarious at the same time. How could it be that I'd only met her properly last night?

'That's what they all say, Seamus!'

'Very funny. You coming, Theo?'

Theo lifted his head off the blanket, squinted at his master, and went back to sleep.

'Take it that's a no, then. Shall we start at the top of the house? Then we can go and look at the buildings outside. Michelle has got her heart set on the garage though. Seamus, you've also already looked at it.'

Emma laughed. 'When you told me about Michelle last night I thought she sounded lovely. Now I know she's getting the best rooms, I think I hate her.'

We laughed but Seamus, who didn't know what we'd been talking about, interrupted us.

'It would be good to get a second look though, and do some

measuring up. Then I can start to get some firm prices together for you. I've also just remembered something I meant to tell you when I arrived. I've just seen cars and moving vans stop outside of the gates of the house next door. Well, you know the one up the road.'

'Great, I won't be the new neighbour now then.'

'You won't. They have some posh cars though. Can't wait to meet them. Right, I haven't got all day to stand here gossiping about the neighbours. I'll crack on, shall I?'

Emma and I left Seamus with his tape measure after she'd oohed and aahed at the view from the Juliet balcony.

The second floor was as big as the top, probably more so as the gabled roof took some of the room off the top floor. Behind each door were boxes and boxes of stuff. Some were marked with labels, indicating that Aunty June had clearly been trying to have a sort out. There was a TV that looked like it had come from the seventies and what looked like an old record player too. I couldn't quite work out which bedroom Aunty June used for herself.

'This furniture is quite something, you know, Jo.' Emma was running her hands across a kidney-shaped dressing table and when she pulled out the top drawer, it quirkily folded back in on itself. 'G-plan at a guess. These could be collectors' items. Especially if they have the stamp on the bottom. Do you mind?'

Before I'd given her permission, she was down on her hands and knees scrambling around underneath.

'God, I'm good. Yep, G-plan for sure. It was all the rage in the seventies. This is good-quality stuff. I've got a book at home that has all the furniture listed. There are people out there that might pay good money for stuff like this.'

'Really?' I found it hard to believe. It was old, and needed a bloody good clean above anything else. I just couldn't see past the film of dust that was lying on the top.

'Yep, I promise you.' She got her phone out and started to snap photos from all angles. 'We'll be able to get more of an idea when it's clean and then we have a couple of options really. We could dress it properly and then put some pictures on Facebook – there are specialist groups on there. Some people might buy the stuff and strip it back and do it up if it's needed. It's the framework more than anything that they need. That'll take a bit of time obviously.'

'Or?'

'Or we take them to auction and see what they fetch. Ooh, this is the most fun I've had for a year! Show me more!'

22

By the time we'd seen nearly the whole of the house, I decided to show them both my favourite place of all, which I'd recently discovered underneath a load of weeds, which, once I started pulling, uncovered a heavenly little area. To the left of the cottage, the French doors led out to a wonderful patio area, around a garden pond. It was probably ahead of its time, because you could almost call it an infinity pond, with a cascading waterfall. When I first discovered it, the water didn't flow, but I filled it up using an old hosepipe and cleared out all the blockages, and the water now cascaded over the slate levels. The patio area was still overgrown with weeds, and would need a lot of hard work; old broken plant pots with bits of crumbled terracotta strewn around. There was all sorts of rubbish from old bin bags, holding God knows what as I hadn't been brave enough to open them, to broken furniture, and it looked like it had just been used as a dumping ground.

'Christ, Jo,' Seamus whispered from behind me as I led them both out and he made to step ahead of me.

'Tread carefully.' Instinctively, I reached out to touch his arm to stop him going further. 'I honestly have no idea how safe this is.'

'Not bloody very, I reckon. Specially with all this shite up here.'

'Who cares though? When you have a view like that.' Emma put her hands above her eyes and looked out to the horizon.

The most amazing thing about the whole house was that it was higher than the sand dunes and looked out over the whole bay. It was as I imagined it would be if you were in heaven, looking down.

'Wow. That is stunning. Do you know how amazing this could be?'

'Yeah, I know. But I think this has to be the lowest of priorities really. However, if you thought the view from the decking below couldn't get any better, this beats it hands down.'

'Oh, Jo, you are so lucky. This is like my dream home. Sell it to me.'

I laughed. 'I might have to. Don't joke about it just yet.'

'OK, here's a suggestion for you. Don't sell it to me. But let me live here.'

I turned to Emma and laughed again, but her face was deadly serious.

'I'm not kidding. I would move here in a heartbeat.'

My brain was starting to tick over. I looked at Seamus and he raised an eyebrow at me.

'How would that be possible though?'

'Well,' he said, 'there's such a lot of work that would need doing but it's doable.'

'I'm not sure I have enough money to do all of that.'

'Well, we could start with one building and get someone

living in that and then start on the other. It would be doable as long as you are not in any rush.'

I sat down on a broken bit of wall and steadied myself.

'I just don't know.'

'Think about it, Jo, it could be the perfect answer. And just think about the fun we could have.'

I looked across at Seamus and he shrugged.

'Your decision, Jo Jenkins. No pressure from me at all.'

'Me neither,' laughed Emma, 'but when can I move in?'

Seamus laughed. 'I know it's probably blowing your mind right now but we could probably sit down and map it all out. Do some brainstorming. Even just thinking about it might make you decide whether you want to do it or not. What I do know though is that you're going to have some upheaval whatever happens. We could do this, Jo. You could make this happen.'

I stared into his big brown eyes. He seemed so trustworthy. So nice. He was so different to Michael. Michael was all talk and no action and got other people to do things for him, never getting his hands dirty. Seamus was considering getting stuck in and helping me. I just didn't know how I could pay him. A tradesperson wasn't cheap these days.

'Don't overthink it,' he urged. 'Just consider it.'

'Much as I'd love to stand here admiring that view all day,' Emma declared, breaking the tension, 'I've got to get off to the auction house via my house for a quick shower. I smell like a badger's arse.'

My head was swimming with ideas. I'd even got an image of Seamus and me drinking wine here while watching the sun set over Sandpiper Shore. There was almost a 360 view from this area and I reckoned that you might even get a sunrise here too. Imagine watching the sun rise every morning, sitting on a chair snuggled in a huge warm blanket, hands around a steaming cup of coffee.

'Hello. Jo. Did you hear me, love? I'm going to have to get off.' I turned towards her voice. 'I've got loads of photos so I'll let you know what the auction house says. That OK?'

'That would be great, thanks so much.'

She leaned across and kissed my cheek.

'Thanks so much for having me, love. I haven't enjoyed a night so much in ages. Just what I needed. I'll call you later.'

'You're welcome any time, Emma. Now you know where I am, feel free to pop by.'

'You may regret saying that, my friend.' She tittered as she tottered off on her high heels down the hallway.

'Fancy another cuppa, Seamus?'

'Ooh, you know the way to a man's heart, Jo Jenkins.' There was that eye contact again and that little skip in my tummy.

The trill of the phone ringing brought us both back to life and I answered it before even checking who it was.

'Jo darling. Good morning!' The feeling in my tummy turned into one of gloom.

'Michael. What can I do for you?'

'We need to finalise details about the wedding.'

My heart sank. I knew this day was coming and was dreading it. My stomach felt like lead and nausea swept through my body.

'We'll both be there and of course you will too. We've been waiting for this day for years. Claudia and I are so excited.'

'Right. Yes.' I needed to get off the phone as soon as possible. I needed time to seriously think about how this was going to work. I couldn't put it off any longer. There had been a little part of me that thought Michael would never be so insensitive as to bring Claudia with him. 'Sorry, Michael, but there's someone at the door, I have to go.'

I disconnected the call before he had a chance to say anything else.

I carried on making the tea, aware that Seamus was standing behind me, watching my every move. My hands began to shake, which he must have seen because he came over and lifted the spoon from my hand and took over.

I went over to the window at the edge of the kitchen and gazed out into the distance. How could I possibly go to that wedding? How could I be in the same room as my ex-husband and that floozy that he went off with? They'd already taken my future from me, then my holiday home. And now I was expected to go and be part of these celebrations and be civil to them both. I simply could not do it. I had been putting it off for so long, hoping it would go away, but now realisation was setting in. I'd never felt so sick. Well, apart from when Michael and Claudia sat me down in our house and told me that they were in love and that he was leaving me. That was horrendous.

A cough behind me alerted me to the fact that I was no longer alone with my thoughts.

After placing the mugs down on the coffee table, Seamus put his hands on my shoulders and guided me to a chair where he practically forced me to sit down.

'So, Jo Jenkins. Are you going to tell me what that was all about then?'

'N... nothing.'

'Doesn't look like nothing from where I'm standing. A problem shared is a problem halved. Or something like that.'

I sighed loudly.

'My daughter is getting married. Well, our daughter. And I'm dreading the whole day because we'll all be together for the first time.'

'So you, your daughters and your ex-husband, you mean?'

I nodded. 'His girlfriend too.'

'Do you want to go?'

I chewed the inside of my cheek.

'If he wasn't going, I'd be there in a heartbeat. My children are my everything. It will be a fabulously lavish affair. I should know. I've paid for most of it. I know it will be a wonderful day. But I honestly don't know how I can go through with it.'

'Is there any chance that he'd go alone? Maybe he'll be tactful and leave his girlfriend behind.'

'That'll never happen. He's already said that she's looking forward to it. She's like a limpet and won't let him go anywhere without him. But that's half the problem. If she knows I'm there, I'm a bit concerned that she'll try to be friends with me. It'll feel like they'll just be rubbing my nose in it.'

'Maybe if you told him how you felt, and asked him to leave her behind, he might?'

I scoffed.

'Absolutely not. He'd tell me I was being ridiculous. I've been married to him for long enough to know exactly what he was thinking.' I was aware of how ironic this might be, considering the shock I'd had when he and Claudia had confessed all.

Seamus leaned forward in his chair, slurped at his tea and ruffled Theo's ears.

'There is one thing you could do.'

I looked at him and raised an eyebrow. I couldn't think of anything that would make the situation any better.

'Hear me out before you say no!'

I stared at him, my second eyebrow meeting my first, inviting him to continue.

'Go with someone else and make him feel jealous.'

'Ha!'

'Would it work?' he asked.

'I honestly don't know. And even if it did, I'd have to find someone first to come with me.'

'Maybe you could try an escort agency?'

I laughed.

'Do they still have those? I know they used to be all the rage, but I've not heard of that expression for ages.'

Seamus grinned. 'It's probably been replaced by Tinder or Bumble.'

'Bumble? What the hell is Bumble?' I asked.

'Another dating app.' This time it was his turn to raise his eyebrows. 'Apparently.'

We both grinned. My heartbeat had started to slow down again and I felt a little calmer.

'I don't want to join a dating app though. The thought of doing something like that scares the living daylights out of me. Have you ever done anything like that?' I realised as soon as the words were out of my mouth that it was a much too personal question to ask someone I hardly knew. 'Sorry, I don't mean to pry. Wipe that.'

'I don't mind telling you that I have. When my last partner Al dumped me, I was a bit down in the dumps and one of the lads on the building site signed me up and made me a profile. Al was a Sky engineer and was working away a lot, or so I thought. I didn't realise working actually meant having an affair behind my back. I was gutted and felt a bit of a fool. And with the dating app, to be honest, my heart wasn't in it. I met a few people who I thought might be suitable for me to get to know a bit better, but then I got ghosted a couple of times so I didn't bother again.'

I had never felt more foolish in my life and recently there had been many occasions which could have competed. I didn't realise how much what he'd said would affect me. He'd been flirty with me, yet what he was saying now made me realise that it wasn't even flirting to him because I wasn't sure any longer that he was even into women. I'd started to think that maybe there was something more than friends between us. I was shocked. How could my self-esteem have been so low that just because someone was being nice to me meant that they were thinking of me romantically? How had I managed to get it so wrong? I was such an idiot.

23

I had a massive job on my hands getting prepared for the major work to begin and it was a good thing that I did because it meant that the conversation that Seamus and I recently had wasn't my main priority. I was still trying not to think about the looming wedding. Michelle did ask me recently what I was planning to wear and was stunned when I said I hadn't a clue yet. My way of dealing with it was to pretend it wasn't happening and that was quite easy while there was so much going on within the grounds of the cottage.

Luckily there were another couple of smaller brick buildings, probably one once a coal shed and the other an outside loo, so I was able to dump a lot of the rubbish in there. I'd spent a couple of weeks where I filled the recycling bins ten times over and hired numerous skips, cursing myself for getting rid of the Range Rover before I tackled this part of the project. Whilst I was sure Aunty June might have been turning in her grave to see all the things she'd been keeping over the years get thrown out, it just had to go. It appeared that she'd saved every single butter tub she'd ever used since the 1960s. Mum said it was probably because she came from an era when they didn't have lots of money, so literally saved everything just in case they ever needed it.

While throwing away her things, it also gave me the courage to get rid of some of the items that I'd been saving too; things that I hadn't looked at for years from when the girls were at school and wedding presents that had been in the loft for years, never touched. While I'd had a good sort out when I left Staffordshire to come to Cornwall, there was still a lot from my previous life that I was hanging on to, which I now realised was unnecessary and not helpful. It felt cathartic and refreshing. At the end of each day my body ached like never before, but I was invigorated and raring to go every morning when I woke up.

Theo kept me company most days, which was nice in that I had someone to talk to, or probably at. Seamus came round and helped me at the weekends but was finishing off the electrical jobs that he had in his schedule, so that it freed up some time for the work I needed doing. We worked so well together, the flirty banter between us gone now but still plenty of jokes and laughs. I loved being in his company and had resigned myself to the fact that we would only ever be friends. And that was enough for me. After all, I didn't need a hero in my life. I needed friends. It had taken me till now to realise that it was up to me to make myself happy. That was my job and no one else's. I felt whole and felt like I'd come a really long way in the last few weeks since moving to Sandpiper Shore. And once the wedding was out of the way, along with the guilt I felt about trying not to think about what should be a really happy day and the best day of my daughter's life, I really did feel that this move was the best decision that I'd ever made.

Emma and Michelle had come over a few times over the last couple of weeks and got on like a house on fire – I knew they would – so it was looking more and more likely they'd both be moving in eventually.

I wanted to have a move around in the main house too, as Mum had mentioned that she might visit soon. Whilst I tried to move everything I could myself, I did have to ask Seamus to help me with the room that Emma had previously stayed in. As we moved the big old wooden bed to make the most of the view, I kicked something with my foot and realised that it must be the old suitcase that Emma had mentioned.

'Bear with me one sec while I just go and put this downstairs. Won't be long.'

Heavy and awkward, it was cumbersome to carry, and not knowing how strong it was I carefully placed it on the wooden chest which sat to the side of the French doors in the lounge. I was wondering if the rusty catch still worked. I fumbled with the lock, working it loose with each wiggle as it was stiff at first and it was just starting to budge a little when Seamus shouted down.

'You haven't forgotten me, have you, Jo Jenkins?' I still loved the way he said my full name. It made me feel like it was his little nickname for me. I felt special, even if it was just as a friend, and I hadn't felt special to someone for a long time.

'On my way,' I yelled back, as the catch sprang open. 'Bingo!'

I lifted the lid, and the strong musky smell of something having been stored for years got right into my nostrils. I wrinkled my nose, willing the sneeze to go away.

Inside, under the paperwork that I'd previously seen lying on the top, were bundles of old envelopes tied together with lilac ribbon and underneath them a pile of old photographs, of all sizes and shapes.

'Jo Jenkins. Are you really on your way?'

I wasn't being fair to Seamus to keep him waiting but I was

drawn to the case. An invisible force was willing me to delve further into its contents.

But knowing that this would have to wait, I closed the lid and patted the suitcase on the top, saying, 'I'll see you later!' as I did so. I was laughing to myself as I walked back upstairs, clearly going a little bit bonkers if I thought that talking to a suitcase was a sane thing to do.

'Seamus? You do know that if you have anything more exciting to do, each time I call you to ask for your help you only have to say so.'

He laughed back at me.

'This *is* the most exciting thing I do. Have you not yet noticed that there's not a great deal going on in this little seaside town?'

'Well, I've heard there's a carnival coming up soon. That sounds like something to look forward to.'

'You've clearly never been to the Sandpiper Shore carnival then. The locals all dress up in silly costumes, all have too much to eat and drink, someone normally ends up in the sea in the middle of the night and the lifeboat has to go out and rescue them. Happens every year. It's almost part of the tradition.'

'Wow. Sounds like a bundle of fun. Can't wait.' We both laughed.

'It is something to do, I suppose. It brings the community together. Even those who we don't see very often come out on carnival day. The local council arranges for the main promenade to be cordoned off so the floats can be driven down and if you're lucky you might get to join in with the local Morris dancers.'

'An opportunity not to be missed,' I said seriously. 'I used to be a Morris dancer, Seamus.'

Seamus's head swung round so quickly, it made me laugh.

'I love a bell,' I added. 'I joined a bell-ringing group at our local church once too but I got kicked out because I kept on getting my ding and my dong mixed up.' I turned away, trying to hide my smile.

'Oh my God, Jo! Really? You never cease to amaze me, you know.'

I turned round to face him and burst out laughing.

'You muppet. Of course I didn't. And I wasn't a Morris dancer either. I was pulling your leg.'

'I proper believed you then. I couldn't imagine you in a bell-ringing group. I could maybe see you Morris dancing though. Honestly, Jo, you crack me up.'

Seamus always seemed to find me funny and I loved winding him up so that he did. It made me happy to see him laugh. I really enjoyed being in his company, though I had to be careful that I didn't enjoy it too much as we were just friends who got on like a house on fire. I was glad that I knew where we stood before my already bruised heart got even more damaged.

When Seamus left later that evening, I went straight to the suitcase. It was almost as if it had been tapping away at my brain all day and part of me felt bad that I couldn't wait for him to go so that I could delve into it. I knelt down beside the wooden chest on which it was resting and took out the photographs, trying to put them into order from the dates on the back.

Most were of two women, evidently friends. Right at the bottom of the pile, I pulled out two photos larger than the rest. The first was a wedding photograph and I flipped it over but couldn't make out the names on the back, worn away years ago along with the date. The couple were smiling at each other and holding hands, clearly head over heels in love. He was a handsome man, tall, broad shouldered in his forces uniform. The woman was dressed in a smart suit with a huge hat which partially covered her face. The only thing glaringly obvious about her was she undoubtedly adored the man that she had just married. Her eyes looked familiar but I couldn't quite place her. I did wonder if it was Aunty June, or even Tessa.

The other was of the same couple but this time they were flanked by another pair: a very glamorous woman, also in a pale-coloured dress and matching jacket, and another handsome uniformed man. When I turned over this photo, I saw there was nothing written on the back but it was taken on the same day. I wondered who the couple were and whether they were still alive today.

This sent me off down a rabbit hole, cracking open a bottle of wine and fetching my own wedding album. I'd tackle June's photographs another day.

As I looked through my own wedding photographs, a few tears threatened, as I thought over the way things had turned out. What would I do with this album now? I couldn't imagine the girls would want it. And Michael certainly wouldn't. Maybe it was silly to hang on to these pictures. I put the album on the sideboard where it taunted me for a couple of hours, and after I'd finished my dinner that night, I jumped up with steely determination.

'Right. Off you go.' I headed outside and threw it into the wheelie bin, happy to hear the thud as it hit the bottom. My wedding dress could go too, I decided. And so, fuelled by Pinot Grigio, I stomped up the stairs to fetch that, and it followed with a hearty shout of, 'Have that, you motherfucker!' as the lid slammed shut.

'Evening, Jo.'

I clutched my chest and caught my breath when I saw Kate from next door standing at her front door, the telltale orange glow from the end of a cigarette and the smell of smoke wafting across the front garden.

'God, you scared the life out of me.' We both laughed at the shock she'd given me.

'Well, you were clearly having a moment and I wanted to check that all was OK.'

'Ah, yes. Just decluttering some memories.' Not sure why I felt the need to explain but if I didn't she'd probably think me a complete and utter nutcase.

'Good for the soul, Jo. A good clear-out sometimes does you the world of good.'

'You OK?' I asked. It wasn't like her to be standing out here. I usually found her sitting on her chair on her decking. 'What are you doing out the front?'

'Mum's here. Just having a crafty fag. I'm forty-seven and she still doesn't know I smoke. How ridiculous is it that I'm not brave enough to tell her?'

We both laughed again.

Before I went to bed, I went back out to the wheelie bin, this time making sure that there was no one around, and made sure that I put the remnants of my salmon dinner right on the top of the contents, so I didn't change my mind and try to retrieve them. When I woke the following morning, with a thumping hangover, and heard the refuse collection wagon outside, my heart gave a little jolt, as I wondered whether I'd done the right thing or not. However, as I stared out of the window as it pulled out of the road, it was just a little bit too late to change my mind.

24

Seamus had said that he'd pick me up around eleven o'clock the following morning, to go to the local timber merchants. I had a very leisurely start to the day; my plan was to sit in bed drinking coffee and reading but the view from my window was just too good, and to sit and watch the grasses gently sway in the wind and the ebb and flow of the sea beyond was totally mesmerising. Would I ever take it for granted? I sincerely hoped not.

By around ten o'clock, I'd showered and left my hair to dry naturally, which meant it should fall into tousled waves, but there were times when it just went into wild curls instead. Today was one of those days. But as I wasn't trying to impress anyone, I had decided that I didn't actually care. I had about an hour to myself and so I sat at my sewing machine and continued with another of the cushions that I'd made last weekend. Even though I said so myself, it was a good effort. When you had a massive house to buy soft furnishings for, to buy all new would have cost a fortune, so this was my way of keeping costs low. I'd ordered one roll of material online in the hope it would do the job and when it arrived it surprised me by being absolutely stunning. The photographs on the website didn't do it justice and it was incredibly reasonably priced too.

Lost in a world of my own, I was humming along to a tune on the radio from the eighties which I hadn't heard for years, when I had the shock of my life by a hammering at the front door. Looking at my watch, I could see it wasn't yet eleven. Was it Seamus and he was early? He was normally bang on time.

The hammering continued.

'All right. I'm coming.'

When I opened the door, Michelle was leaning against the doorframe with a big smile on her face.

'Get your gladrags on, Mrs. We're heading out.'

'I can't, Michelle. Seamus is coming to pick me up shortly. We've got some errands to run.'

'Actually, you haven't. We got Seamus to tell you he was coming but you're actually coming out with Emma and me for the day.' She thumbed behind her, to Emma who waved from Michelle's passenger seat.

I was now totally confused. 'Where are we going?'

'Now if we told you that it would spoil the surprise, wouldn't it?'

'I hate surprises though.'

'Tough. Go and get your bag and your coat if you need one. We promise it's a nice surprise, by the way. You just have to trust us.'

I'd hated surprises since Michael organised a last-minute weekend away to Paris. He'd arranged for the girls to stay with my mum and I was excited about how thoughtful he'd been. It was somewhere I'd always wanted to go. But when we arrived, he revealed he'd arranged a meeting with a potential client and the two of them spent the afternoon getting drunk in the hotel bar, while he packed me off to explore Paris on my own. I tried to make the best of it, but when I got back to the hotel, Michael was so drunk he passed out and spent the evening in bed, and so I spent the evening staring at the hotel room wall. So despite it being one of the most romantic cities in the world, I always cringed whenever anyone mentioned it. It certainly didn't hold special memories for me and there were certainly no ooh la las coming from our hotel room.

I slammed the front door behind me and, despite feeling sorry for myself due to a slight hangover, just being in the company of these two ladies soon lifted my spirits. Even though I should probably have been feeling a little apprehensive as I had no clue where I was going, I knew that it would be somewhere good. I knew in my heart that they would never let me down.

We literally only drove to the house which was next door, even though it was up the lane a little from me, which confused me even more. When we reached a pair of big automatic wrought-iron gates and Michelle pressed the buzzer to seek admittance, the girls declared that we'd arrived at our destination. As we drove through the gates, the house that stood before us took my breath away. A big glass-fronted stone house, which might possibly have been an enormous barn in a previous life; modern architecture mixing old and new in true style.

The car's tyres crunched on the gravel drive as we came to a stop beside a huge stone fountain.

As we climbed out, the double entrance doors were flung open and a vision dressed in cream from head to toe appeared before us in the form of one of the most glamorous women I'd ever seen. Her hair was pulled back in an elegant chignon with soft wavy tendrils framing her face. She was wearing subtle but beautiful make-up, and a scarf tied tightly around her neck in a small side bow completed her chic and stylish look. I couldn't take my eyes off her as she raced across to Emma and flung her arms around her.

'Emma darling. It's been way too long.' She pushed her away to arm's length. 'Let me look at you. Yes, gorgeous. You'll still do. How are you, my darling? How are you coping with life on your own? Have you adapted?'

They clearly knew each other well and Michelle and I looked at each other and grinned. It took a while before they remembered we were there as they chatted amongst themselves.

'God, I'm sorry. Jo. Michelle. I'd like you to meet my very good friend Agatha Nightingale.'

'Oh, please call me Aggie. My full name makes me sound like a ninety-year-old cosy crime writer.' We all laughed at that. 'Do come in. I'll show you around the new house in a bit, ladies, but you'll have to excuse a lot of it. There's shite everywhere.' I laughed, always finding it funny when posh people swore. 'But first, let's have tea on the patio.'

She guided us into the house, her heels click-clacking on the tiled floor of the very impressive entrance hall, with high apex roofs and floor-to-ceiling windows. All I could think about was how she kept them clean and that she couldn't possibly have any children or animals. The door to the left led up three small steps into a lounge area where trifold doors opened straight up onto a gorgeous patio area with a huge swimming pool. I thought I'd died and gone to heaven. If I could have dreamt the perfect house, this would be it.

'Under here OK?' She guided us to a rattan seating area, under a gazebo, the focal point being the sea in the distance.

'It's beautiful, Aggie. Thanks so much for having us over.'

'You are so very welcome, ladies. It's lovely to have you. Ah, here's Calista now.'

A young stylish girl, I would have placed in her late teens, early twenties at a push, placed the tea tray on the coffee table after wishing us all a good morning.

Aggie shuffled forwards towards the tray. 'I'll pour. Thank you, darling. Is Scott back yet?'

'I haven't seen him yet, Aggie.'

The girl smiled sweetly and almost glided out of the room. What was it with the people in this house? They all seemed to have had the elegant memo.

As Aggie sat back in her chair after dishing drinks out to everyone, her shoe dangling off the edge of her foot, I caught a flash of a red sole.

'Scott is my husband,' she explained. 'He's gone out for a run with the dog. Poor man doesn't know what to do with himself these days. I do wish these football clubs looked after their ex-players a bit better once they've retired.'

I wasn't a huge football fan, so had no idea who she was married too, but hadn't heard of a player called Scott Nightingale. The slam of a door and the woof of a dog signified that we might be about to meet him.

My mouth must have literally dropped open when one of the most gorgeous men I'd ever seen walked into the room, swigging from a water bottle. It was only Scott Foster. He had been a goalkeeper for one of the top London premiership teams. Even I recognised him.

'Sorry to interrupt, babe. I just thought I'd come and let you know I was back and see if anyone wanted a cuppa but I can see you're already sorted.' He smiled at Aggie, leant down, kissed her tenderly and then nervously raised a hand in a wave to the rest of us.

'Urgh, get your big sweaty gorgeous body away from me and go and shower.' She grinned back at him and slapped him on the backside as he walked away from her and shouted, 'Bye, ladies.'

Still gaping, Emma laughed at me.

'You OK there, Jo? You're dribbling a bit.'

'Ha. Not quite, but it's not every day Scott Foster offers you a cup of tea!'

'Ah yes, I forgot to mention that I'd discovered recently that Aggie and Scott had moved in next door to you.'

'Probably not helped by the fact that we have different names. I wanted to make sure I kept my own identity and people didn't think that I was only useful because I was married to a famous footballer.'

'And how is he doing now?' Emma asked.

Aggie sighed. 'Getting there, I think. Not a discussion for today as we'll be here all day. Anyway, it's time to talk about why you ladies are here. What magic can I weave for you today, Emma?' she asked.

'Well, our friend Jo here has a wedding to go to soon. It's her daughter's wedding and her ex-husband and his girlfriend, who also used to be Jo's best friend, will also be there. So Jo wants to look like a complete and utter knockout in their presence. Can you help with that?'

'Thanks, friends. I love you both very much but you've made me sound like a right blooming loser.'

'Well... if the cap...'

'Thanks a bunch, Michelle.'

'Ah, you know we're only joking with you. Aggie, why don't you tell Jo a little bit more about what you do and it might start to make a little more sense.'

'Great idea. So, Jo.' Aggie leant forward in her chair and whispered, 'I groom girls.'

25

'What the fuck? You groom girls? What the hell is going on here?'

When I turned, each of them was laughing till tears ran down their cheeks.

What the hell was in fact going on here? Was I the only one not in on this clearly hilarious joke? I was getting more furious by the minute.

'I'm sorry. We're joking with you. I do kind of groom girls but not in the way that's all over the news these days. I help people who would like to look, feel and be different to do just that. Calista, for instance, is hoping to get engaged soon. The love of her life, Hugo, is landed gentry and she's just a, according to his mother, commoner. Most of us are compared to them, to be honest. Which I know is funny coming from someone like me.' She laughed but it didn't reach her eyes and I wondered what was behind this sad smile.

'So I'm helping her to fit in with them. I'm teaching her how to use the right cutlery, wear the right clothes, use the right make-up, use the right words even. Hugo adores her the way she is, but teaching her the things that I'm teaching her will allow her to fit into his life in a more comfortable way for them both. I suppose I'm a style and image consultant or coach – a cross between Professor Higgins and Gok Wan.'

It took a moment or two to sink in. And eventually, I felt calmer and became more understanding about how this might affect me.

'So I'll be able to help you find something fabulous to wear to fit in at your daughter's wedding. You'll look amazing and that will give you the confidence to feel amazing too. We can try different hair and make-up styles to suit you and when we find the best look, I'll teach you to do it yourself.' Aggie reached forward to click the mousepad of the MacBook Pro which was sitting on the table in front of us. 'Watch this. This will explain a little more.'

A promotional video popped up of a lady who looked quite plain in jeans, T-shirt and trainers. A banner at the bottom of the screen showed that her name was Wendy. Wendy talked about applying for a job interview and whilst she knew she could do the technical aspects of the job, she worried she wouldn't fit in with all the glamorous young people who worked at the company. In an interview-style format, Aggie chatted with her and they talked about why she lacked confidence: a divorce, menopause, the loss of her mother to dementia and kids fleeing the nest. Aggie brought out the reasons why Wendy deserved a second chance at life and they went on to choose outfits that would give her confidence, along with the body parts that she did and didn't like. At the end of the interview, Wendy went off into another room to get a facial, and her hair and nails done, while Aggie went shopping and brought back a number of outfits for her to try. The video ended with Wendy entering a room full of mirrors and bursting into tears when she saw herself. She couldn't believe that she was looking at herself.

I felt my heart swell with love for Wendy and it brought both a tear to my eye and a flutter in my belly. This was what I wanted for me. This was the feeling that I wanted when I went to my daughter's wedding. I wanted to hold my head high and show that I wasn't adversely damaged by my recent divorce and the loss and deception of both my husband and my best friend. That the situation had given me the opportunity to grow my mindset and change my ways. To have the confidence to rightly sit there with the rest of my family and know that I would look bloody fabulous while doing it. And if I could have an ounce of Aggie's grace, sophistication and style, I would be one very happy lady.

I looked at Michelle and she smiled at me nervously. When I looked at Emma, she asked, 'Did we get it right, Jo? We only want the best for you. I hope you know that.'

I reached across for both of their hands.

'I don't think anyone has ever done anything so kind for me in my life.' I heard my voice break when I whispered, 'Thank you.'

Aggie stood and clapped her hands twice.

'Right, come on then, ladies. Let's crack open a bottle of Prosecco. We have work to do.'

26

'So, are you ready for the big reveal?'

I made a very strange noise and blew air out of my cheeks.

'You won't do that on the day, now, will you? It's not a good look.' Aggie winked at me, taking away some of the tension I was feeling.

After a very deep breath, I nodded. Aggie grabbed the door handle.

'OK, let's go. Now remember the three t's I taught you. Tummy in, tits out, and flash those teeth. Ladies, may I introduce you to the mother of the bride.'

I walked into the adjoining room with the widest of smiles, while Michelle and Emma stared back at me with the hugest of grins.

There were floor-to-ceiling mirrors on the opposite wall and as I looked at myself I gasped and clutched my chest. I looked round at Aggie. 'Is that me?'

'It is, my darling.'

'Are you sure it's me?'

She laughed.

'I'm very sure. What do you think?'

I looked across at my friends, who were literally both holding their breath. Michelle took her hands away from her mouth first. 'You look incredible, Jo.' There were tears in her eyes.

Emma walked over to me and held my hand. 'You, lady, are going to knock their socks off.'

'You think so?' I was nervous but as I twirled this way and that, checking out how I looked from all angles, I was starting to believe that it really was me.

'I know so! God, if Seamus wasn't gay he'd have trouble keeping his hands off you.'

'Ah, who is this mysterious Seamus and is he gay?' Aggie looked puzzled.

Michelle, Emma and I had discussed the situation with Seamus a lot over the last couple of weeks and we'd analysed and very probably overanalysed much of the situation. All three of us were still surprised to learn that he was gay. Michelle particularly, who said that her normally brilliantly accurate gaydar hadn't been going off at all around him.

'Well, we don't really know, to be honest. But he and Jo hang around together a lot.'

'Yeah, but only because he's helping me with my house,' I chipped in.

'But you get on like a house on fire,' Emma answered.

Aggie was frowning, lost in this conversation.

'I'm confused? Why do you think he is?'

'He said he had a boyfriend called Al,' I explained.

'Has he shown an interest in you, Jo? He could just be bisexual. How would you feel about that?' Aggie was well into the discussion at this point.

I pulled an 'I'm-not-really-sure' face as I tried to think about whether he had or not recently. At first he had flirted with me, a lot, but it seemed to have stopped lately. Although I'd probably stopped flirting back since he'd mentioned Al to me. Relationships in this day and age were so very different to when I first got together with Michael. All those years ago, there weren't that many people around who were gay. Or certainly not openly like now. It was lovely that people could truly be themselves, but I wasn't sure whether I was as open-minded as I possibly should be. And now it puzzled me to think about how I would feel if he was bisexual. That was a new one on me.

'Why don't you just ask him?'

'No! I couldn't!' I responded to Aggie. It was nice to get a new perspective but I wasn't sure if this was the sort of conversation you had with a new friend. Would he be offended if I asked him? Did I even want to know the truth? Did me caring about this mean that I liked Seamus more than I was admitting to myself, let alone my friends?

'Well then, you'll always wonder, won't you? If you ask, you'll know. It's just words. Just a few words put together to form a question. It's not hard.'

Aggie was a wonderful soul. She made the impossible seem perfectly possible. I sighed out loud.

'Maybe I will build up to it. One of these days.'

'Don't let an opportunity pass you by because you were too scared to ask a question. This is the new Jo, remember. Badass Jo who takes no shit from anyone. Mark my words, Jo. And be brave. One question could change your life.'

That certainly gave me a lot to ponder but for now, I just wanted to lap up my new look. Gone was my mousy-brown bobbed hair that I'd had for years. My new chestnut-brown hair with copper highlights was flicky and funky. My make-up was subtle yet elegant, dewy and glowy at the same time and the main wedding day outfit that Aggie had chosen fitted like a glove, despite me telling her that I was most definitely at least a size sixteen and she said I'd fit into a twelve. I was obviously delighted when it was not only fabulous but so different to what I'd usually choose for myself. I'd never envisaged myself in a trouser suit, but I had to admit that I loved the royal blue number. With a sequinned cerise camisole top to lift and contrast with the blue, the pink strappy sandals and a sparkly pink bag to match, it really was the perfect outfit and I felt like a million dollars.

As she styled my hair, she'd shown me exactly step by step how to do it myself and I felt totally confident that I could. Aggie's demeanour changed as she'd talked a little about her husband and how difficult he was finding life since he'd retired from the game. It was clearly a huge issue of concern to her. I tried not to delve too deeply, after all, we'd only just met, but I was intrigued. She'd also talked about how she'd made sure she'd always kept herself and their children out of the public eye.

She also showed me how daytime make-up could be used to look natural and then apply more layer by layer for a more dramatic look. I'd chosen a couple of other outfits too. Two casual but elegant daytime looks, very similar to what Aggie herself was wearing, and another consisting of a pair of well-fitting, bum-lifting, tummy-tucking jeans, a smart cardigan and again a camisole top which showed off my favourite part of my body: my cleavage.

'Honestly, Jo, you are going to knock them dead. They won't recognise you.'

'Thanks, I think, that's the idea.' I repeated back the words that Aggie had taught me to say to myself earlier. 'I am a strong and confident woman. I'm not only surviving without them but thriving too.'

'Woohoo! I feel like I'm in the female version of *Braveheart*.' We all laughed at Michelle and her ability to always lighten the mood.

'Right, are we all ready to go? I'm going to get out of this clobber, settle up with Aggie for what I owe her and then I'm taking you two to the pub for tea to say thanks.'

'To be honest, after you've settled up with me, you might not be able to afford to take them to the pub.' We laughed, but as Aggie told me how much I owed her and I tried not to let my eyes pop out of my head, I knew that the feeling I got from the day I'd spent with her was actually something that money couldn't buy. She'd been kind enough to throw in the consultation as a favour to Emma, which was very generous and most welcome, as this was all going on my credit card. I knew it was extravagant considering my circumstances, but I'd worry about that another day. After all the hard work I'd been doing lately, I deserved a treat. And I was mother of the bride, after all.

When we arrived at the pub after dropping all the clothes off at my house, we caused quite a stir, laughing as we walked through the doors. Gone were the elegant clothes I would be saving for the wedding weekend and the jeans, T-shirt and fleece I'd left the house in this morning. In their place were the figure-shaping black jeans I'd bought, with a plain cream blouse and a cashmere cardigan in a similar tone with a gorgeous multicoloured scarf that brought out the blue in my eyes. A pair of high boots finished off the outfit. Aggie really did have impeccable taste and even though this was quite a casual outfit, I felt all the same confidence that I'd felt earlier.

'I told you you'd lost weight too. It's all that hard work you're doing at the house,' Michelle said as we approached the bar. She ordered a bottle of wine and three glasses before noticing who was sitting with his back to us.

'Oh, hello, Seamus. Have you met our new friend Jo?'

Seamus swivelled round on his bar stool. When he saw me, his jaw visibly dropped and his eyes widened.

He scratched his head. 'Err... wow, Jo. You look...' He seemed at a loss for words and there was an awkward silence while he tried to find something suitable.

Emma filled the gap in the conversation.

'Come on, you two. You grab the table in the window. I'll grab the drinks.'

I turned to walk away but Seamus grabbed my arm and gently pulled me back.

'Stunning. Incredible. Amazing. Not that you didn't... erm... already... you know...'

I laughed at him, knowing that I was blushing. I wasn't sure why I still did this, knowing that I wasn't his type.

'You don't have to say that but thank you. And thank you for helping the girls to trick me this morning. What an amazing bunch of friends I have. Thank goodness for the people I've met since I came to live in Sandpiper Shore. I'm a lucky girl.'

'Maybe we're the lucky ones,' he whispered back.

27

Two days later, I was taking Theo for a lunchtime walk on the beach, while Seamus was out on a couple of small jobs, when I bumped into Dame Tessa down at the water's edge. She was walking without the dogs so I thought I might take the opportunity to ask her some more questions about the habitat in an effort to engage her in conversation.

'I'm so glad I've seen you,' I said. 'I wanted to ask you about these plants that I saw the other day and wondered if you'd know what they were. I took some photos to show you.' I fumbled with my phone and eventually got the photos up.

'Ah, yes, that one with the purply-pink flowers and the oval leaves is wild thyme. Otherwise known as elfin thyme or creeping thyme. A member of the mint family. Normally found in the short areas, along with another plant called eyebright. That one has white flowers with purple veins and yellow centres and keeps the grasses at bay encouraging the wildflowers to grow. They all have a purpose, you know.' She really came alive when she was talking about these things. She flicked across to the next photo. It surprised me that she knew what to do.

'Don't look so surprised. I'm quite up on my technology. I have the latest iPhone and iPad myself and there's not much I can't do on an Apple Mac, you know.'

I laughed. You really should never judge a book by its cover.

'So this one I don't think is anything at all. I think it's just a daisy that's dying off.' I was rather proud of myself for recognising that it was just a weed.

'Now that's where you're wrong. This, my dear, might look like a dead daisy, but it's actually what's called a carline thistle. If you catch them in the bright sunlight, they glisten silver and gold. Beautiful.'

Gosh, that showed that I still had a lot to learn. I swiped across to the final picture of a yellow flowered weed, but I daren't say that's what I thought it was.

'Ah, yes, the lovely lady's bedstraw.'

'Gosh, that's a funny name.'

'It's a very clever plant, you know. Used to curdle milk in the old days when making cheese and they say that the name comes from the fact that it used to be dried and stuffed into mattresses for women when going into childbirth. And if you look closely you'll see elephant hawk moths not too far away. Apparently, it's the sweet honey-like scent that it gives off.'

'You're so knowledgeable.' I didn't know whether to call her Tessa or Dame or anything else. Aggie's words popped into my head: why don't you just ask? But, with Tessa's age, I wasn't sure if it would come off as rude so I just didn't call her anything.

'I've been around a lot of years, lass. And I've always been good at the small details.'

She stared at me for longer than I thought was necessary, and I still couldn't figure out whether she liked me or not. I also didn't know why I cared so much. Maybe it was just because she was

Aunty June's best friend that I wanted to make a good impression. Wanted her to like me. Maybe even we could be friends one day.

'I don't suppose you'd... well, you know...'

'Spit it out, dear.'

'I wondered if you'd like to join me for a cup of tea up at the house.'

She seemed to deliberate on the question, not immediately answering, but still those eyes seemed to bore into my very soul.

'I thought you'd never ask.'

'I baked a lemon drizzle cake this morning too.'

Her face lit up. 'Ooh, that's my favourite. You must have known.'

I didn't have the heart to say that it was just coincidence but I smiled and led the way up the beach path to the house.

When Tessa came in, it felt kind of weird. She'd clearly been in this house before, way more than I had, and I really wanted her to like what I'd done but more than that, I wanted her to think that Aunty June would have liked it too. There felt more pressure with her being in the house than any other visitor I'd had and I could see her looking around from the moment I opened the French doors and saw her roving eye. There was nothing I could do about it though, so I left her to mooch while I put the kettle on. Inspired by the fact that when I'd visited Aggie's house, we'd been presented with a tea tray, I decided to do the same.

As I returned to the lounge, she was sitting in one of the chairs by the side of the French doors and she was smiling.

'I wasn't sure what you'd be doing inside the house, but you seem to have kept some of the character while at the same time making it modern, warm and inviting. She'd have approved, you know.'

'That makes me so happy.' It filled my heart with joy and

made me feel a tiny bit brave too. 'And I'm sorry to ask, but what should I call you? It's just that someone said that you were a dame so I wasn't sure if I should call you Dame, or Dame Tessa, or…'

'You're overthinking things, m'dear. Tessa is just fine. It is my name, after all.' She peered at me over the top of her china cup. 'So, Joanna, tell me about your life. Has it been a happy one?'

Her question threw me a little. Unusual, really.

'Well, nothing much to say really apart from that I was married to Aunty June's nephew for nearly twenty-five years. I have two daughters, both with their own lives, one due to be married shortly. Lucy is a vet and Melissa is a doctor so they've done very well for themselves. They both earn plenty of money and have everything they want.'

'But are they happy? It's not what we have in life but how we feel about it surely?'

'You're probably right.'

'Oh, I am, dear. I learnt that a long time ago. The hard way.' She stared out of the French doors to the garden and the sea beyond, somewhat lost in her thoughts, and I drank my tea, although the silence was going on for so long it was becoming uncomfortable.

'Can I ask you something, Tessa?' I said. 'It's quite personal.'

'Go ahead.'

'How did you become a dame?'

'Ah, well, that's a very long story but one that I choose not to talk about, to be honest. Only June knew the truth and she took my secret to the grave with her. I'd rather you didn't ask, if you don't mind.' She became quite huffy which came as a surprise. A complete turn-around in her demeanour.

'Apologies. I didn't mean to pry.'

'That's OK. It's just something I'm quite touchy over. And I'm finding life hard without June. We knew all of each other's secrets. She was truly the only person that I could be myself with.'

'I'm so sorry to hear that. I'm always here if you feel like talking.'

'Thank you. That's kind. I must be off now, dear. Thank you for having me. And letting me look at that wonderful view. It's like a photograph.'

'Oh, that reminds me. I was actually wondering if one of these days, you might have a look through an old suitcase I've found. There are lots of old photographs, a sealed envelope, and a bundle of letters.'

Bizarrely Tessa snapped. 'Throw them away. No good will ever come of dredging up the past. We have to live in the present. Throw them in the bin, Joanna, please. For all our sakes. Don't go rooting through them. It'll do more harm than good.' She started to go a little red in the face, clearly flustered by my request, and she grasped my hand. 'Promise me, Joanna. That you'll throw them out. June would turn in her grave if she thought someone was looking through her private things. Promise me.'

Those eyes bored into my soul and I felt compelled in that moment to tell her I promised.

'Would you like me to walk you home? You look really peaky.'

'I'm fine, lass, thank you. I've walked these streets for years and nothing has ever happened to me yet. I'll be fine once I get some fresh air in my lungs.'

'OK, but let me scribble my number down for you and if you need me, just give me a call. OK?'

Totally and utterly out of character, she lifted her hand and cupped my face, stroking my cheek with her thumb. 'Such a sweet girl.'

Then she seemed to pull herself together, realising what she'd done, and abruptly said, 'Goodbye and thank you. You're very kind.' She turned and departed through the French doors, waved a hand in the air and walked through the dunes down to the coastal path.

When she'd turned the corner and I could no longer see her, I rubbed at the place where she had touched my face. What a very strange old lady.

28

On a Friday morning two months later, my life changed dramatically. Seamus and I had spent every minute of every day working on the house. While Seamus was at work, I did the bits that I could. I'd become a dab hand at sanding floorboards, staining and painting. The shutters had been restored back to their former glory and I was incredibly proud of all that I had achieved on my own. Teamed with the amazing work that Seamus had been doing, not only had he rewired the entire house brilliantly, he'd also become an expert in plumbing (with a little help from a friend of his who he said owed him a huge favour) and plastering. Between us, we'd performed nothing short of a miracle. I was completely and utterly knackered, woke up most mornings aching from the work done the day before, and fell into bed each night exhausted. Every spare moment Seamus had was spent at the house with me and I can honestly say that I'd never worked so hard in my life. I could also say that it had probably been the best time of my life.

I had almost trained myself not to have romantic feelings towards Seamus any more. There was still a spark between us and we had become the best of friends and got on like a house on fire, settling into a companionable way of working together, each knowing exactly what the other was about to say. I had never enjoyed myself more.

We'd celebrated with a cup of coffee and we sat on the decking in the warmth of the evening sun, knackered emotionally and physically.

'Congratulations, Jo Jenkins. Here's to you and your new home and the next adventure.' We chinked mugs.

'Oh, Seamus. Here's to you. There was no way in the world I could have done this without you. You've been...' I searched for a word to sum up everything that I felt in my heart about him right now. If there had been something romantic between us, I know I would have said perfect, but it wasn't so I had to find something else. 'A marvel. An absolute bloody marvel.' Maybe it was better this way. Better that I wasn't linked romantically to him, because the feeling would have been utterly overwhelming.

'Get off with you. If you hadn't been as willing to try the things I'd suggested, and we hadn't worked together to make it all work, it wouldn't have been half as much fun. It's been a real blast. I've enjoyed every single minute.' He grinned at me and his nose twitched. I had noticed this little habit more and more and it was just one of the many things that I loved about him.

'*Every* minute?' I tipped my hand to one side.

'Well, obviously I didn't enjoy the part when you hit my thumb with the hammer. God, that hurt.'

'Ah, really? You should have said.' We both laughed.

On that particular occasion, Seamus turned the air black and blue coming out with expletives that surprised us both but was still so kind towards me and never once blamed me. He was an incredibly kind soul and I was so lucky to have him in my life.

The slamming of a van door broke into my thoughts and the

normal peace and solitude was shattered. Because Michelle and Emma had arrived, with all of their worldly possessions, ready to move in.

And within seconds, my house was a hive of activity. Outside, removals vans blocked the street, and inside, it was like Piccadilly Circus. I'd never made so many cups of tea in one day in my life or seen so many people in my home. It was total and utter chaos and I loved every second.

That evening, to celebrate, we decided to have drinks on the terrace. This was the area that I had been working on clearing myself while Seamus had been dealing with the important stuff on the inside that he didn't need help with. I was determined that it was going to be our little sanctuary of tranquillity, where – thanks to the panoramic views over the sand dunes – we could watch the sun come up from one direction and go down in the other.

As I looked around me, I was super proud of all that I had achieved on my own. Well, mainly on my own. I'd only had to call in a bit of support from Seamus a couple of times once the landscaping company had erected the large aluminium pergola. It was an expense that I'd thought very carefully about splashing out on, but it seemed a shame to only be able to enjoy a magnificent view like that in the dry weather. At least this way, even if it was chucking it down, I could still wrap up in a blanket and be dry under the slide and tilt roof. I hadn't realised how much I enjoyed being outside until I'd moved to the village. I'd spent more time outdoors than I did in these days.

I'd built the rattan lounge furniture myself, and struggled at first with the matching sun loungers but I persevered, and once I got the hang of the first one, the other two didn't take too long at all. I removed the multi-coloured Moroccan-style cushions and throws from a big rattan box and decorated the furniture so that it looked colourful and bright. Festoon lights ran from one side of the pergola to the outside wall of the cottage and there were some huge palm plants in brightly coloured ceramic pots which complemented the Moroccan lanterns which hung from the canopy. It was the sort of terrace that I would have thought I was only capable of dreaming about in the past. But now, it was all mine. And my very special surprise for these two important ladies in my life.

'Hell-ooooo! Oh! My! Fricking! God! Jo! I know you said you had been working here but who knew you'd created this little haven? You are so lucky to have this, you know.'

'Thanks, Michelle, but this is what I created for us. I thought it could be like a little community place for us all to come together if we want to. We'll all live individual lives in our own homes, but if we do feel like a bit of company then this could be the place to do it. I hope you like the idea.' I handed her a glass of chilled Prosecco that I'd just poured.

Emma strode across the terrace to us and took the glass I offered.

'Thank you, darling. Sorry for earwigging but I heard that and I think it's a wonderful idea. We're all used to living on our own nowadays, so this is the perfect compromise. And honestly, Jo.' She swept her glass free arm around. 'It's bloody gorgeous. I don't think I want my flat any more. Can I live on this terrace instead? Oh, you know what we should do? Cocks on Friday!'

We both spun round. Emma laughed at us. 'Your faces. Honestly. I just thought we could do regular cocktails on a Friday night. We could all come together and tell all about how our weeks have been. The good parts. The bad parts. One of the many things I've missed since I've been a widow, apart from the sex of course, is sharing how my day or my week has been. It'll be so nice to have someone who gives a shit about me.'

I grinned back at her. 'I think it's a fantastic idea. Here's to Cocks on Friday.'

Michelle guffawed and shouted loudly, 'To Cocks!'

As our glasses clinked together, we heard a little cough in the background.

'Gosh. Have I come to the right place? I thought there were three sensible middle-aged women living together in this big old house, not three old slappers from *Love Island* toasting to, well, you know...' Seamus seemed to struggle to use the word in front of us.

'Oi! Less of the old, if you don't mind.'

I laughed at the fact Michelle was more upset by the fact he'd called us old than the fact he'd called us slappers.

'You can come and join us if you like,' I said. 'I can go and grab another glass.'

'That's very kind of you, Jo Jenkins, but I was just coming to find you to say that I'm getting off now. I've finished up in the kitchen and will be back tomorrow if that's OK. I'll leave you ladies to celebrate. I reckon you'll all be very happy living here together, you know. Have a good evening, all.' He mock-saluted and gave me a cheeky little wink before he went back through the side gate, Theo trotting along by his side.

Michelle came and stood next to me and nudged my shoulder.

'Talking of cocks, I'd quite like to...'

My head snatched round to face her.

'Too much?'

I nodded. 'Yep, too much.'

She slung her arm around my shoulder. 'Come on, did I see some nuts to mop up some of this Prosecco? It's making me feel quite squiffy. Do you think we should rename our little group The Lonely Hearts Club?'

'God! That just makes us sound like a bunch of losers,' I replied.

'On the contrary, Jo.' Emma grinned. 'I think it makes us sound like a wonderful group of people who, despite having really big hearts, are alone in life for different reasons, who have found friendship and solace and who are helping each other to overcome their loneliness.'

'Well, when you say it like that, it doesn't sound so bad and probably is better than Cocks on Friday.'

'Oh, I don't know.' Michelle laughed. 'That has a certain ring to it.'

Laughing with friends is one of life's best therapies. Originally, I'd been wondering if I was doing the right thing by inviting two women that I hardly knew into my home. Yet at that moment, I was so very pleased with my decision. My world had once again spun and I had finally started to believe that everything was going to be OK. Better than OK in fact. It was feeling really good. The friendship that we'd formed, three strangers who had become firm friends, you could even say had been life-changing for me.

I wondered how many other people there were out in the world who felt the same way. We were literally three women from different walks of life, who would probably never have met under different circumstances. How many other people woke up every day, wondering if they'd speak to another person that day? Have any contact with the outside world? You just assumed that everyone was OK really. What if they weren't? What if they were all experiencing some sort of mental health crisis and were terribly lonely and too afraid to tell anyone?

For some reason, Dame Tessa sprang to mind. She'd been alone for years, living in that big old house on the hill. I wondered if she had days when she felt that they would go on forever. When she'd love to go out for a meal with friends but, now she'd lost Aunty June, had no one to go with and must be feeling it even more. How would someone of her age cope? Maybe I would have to make more of an effort to get to know her.

Before I came to Sandpiper Shore, I didn't know if I'd ever be able to work through my feelings of loneliness; how I could ever start afresh and change my mindset. However, since I'd met these two special ladies, I felt like maybe the tide was turning and that I did have a fine future ahead. I could sit and wait for the future to happen to me, or I could put myself out there and make things happen *for* me. And maybe not just for me too. Maybe I could not only change my own life, but change others' lives too. I just had to find my 'brave'.

'Err, Jo. Did you hear me?' Michelle's voice brought me back to the present. 'You OK there? You drifted off for a minute.'

I smiled, my heart suddenly filling with joy with a feeling that I'd finally found a purpose.

'Do you know what, ladies, I actually am fine. And I think I've just had a really good idea that I might need your help with.'

29

'I love it, Jo. What a lovely thing to do.' I was delighted that Emma liked my idea. I looked over at Michelle, who had a great big grin spread across her face.

'It's genius. It's like a dating service for friends.'

I breathed a sigh of relief that they didn't both think that I was completely bonkers.

'There must be loads of people like us. Good people that want to still have a life, but don't have anyone to do it with. I'm going to do some research and work out how to start everything off. Maybe I just do a Facebook page or a membership group or something like that. We could even set up a few organised events, maybe some meals out to start with and promote them locally.'

'So when you say we, I presume that we're being dragged into this too then?' Emma grinned and grabbed my hand. 'I am in, by the way. I think you've really hit on something here. And I think we need to aim big too. Other events that people are missing out on. Dancing, theatre trips, days out; the world is our oyster. We just need to think about all the things that are hard to do on your own. Are we just limiting it to women, or including anyone?'

Michelle was nodding so hard I thought she'd make her neck ache. 'Yeah, I'm in too. However I can be involved, count me in. It took me so long to admit that I was lonely to myself, let alone to others. I know there are tons of people who must feel the same. I watched something on TV recently and there was a huge amount of people who admitted to feeling lonely at times in their life. It really surprised me. And women are more likely to be lonely than men, but I reckon that's only because women would admit it more. There were some incredible statistics that have really stuck with me since I saw the programme.'

'I think you're right about women and men. Women are just better at talking about it rather than men. Men definitely need to open up more. There are more programmes about men's mental health than ever on the TV. There was something on the other night that said males are three times more likely than women to take their own lives. I definitely think we should be totally open to everyone of any age too. I think there are as many young people now who are lonely, especially in this digital age that we live in. And probably those who are older too.' Once again, Dame Tessa entered my head. 'Those who have lost friends and partners. Just imagine if what we did could make a difference to just one person's life.' I felt a sense of pride in what we were about to do. 'It would be so worthwhile.'

We all fell silent, alone in our thoughts. I felt a little fire in my belly. My feeling of purpose and also excitement was growing bigger and bigger the more we talked about it. I knew in my heart that we could change some people's worlds.

'I think calling it The Lonely Hearts Club sums it all up. We might need a strapline, though, to go with it.'

'What do you mean Michelle?' I'd heard the expression strapline many times but never really knew what it meant.

'Something to sound positive to go alongside it. "Helping

friendships flourish", "finding friends" or "fabulous friendship group". Something like that so people know what to expect from the group. Otherwise it might just sound like a dating site, which is not what it is.' Michelle was clearly very good at her job. I knew she worked in marketing but didn't realise just how integral to this project she could be.

'It absolutely isn't, but wouldn't it also be wonderful to know that we'd enabled two people to meet and develop more than just friendship?' Emma clutched her hands to her heart and laughed. 'God, I'm such an old romantic.'

Michelle, clearly enthused, was speaking so fast she could hardly get her words out. 'Honestly, the more I think about this, the more I know it's the right thing to do. Why hasn't anyone else really thought of this? There are loads of dating sites and apps out in the world, mostly full of pervy men who just want to send pictures of their anatomy to poor unsuspecting females. But maybe that's just my experience.'

We all laughed at her. The thought of going through some of the things I heard about horrified me. I'd never find love again if apps were the only way forward.

'They could just be really simple things,' I was becoming quite excited by this idea, 'like a group walk, keep fit classes, group swimming, some meals and evenings out to start with, and maybe in time we could even do holidays. There must be hundreds, even thousands of people who miss out on holidays because they don't have anyone to go with. I haven't had a holiday since Michael and I split up. I'd feel ridiculous sat in a hotel on my own. I'd feel as if everyone was staring at me even though they probably wouldn't be.'

I thought back to the wonderful family holidays we'd had over the years until the girls became too old to want to come with us. And then Michael had been working so hard that he didn't feel he could take time off. Although now I knew that he wasn't actually working that hard but spending that time with Claudia.

Much as I would have loved to lie around a pool in the sunshine, I'd not plucked up the courage in the last couple of years to go it alone, despite feeling like I really needed it.

'So come on then. Jo, go and get some paper and pens. Emma, go and grab us another bottle of Prosecco out of the fridge. We have lists to make and jobs to allocate. We need to think of things that cost money and some things that don't. Not everyone can afford to go out eating all the time or paying lots to go to things so we definitely need to think of some no-cost and low-cost things to do. However, I think we should start with a launch party. I'm going to share the arse off this on my social media profiles.' Michelle clapped her hands at Emma and me. 'Come on, girls. Get to it.'

'God, I love how bossy you are, Michelle.' Emma laughed as she went off to the outside wine cooler and grabbed us another bottle. It made me smile to think about how easily the three of us had fitted into each other's lives without being too intrusive.

'You say bossy. I say assertive. At least we'll get things done if I'm project managing.'

We clinked glasses and toasted. 'The Lonely Hearts Club.'

These women had literally changed my life and at that very moment I could honestly say that for the first time in a while, I hadn't felt lonely or alone. If we could do this for others too, it would be truly remarkable.

30

The sun streaming in through my bedroom window was a little bit too much for even me the following morning. I was feeling the aftereffects of way too much booze last night and my bravery had definitely dwindled after a dream I'd had about the wedding and me chasing my family down the aisle as they all left me behind, and me tripping and falling down in a muddy puddle in front of the whole congregation. My heart was pounding when I woke up and I couldn't get back to sleep. I was grumpy, tired and discombobulated, with the huge reminder of the fact that the wedding was looming.

When Seamus arrived, he seemed a little nervous. It was almost as if he kept going to say something serious and then stopped himself. When he asked me if I'd consider looking after Theo for the day, and I agreed, he didn't give me the normal enthusiasm.

Hovering around the door, he said my name in a strange way. A question almost.

'Jo? This wedding of your daughter's? Is there not someone you could ask to go with you?'

I snapped. I didn't realise how much it had been playing on my mind. 'Of course I would. But it's not an option, is it, at this short notice?'

'It's just that... oh, never mind. It doesn't matter.'

I stared at him, my brain going into overdrive. I had thought a couple of times about asking him to come with me but then with everything else going on and then since him mentioning Al to me, I'd dismissed it again.

The short, sharp trill of my ringtone brought me back to the present. I groaned as Michael's name flashed up on the screen and I dithered over whether to answer. I wasn't sure if I'd had enough coffee to deal with him yet.

I pressed the red button to bounce the call.

'It's definitely worth a thought. Maybe... you might know someone you could ask. That's all I'm saying.'

My phone started to ring again. There was obviously something that Michael wanted and I knew he wouldn't go away unless I answered him.

'I'm sorry, Seamus, but I have to take this. Let's talk later when you pick Theo up.'

'Fine.' He spun round and walked out, mumbling and slamming the door behind him.

Michael had been asking lots of questions about the wedding. Things he should have been asking Lucy not me and I couldn't concentrate and said I'd call him back later.

What Seamus had said was on my mind all day. It made perfect sense, really, but I didn't know if I could pluck up the courage to ask him. At least if he came with me, I wouldn't have to worry about it being someone that I'd met on a dating website and hardly knew. Anything could happen. A friend of mine had met someone recently, and they'd turned out to be a right weirdo. At least with Seamus, I did know him and I did like him. We got on really well and I knew that he'd be someone that I would enjoy spending time with. And he wouldn't, because he wasn't a 'proper' partner, put any pressure on me for anything at all. At least I knew that I wouldn't have to be second guessing when I was supposed to do things that couples in relationships do. Whether they might expect something more than I was willing to give. There were going to be times when Michael and I would have to be together. Some of the photos would probably be of the four of us, so at least there wouldn't be a jealous partner on my side who might make things a little bit awkward. Seamus would be perfect. I pulled back my shoulders and sighed. I just needed to get over myself and take a leap of faith and just ask him.

At around 6.30 p.m. I heard the loud engine of his van pull up outside and Theo ran to the window, jumping onto the windowsill and wagging his tail when he saw his master get out. I felt like I was hopping from one foot to the other and didn't realise until I looked down that I was clenching my fists. I tried to relax and think about another random thought instead.

How was I even getting to the wedding? Now I didn't have the Range Rover, I realised that I'd have to think about hiring something for the day. If he did agree, then the last thing I wanted was to turn up at my daughter's posh hotel wedding venue in a dirty old van which had 'I wish my wife was as filthy as this van' written on dirt in the back.

Seamus knocked on the door and walked in without needing me to answer. He was still wearing his sunglasses.

'Hey. Cuppa?' I asked.

'I'd love one. I'm knackered. It's been a long day.' He bent down and ruffled Theo's head.

'In that case, would you rather have a beer?'

He dipped his head and looked at me over the top of his Ray-Bans, eyebrows raised.

'My way of saying sorry for being a bit grumpy this morning.' He gave me that lopsided grin of his as he followed me through into the kitchen, Theo a shadow at his side.

'Aw, mate.' He perched his sunglasses on the top of his head and bent down to Theo. 'I'm sorry I'm late. I bet you're hungry. Do you want your dinner?'

Theo spun round and sat to attention, thumping his tail on the floor.

'Maybe you should leave an emergency stash of food here for occasions like this if you get held up. It might have been easier if I could have fed him.'

'Yeah, I might have to forgo that beer, Jo Jenkins. I didn't realise the time, to be honest, and it's not fair on this one if I don't feed him.'

I started to mooch through the cupboard I kept all the tinned food in.

'I might be able to rustle up a tin of tuna or something. Would he eat that?'

'You'd be his favourite person in the world if you did that. That's his treat food.'

'OK, why don't you go and grab a seat on the decking with this,' I handed him a bottle of Beck's, 'and we'll go and see what we can find for you, shall we, Theo?'

Theo padded into the kitchen after me and waited patiently while I put a bowl of tuna on the floor next to the bowl I used for his water.

Watching Seamus on the decking felt a little voyeuristic. He stared out to sea and occasionally rubbed the bristles of his chin. I coughed before approaching, and sat beside him. After a moment's silence, we both spoke at the same time.

'About this morning.'
'About this morning.'

We both laughed out loud.

'Ladies first.' He pointed his bottle at me to indicate I should speak. I rushed through the next words before I stopped myself saying them.

'I just wanted to say that I've been thinking about your idea about me asking someone all day and I wondered whether...' I took a deep breath '...you'd consider coming with me.'

He laughed and I tipped my head, feeling myself frowning.

'I was going to say that I wouldn't be insulted if you wanted to say no but that I was going to offer my services...' He blushed. 'As an escort I mean... Oh gosh, that sounds even worse. I've been dithering all day about offering because you might think it's a daft idea and you probably thought I was an idiot to even push myself on you and your family in this way.' He sighed as if grateful that he'd got his words out.

'Honestly, Seamus. It seemed like a better idea every time I thought about it. Your support would be amazing. I would feel such a failure going on my own. I'd feel ridiculous in front of all of our friends.'

'But why? You are far from a failure. Look at you.' He looked deeply into my eyes and held my gaze. 'And this, look at what you've got and what you are doing.'

I looked away, suddenly finding the label on the bottle quite interesting.

He turned to face me and reached out, lifting my chin up so our eyes met again. My heart missed a beat.

'Jo Jenkins. You are strong and you are kind and you are funny and you are...' He sighed. 'You're beautiful.'

As I stared back at him, I thought that this was just my bloody luck. The nicest, most perfect man I wasn't even looking for had unexpectedly come into my life. It had taken me so much courage to give way and admit my feelings to myself. I had liked him a lot.

And then to find out that I was not his type and that he was clearly just being nice to me would take a lot of getting used to. But it was better to have him in my life as a friend, knowing that it could never be anything more than sitting wondering whether he might kiss me, or whether he liked me. I supposed it took all the pressure away, which right then could only be a good thing.

'Thank you. You're very kind and you're very lovely and I would *love* you to be my plus one. And at least you know that you're safe with me and that I'm not going to make any advances towards you. With us just being the best of friends and all that.' I grinned and immediately felt lighter. 'Seamus Shaffernakker. Will you do me the honour of coming to my daughter's wedding with me? Please?'

'Can I wear shorts?'

It struck me then that I'd never seen Seamus wearing anything but shorts. But I could easily imagine him looking dapper in a suit and tie. He would scrub up really well.

'Absolutely not.'

He chewed the inside of his cheek before breaking into a wide grin and raised his bottle to me.

'I will.'

We chinked drinks before he spoke again.

'This is going to be so much fun!'

31

Because my daughter had booked her wedding in the Cotswolds for a Monday, I didn't think it would take us too long to get there. What I didn't account for, however, was the volume of traffic which would be on the motorway coming away from Cornwall on a Sunday afternoon.

My heart was thumping in my chest as Seamus's car pulled up in the car park of the Grove Country House Hotel and Spa. While I was trying to compose myself, he got out and came round to my side, opening the door and offering me his hand.

He winked. 'Just in case anyone is watching.'

I took a deep breath and got out. When I mentioned hiring a car, he said to trust him. That he'd got it covered. What I didn't realise until this morning was that his van was what he used for work. His flame-red Jaguar two-seater sports model was his pride and joy and what he'd turned up in to pick me up.

His breath brushed my skin as he leant forward and kissed my cheek while whispering in my ear. 'Smile, Jo Jenkins. Remember we're meant to be in love.'

A shiver ran down my spine when I felt his hot breath on my

face. I had to pull myself together and not imagine something that wasn't there; reminded myself that this was just an act that we were performing. I turned to him and it was probably more of a grimace than a smile.

'Relax, Jo. It's going to be OK. I've got you.'

We stared at each other for a split second, before he took my hand firmly in one of his, and slammed the door shut with the other and then we walked round to the boot which he sprung open with the key fob, our hands disconnecting so that he could retrieve our luggage.

When he was holding my hand, I felt safe. Now he'd let go, I felt vulnerable and small, not knowing who was looking at me from the hotel windows. As I turned towards the imposing reception foyer, with huge stone pillars either side of the glass doors, Seamus grabbed the two bags and winked again. Even though I was apprehensive about the whole day, I did feel safe with him around me and was really glad he had come. I reached up and kissed his cheek.

'Thank you for doing this.'

'You're so welcome. Ready?'

As we headed for the foyer, my larger-than-life ex-husband came bowling out. I took a long deep breath to prepare me for what came next. Michael had never been a particularly quiet person, he was one of those that I constantly wanted to say 'inside voice' to, so that he didn't show us all up. When the kids were growing up, they had to learn to accept him for who he was, yet I still found him loud and embarrassing at times and just wanted him to turn it down a bit, but he was more of a 'I'm here, look at me' type of personality. They say that opposites attract and maybe that's why we'd stayed together so long. Either that or a sense of duty for me – that that's what married couples do.

Michael's feet crunched across the gravel driveway as he

approached us, and he shouted over his shoulder, alerting me to the fact that *she* was right behind him. She followed in his shadow while wobbling precariously on three-inch-high strappy sandals.

'Joanna, darling. So great to see you. Looking as gorgeous as ever, I see.'

He wrapped me in a bear hug and, despite my stiffness, my senses betrayed me and rapidly reminded me of everything about him. How he felt. How he smelt.

When he stepped back, I saw how he looked too and it was hard to admit it to myself but he looked good. The golden tan suited him, although he had more laughter lines around his eyes than I remembered. *She* obviously made him laugh more than I ever did. His open-necked pale blue shirt and beige chino trousers gave him a relaxed look. Even the no socks and boat shoes looked good on him. Not that I'd ever say that, of course.

'Hello, Michael.' I was determined not to ask questions like 'How are you?' just to be polite.

'And you must be... Sean, was it?' Michael smirked, purposely using the wrong name, I guessed, to put my friend on the back foot.

'Seamus. Nice to meet you, Mark. What a stunning venue. A fabulous choice for a wedding.'

I coughed to cover up Seamus's deliberate faux pas.

Seamus stepped forward into his space and held out his hand while beaming at Michael, whose smirk had immediately disappeared. The two men shook hands and were quite obviously sizing each other up. Michael then seemed to suddenly remember that Claudia was behind him and he turned and grabbed her wrist, pulling her towards him and proprietarily throwing an arm around her shoulders.

'And of course, Jo, you already know Claudia.'

He laughed. I didn't.

I gave her a nod. I wasn't going to be rude, but I also wasn't going to treat her like she was still my best friend. She gave up the right to that title when she shagged my husband.

'Hi, Jo, lovely to see you.'

My heart was pumping ferociously and I was betrayed again when I realised that it *was* almost lovely to see her face. One which I knew every part of. That was so familiar to me. I had to fight the urge to say, 'Nice to see you too,' which I would have said to *anyone* in a meet-and-greet situation but kept my mouth shut for once and instead smiled falsely.

We all stood and looked at each other uncomfortably until Seamus took control of the situation, saying, 'Shall we go and check in then, babe?'

I raised an eyebrow at him and he kind of grimaced back, before picking up both of the bags and the suit carriers.

'Here, let me help you, Seamus. Nice motor, by the way.'

Michael had and always would be a total and utter charmer. People who had met him over the years adored him. I had always felt that he exhausted himself being so nice to others, that when I got him at home at the end of the day, he had nothing left for me. And after taking care of the girls single-handedly, I hadn't got a lot left to give either. Running our daughters to school, keeping house and running errands, picking them up, taking them to two different classes, to meet their friends, to parties when they got slightly older, kept me as busy as having a full-time job. That, along with a constantly filled washing basket, which I was convinced actually had more clean clothes in it than dirty, which had just been discarded from the wardrobe and chucked in the washing because they couldn't be bothered to pick them up, left me with no time for myself.

I didn't realise until after we'd split up and I'd had hours and hours to myself, micro-analysing our lives, that our marriage *had* stagnated, hard though it was to admit. It was no wonder he went off with someone a few years younger, more beautiful, more confident. More exciting. Someone who put him first and clearly made him smile more than I even did, because he really did look happier than I think I'd ever seen him. Maybe I should want that for him, I thought, but there was quite a large bit of me that wanted him to have thought he'd made the wrong decision and want me back. He clearly did not.

Maybe having someone who probably shaved her armpits and legs every time she had a shower, prepared with her best undies on at all times to have spontaneous sex at any time, was what every man needed. I was someone who was constantly knackered after doing everything for everyone else and only made the effort to do it if I thought there might be the remote chance of some bedroom action. And even then it felt a bit more like a tick off on my mental to-do list, rather than something that we were doing because passion took over.

As Michael grabbed Claudia's hand to walk back towards the entrance of the hotel and she turned to smile at him, it made me think of all the times that he used to do that with me. Despite what had happened between us and all the things that I felt were wrong in our relationship, seeing him now made me remember that there were amazing times along the way too. I recalled the times when he did make me feel like I was the only woman in the world for him, and how we were a team in everything we did. It's almost like your brain wipes out the bad times and replaces them with the good and those times seem to be multiplied by one hundred to make them the only things you can think of.

Michael turned, dropping her hand, and took the suit carriers from Seamus. Then they walked ahead of Claudia and me. As we made our way into the hotel, she was constantly chattering to me, about the building I think, but to be honest I didn't really pay any attention to what she was saying. My head was aching already; a buzzing in my ears; the stress getting to me. All I was thinking was that Michael would see straight through mine and Seamus's fake date for what it really was. One good man, supporting a friend in need.

As the automatic glass doors opened into a minimalist foyer where the modern furniture perfectly complemented the character of the old gothic building, giving a trendy but sophisticated and luxurious vibe, I could absolutely see why Lucy had picked this hotel for her special day.

The young receptionist, who was standing behind a part-wood, part-glass desk, raised an eyebrow when she saw Seamus, clearly appreciating a good-looking man when she saw one. A tinge of jealously struck me. How bloody dare she? If we were actually together she really would have been openly flirting with my man. I could feel my nostrils flaring, feeling properly riled.

'Can I take your name, please?'

Michael boomed from behind. 'Mrs Michael Jenkins and partner. This is the booking where I asked you to upgrade the two rooms to a suite. On me.'

'Oh, you didn't have to do that,' I said, secretly cursing him for putting me in this predicament, which now sounded like Seamus and I would now have to share. I just hoped that they'd respected that we'd originally asked for two beds.

'My pleasure,' he replied to me. 'Can't have my former wife and her,' he indicated speech marks in the air, '"boyfriend" in a shitty room now, can I? What sort of man would that make me?'

Resisting the urge to tell him what sort of man I thought he really was, I smiled sweetly again, wondering if a genuine smile would appear on my face.

'Why don't you go up to your room, freshen up and meet us in the bar shortly?' Michael said. 'We've already got Lucy with us and I've told them you'll join us in there.'

I nodded and the receptionist informed us that she'd get a porter to take our luggage up immediately.

The large sweeping wooden staircase seemed like a mountain as we began to climb and I could feel eyes boring into me from behind but was determined not to look back. My head was already hurting and we'd only just arrived. I could feel a huge pressure hanging over me, even though I'd been telling myself that I just had to stop stressing about the whole situation and enjoy the occasion.

The porter came to a stop outside the room and Seamus stood back to let me follow in first. I smiled at the porter as he doffed his imaginary cap and stepped out before Seamus entered. We looked towards the huge bed in the centre of the room and mouthed the word 'Oh!' at exactly the same time but mine in an 'Oh-my-God!' tone and his in a 'Look-at-the-size-of-that' voice.

I looked around the room for another door and, on finding two facing us, I let out a sigh of relief. But when I approached it, and tentatively turned the handle of the first one, it opened into a huge bathroom, with an enormous bath as the central point and beyond it, a window which overlooked the rolling Cotswold hills. There was a double sink set in granite countertop, a shower big enough to have a party in and a toilet in the corner.

Moving back out into the other room, I opened the other door, looking forward to seeing what Seamus's room was going to be like. Unfortunately, that door opened up into a huge dressing room and nothing else. My heartbeat sped up and I turned to Seamus, who was biting his lip, trying not to laugh.

I huffed louder than I'd ever done in my life. And that was hard because I was a good huffer!

'It's like the scene from a romcom movie. There's only one bed.'

He managed to keep his face from breaking into a grin.

'And you know what always happens in those romcoms, don't you?'

'That's really not helping my anxiety at the moment, Seamus.'

'I'm sorry, Jo. I'm just trying to make light of the situation. I'll go and see the receptionist and see whether we can change rooms. I'll be back in a mo.'

Managing to mutter my thanks at him, I plonked myself down on the sofa which overlooked the main bedroom window, the beautiful greenery outside calming my nerves slightly. Opening the window, I breathed in the fresh air and the sound of the birds singing in the garden below calmed me a little, and I started to feel myself relaxing once more.

A cough from behind me alerted me that Seamus was back and when I turned, his face looked quite dejected.

'They're fully booked, this is the only room they have, Jo. There's nothing more that we can do.'

32

'Share? We can't share.'

The thought of even getting changed in front of someone new horrified me, let alone sharing a bed. The last year had not been particularly kind to me and through comfort eating, which had been the only thing that made me temporarily happy, I'd put on just under a stone. Mum had commented on it recently, and said that at my age, life was too short not to eat the biscuit, or the cake that I wanted, but I don't think her permission had really helped me to control my recent food habits. Just thinking about taking my clothes off and someone seeing the roll of fat which had developed around my belly which I'd never had before made me cringe. Thank you, menopause. You're so kind to constantly gift middle-aged women these wonderful qualities. Not only the weight but the constant brain fog and other unexpected things which crop up on a weekly basis. Only the day before, when I was waxing my faint moustache, I noticed a huge coarse hair had sprouted from my chin.

'What the hell are we going to do now?' I asked as I plonked myself down on the bed.

I felt an arm come around my shoulders at the same time as I felt the weight of Seamus sitting next to me on the bed. This was way too intimate. For the last thirty years or so, the only people I'd been in a bedroom with were my husband or one of my daughters and even then I'd always managed to cover myself up. I wasn't one of those mums who flaunted everything they had in front of the whole family. In fairness, Michael didn't get to see me often without my clothes on and when we did ever get around to being intimate it was always strictly with the lights off. Also, I slept in a Marks and Sparks nightie these days and was dreading the thought of only having the strappy negligee I decided to treat myself to for this trip because I wanted to feel at my best at all times. I wasn't sure that it would hide an awful lot.

'We'll sort it later. Don't worry. There'll be a solution. I just need to give it some thought. I saw Michael downstairs and he said that he'd organised some teas and coffees in the bar. They're all waiting for us. I think we should go, Jo Jenkins.'

I resigned myself to the fact the bed situation wasn't something that we could deal with right now and without a great deal of thought, and while I wanted to text both Emma and Michelle to tell them what had happened, I was pretty sure that they'd find the situation far more amusing than I had.

'Chin up, babe.'

I turned towards Seamus and raised my eyebrow again – this was the second time he'd used that word.

'Since when have you been a "babe" type of guy, by the way?'

'Since I had to pretend to my friend's ex-husband that she is the love of my life.' He winked. 'Babe.'

I grinned. It didn't seem to matter what I found myself doing, I struggled to look at this man and not be smiley. He had one of those faces that was constantly happy and it was infectious. He had such a lovely energy and was a wonderful presence to be around. Maybe I just had to embrace that and be thankful that he'd volunteered to accompany me on this trip and that I didn't have to come alone.

As we approached the bar, which was opposite the reception desk, the girl behind the desk smiled at Seamus and I could see that he was blushing slightly.

'You OK there?' I asked.

He rested his hand on the small of my back and practically propelled me through the door.

'I am, but that receptionist did offer me a bed in her room for the night. She told me that if we were struggling with the arrangements there was a huge bed in her room and that she'd be prepared to let me "share".'

'Oh! My! God! The cheeky cow. How dare she?' I felt rage creeping up within me.

'Thank you for jumping to my defence, Jo Jenkins. Very kind of you. I did thank her very much and say that you and I would be perfectly fine together, then I practically ran up the stairs back to you. She scared the living daylights out of me.'

My rage quickly subsided. My fake date was back to where it should be.

I turned towards the reception desk and saw that the woman had been watching us like a hawk. I never thought I'd have to be worrying about Seamus being propositioned right in front of my eyes. I turned towards her and smiled, and slung my arm around his waist.

'She looks like she'd eat me alive!' he whispered into my ear, as he reached down towards me and kissed my cheek. I burst into laughter and so did he.

'It's good to see you laugh, Mum. It's been a while. And you are…?'

My daughter Lucy had come across to greet us. She leaned

over and kissed my cheek, an air of coolness about her. It wasn't the reunion I'd envisaged. I thought it would have been a bit more, well, huggy really. Maybe it was because it was a generally awkward situation for all of us. I immediately forgave her.

'This is Seamus, who I told you about.'

She had the good grace to look bashful.

'Oh yes, sorry. I must have forgotten your name. Nice to meet you.'

'You too. Your mum talks about her girls all the time. It's clear to see that they get their good looks from their mother. On the picture above her fireplace you look like three sisters.'

I batted him on the arm and blushed. Lucy looked from one of us to the other and then invited us to join the large group around a couple of small tables. Noticing that she was chewing the inside of her cheek (a family trait!) I smiled at her and noticed that she shook her head as she sat down and looked away.

'Seamus, my man. Joanna, darling. Come and join us.' Michael was reorganising the seating to squeeze us in and was obviously giving it large in front of his friends. As I looked around the room, I realised that these people were actually *our* friends. Some of whom I hadn't seen since we'd split up. It's strange when a couple parts company. Sometimes people take sides, some people stick by you through thick and thin. Michael's charm meant that in our situation, nearly everyone except for my wonderful friend Lisa had gradually dropped away. Clearly he'd kept in touch with them all and as I heard him talk about inviting them over to the villa in Spain, I realised the reason. He was fun. While I'd been wallowing in my loneliness and self-pity, he'd been thriving; living his best life with not a care in the world.

Seamus glanced at me from his seat a couple of times. He'd been put next to Claudia and I couldn't even begin to imagine what they would have in common to talk about apart from us. I hoped she wasn't grilling him too much about our relationship.

I got up and excused myself to go to the loo, and when I came out of the ladies', I found Michael and Seamus standing awkwardly at the bar, arguing about who was going to pay for the wine for the dinner table, and Michael appeared to be winning.

'Trust me, Seamus,' I said. 'When Michael gets an idea into his head, there's no backing down. I learned that years ago.'

'I just didn't want to take advantage of his hospitality. He's already covered the cost of our room.'

The words 'our room' made me cringe but I pushed the thoughts away, thinking that I would deal with that later. Also, I would remind Michael at some point that the wedding budget he was using to cover the cost was coming from a fund I'd contributed to way more than he had.

One crisis at a time though.

'So, how is your room, Joanna, darling? Everything OK for you both?'

'Yes, it's lovely, thank you. Very nice indeed.'

'Excellent. Strangely the woman on reception must have got the bookings wrong because she said you were in adjoining rooms so I told her there was clearly an error when I wanted you to be upgraded. Glad it's all worked well, *mate*.' He looked directly at Seamus and I hoped that both of our pasted-on smiles of gratitude did not reflect what we were really thinking.

'So, how did you two meet?' Michael continued. 'You never mentioned anyone special, Joanna? Surely, as your husband, I should be the first to know.'

I went to speak but Seamus beat me to it.

'You think? I would have thought that really, as her *ex*-husband, you should be the *last* to know.' He forced a laugh. 'Mate!'

The two men stared each other down and I felt that I needed to break the uncomfortable silence between them.

'We've got to know each other while Seamus has been doing some work at Aunty June's house, didn't we?' I smiled at Seamus, proudly resting my hand upon his arm.

'Yes. That's right,' Seamus said. 'I'll never forget the moment I first laid eyes on Jo. She opened the door to her house and she took my breath away. I thought she was one of the most beautiful people I'd ever met, and when I got to know her better, I knew it was both inside and out. I just couldn't wait to spend more time with this wonderful, brave, kind and inspiring lady. I suppose you could even say it was love at first sight for me. And remember, babe, it's *your* house now.'

'*My* Aunty June's house, you mean,' Michael corrected. 'Daft old battle axe. Never did like her but can't believe the old biddy left it to you. That was very interesting to find out. Couldn't believe it when the girls told me. Thought she might even leave it to them if she didn't want to leave it to me. I was her only nephew, after all.'

'To be honest, Michael, the girls will get it in the end anyway, so they'll have their chance.'

He walked away but not until after I'd heard him mutter under his breath, 'They most certainly will. Maybe sooner than you think.'

A shiver ran up my spine.

33

I didn't want to sit around in the bar drinking all afternoon. I'd spent literal years doing this when Michael and I were together. My mum would look after the kids for a night, and Michael would whisk me away for what I thought was a romantic break, but more often than not ended up with us sitting in a golf hotel with his golfing friends.

I looked around the table at the empty glasses already there. I wasn't a huge drinker and the bubbles from the glass of Prosecco that I'd had when we came into the bar had fizzled out a while ago. I laughed to myself while thinking that was a metaphor for my marriage.

Seamus looked a little uneasy so I asked if he fancied going for a walk in the grounds. He jumped up straight away and said he'd love to stretch his legs. Claudia didn't seem to be able to take her eyes off Seamus as he stood and stretched. God, as if taking my husband wasn't enough...

As we reached the foyer, we shimmied past the receptionist, who nearly broke her neck trying to speak to Seamus, and headed outside. The late-afternoon sun was still warm and felt wonderful on my body as I let out all the pent-up tension I'd been holding in my shoulders and neck. Seamus also rolled his shoulders, so he must have been feeling the same.

'I'm sorry. I should never have asked you to do this for me,' I said. 'What was I thinking?'

'Well, firstly, Jo Jenkins, you didn't ask. I offered. And secondly, I get to spend a couple of nights in a hotel with a hot lady. What's to complain about? It's the most exciting thing to have happened to me in literally years.' His eyes crinkled when he smiled at me and reached out for my hand, which incidentally fitted perfectly in his. It felt nice to hold hands with someone after all these years. Another thing that disappears after a few years of marriage and when your children grow up and don't want to hold your hand any more. One day it just stops with no warning. I had missed the warmth of another hand in mine more than I realised.

He dropped it as soon as we walked past the window. Oh. I hadn't realised it was all for show. I tried to hide the disappointment. All of this fake emotion was messing with my head. Here was a gorgeous man, who had offered to pretend to be my date, and he seemed to genuinely like me and find me attractive and funny. Hot, he even said earlier, and that was when we weren't in company either. Yet the last person he lived with was a man. Was he gay? Bisexual? Who knew what people's preferences were these days? When I was last 'courting', as Mum called it, there weren't many gay people around in our little Staffordshire village. In those days, we were very un-diverse. I'm sure it was different in more cosmopolitan cities. But these days, when you met a man, you had no idea about his sexuality.

My mind wandered off to how I would feel if I discovered that Seamus was bisexual. I honestly didn't know how I'd deal with that. It was not something I'd had to consider before but I supposed it could be a possibility. It was all very complicated and I couldn't afford to get my hopes up so pushed it to the back of my mind again. Gosh, this new style of dating in the 2020s was too bloody confusing for a girl like me.

When Seamus stopped and looked at me, waiting, I realised that he had asked me something.

'Sorry, I was away with the fairies then. What did you say?'

'I was just asking what you wanted to do about getting ready to go out. Would you like me to get ready first or would you like to? Or do you want to get ready together?'

Honestly, I didn't know how this was going to go. If he got ready first, where would I go? I didn't want to be left alone somewhere while I waited. And if he got ready first, then it'd be the same for him but worse because he didn't know anyone here. Also, it would look weird. I should have asked Emma and Michelle to come today instead of tomorrow. It would have been so much easier if I could have gone to theirs.

'We could just be grown-ups and get ready together.'

'What? In the same room? At the same time? Wouldn't that be a bit awkward?'

'There's only one way to find out, I suppose. But only if you promise to cover your eyes with your hands when I'm walking around naked!'

I fiddled with my necklace, and could feel my face getting a little hot.

'Don't worry, Jo Jenkins. Come on, let's go and get it over and done with.' He turned to walk away. 'And I don't normally walk around naked. My underwear of choice is a gold lamé thong, so at least the front will be covered up, even if you have to see my arse cheeks hanging out.'

And with that he walked away from me, leaving me with a

very odd expression on my face, wondering whether he was telling the truth or not.

Having a long relaxing bath was now off the menu; a quick shower seemed more apt under the circumstances. As the water cascaded over my body, I realised that I was stressing over everything and really needed to calm myself. I took a deep breath and told myself to be brave, walking back into the bedroom, wrapped in a towel that barely covered me up and another tied turban-style around my head. Seamus was lying on the bed in his clothes, looking mighty comfortable. A sexy little snore indicated that he was indeed very chilled. Watching his chest move up and down was peaceful for me in itself. He really was handsome and I struggled to drag my eyes away.

A knock at the door made his eyes spring open and I immediately went to open it, pretending I'd only just come out of the bathroom and hadn't been staring at him.

My other daughter, Melissa, stood there in the hallway. She'd arrived late, much to her sister's disgust apparently, and was just popping by to say hello. When she saw Seamus lying on the bed, she raised an eyebrow at me, and a look of horror passed on her face.

'Really, Mother. Do you have to be so blatant? I'll see you in the restaurant at 7.30 p.m.' She stomped off, clearly disgusted at the thought that her mother might be even contemplating being in a relationship with anyone who wasn't her father. A clear case of double standards, I'd say.

Seamus, who was now awake, grimaced. 'Sorry, Jo Jenkins. Have I got you into trouble? We must have looked a picture, to be honest.'

I laughed. 'I do think my daughters sometimes forget that I get to have a life too. And forget that I'm a woman, with... you know... needs of my own.'

'Do you indeed? Is that anything I can help you with?' He bit his lip and raised an eyebrow at the same time and I could feel warmth spread through my body. Maybe I was imagining that he'd started flirting with me again. Anyone else might think that he was being totally serious. You shouldn't mess with a woman of a certain age. God only knows what trouble you could end up in.

Totally flustered and getting hotter by the minute, I excused myself and headed back into the bathroom to get my brush.

'Bathroom is all yours.' I couldn't quite meet his eye.

'Thanks, babe.' I turned round but he was gazing out the window. This time it didn't seem like he was putting it on.

Once I heard the shower switch on, I got dressed in super record time, before I heard it go off again. I didn't know how long he might be. Maybe he was being polite by taking a while, or maybe just being thorough in cleaning his body. Oh, gosh, not a time for me to thinking about that. I needed to get myself ready.

I flicked on the TV, trying to distract myself from thinking about his body, and when he appeared, with a towel slung low around his waist, drops of water glistening on his torso, I had to take a deep breath and concentrate hard on the screen.

'Sorry, Jo Jenkins. I forgot to take my toiletry bag and clothes in. Nearly done.' He headed back into the bathroom.

I dried my hair and applied my make-up. I could hear the spraying of deodorant and then he appeared, poking his head around the door.

He whistled.

'You look *amazing*. Sorry, it's probably not the done thing to wolf-whistle at women these days. But trust me. Your ex-husband is going to wish he'd never traded you in for that scutter when he sees you looking like that.'

'Do I really look all right?'

He approached me and took my hands in his.

'You look absolutely stunning and any man would be proud to have you on his arm tonight.'

I chewed the inside of my cheek. I was feeling quite apprehensive about the pre-wedding meal. I knew that a lot of our old friends would be there.

He walked over to the bed and bent to put on his shoes. When he patted the bed next to him, I took the place and sighed.

'Come on. Out with it.'

'With what?'

'Whatever is on your mind.'

I looked around me at the huge room and the bed. The thing that we'd not spoken about since we'd been getting ready. The elephant in the room.

'Where are we going to sleep, Seamus?'

'Well, I'm not sure about you, but I'm adult enough to sleep in a bed with a friend without wanting to jump their bones. How about you? Think you can resist me?'

'Yeah, probably, to be honest.'

'Flattering. Thank you.'

'You started it.'

He prodded me in the side and I poked him back. He fell onto his back and I turned to look at him, his eyes flicking from mine, to my lips, and back again. Our eyes locked. It felt like ages had passed when he pushed himself up.

'What are you really worried about? Is it just the bed?'

There was so much going through my mind right now. I was feeling really confused and it was giving me a headache.

'I don't know how my old friends are going to react when they see me. I'm old, fat and frumpy.' My shoulders slumped.

'You are absolutely none of those things. You are gorgeous and you look amazing. Maybe you should be thinking about how *you* are going to react when you see *them*? How do you want this to go? You can be in control of this situation with a bit of thought.'

'You think?'

'I do. Maybe you'll be happy to see them. Maybe you'll want to stay away. It's entirely up to you and we are going to do this *your* way. You just let me know what you need me to do.'

He dipped his index finger under my chin and lifted my face up to his.

'I wish you could see what I see. You're amazing.' He bent his head towards me and I could feel his warm breath on my face. I closed my eyes and felt his lips brush against my cheek.

I was so confused. This felt like he did like me after all. Had I got this whole thing wrong?

'We should go. Ready?' He held out his hand and mine fitted it perfectly. I took one huge deep breath and then let it go noisily.

'As I'll ever be. Let's do this.'

34

When we arrived in the foyer, we were immediately greeted by Becky, the wedding planner, who informed us, to my absolute sheer horror, that instead of having the family meal that we thought we were having, there had been a change of plans.

'Mr Shaffer... err...'

'Nakker!'

'I beg your pardon!' she exclaimed.

'Shaffernakker. That's how you say it.'

'Oh, my apologies. It's not a name I've come across before. Unusual, isn't it?'

'Not really. I have a whole family of them and you just say it as it looks when it's written down.' He sighed in exasperation. Seamus had explained to me once how he'd been picked on at school for his unusual surname and I knew that he was still quite prickly about it.

I jumped in, keen to change the atmosphere.

'What's happening now then?' I asked.

'Boys in the bar, girls in the orangery. Can't have the bride and groom spending the night before the wedding together now, can we? Don't want bad luck.'

'Oh, OK. I thought all that tradition had gone out of the window.' I patted my handbag, safe in the fact that some traditions were still in place, knowing that I could quite happily pass on my little gift to my daughter shortly. But then very quickly my shoulders slumped at the thought of not having Seamus by my side for that little bit of a comfort blanket. And then at the other thought of him being thrown to the lions, in with a group of men he'd never met before. Then the thought of being with all the girls meant that I'd have to be in close proximity to Claudia. A groan escaped my lips involuntarily which seemed to come from the pit of my stomach.

I turned to him. 'Will you be OK?'

'Of course I will. Will you?'

My faltering smile showed just how insecure I was feeling. However, as a mother and a wife, I'd often had to do things that I didn't want to do. So if I'd done it before, I could do it again. I pulled my shoulders back and took a huge breath, trying to fill my lungs with positivity.

'Only one way to find out.'

He took a step towards me and held both of my shoulders firmly.

'You have absolutely got this, Jo Jenkins! Just have a little bit of the faith I have in you. You're amazing and you just need to go and sock it to them. Don't let anyone get the better of you. You are the bride's mother. You grew her inside your body. You literally made her. And *no one* can take that away from you. Go get the fuckers!'

He winked and a smile spread across my face. He was great at a pep talk, I'd give him that. He leant across and kissed me gently on the cheek and I walked away feeling like I could take on the world.

That wavered slightly when I realised that I was the last to arrive and that the only seat left was next to Claudia, who was sitting next to Lucy, with my own mother on Lucy's other side. But I could do this. This weekend wasn't about me. It was about my daughter and her wedding and I just had to suck it up.

Claudia patted the seat next to her.

'I've saved you a seat, Jo. Mum and Step-Mum together.'

God! The horror.

'Evening, everyone,' I said to the gathered group. 'This looks like it's going to be a whole lot of fun.'

I just wished I was feeling on the inside what I was hopefully portraying on the outside. I wasn't sure where this whoosh of inner strength came from but the next words escaped my mouth before my brain engaged.

'Thanks, Claudia, be a love and swap seats, please. As mother of the bride I am definitely going to be sitting next to my daughter.'

The room fell totally silent and for a moment, when we locked eyes, I could see her nostrils flaring while she decided what to do. I'd known her long enough to know what all her little signs of stress were. I didn't want to cause trouble, but what Seamus had said about me being Lucy's mother was absolutely correct. Lucy was *my* daughter and I *would* sit next to her. I'd been in Claudia's shadow now for long enough and for this weekend, this was my time.

She plastered a smile across her face.

'God, yes, of course. Sorry, Jo. Don't know what I was thinking then. Here you go.'

She moved over into the next seat and I had to shuffle past her. I reached across and kissed Lucy's cheek, and noticed that she was looking at me nervously. I smiled and patted her arm, turning to Claudia.

'Thank you.' My voice came out in a whisper, the words almost catching in my throat as I remembered our very great friendship and what fun we'd had over the years. I nearly crumbled but then I recalled the sheer betrayal I felt when I'd discovered the truth about their affair. The confidence I'd had a moment ago diminished to hardly anything and I smoothed down the invisible creases in my dress, gathering myself together.

'No problem, Jo. Here, let me pour you a glass of Prosecco. I think we could both do with one, don't you?' Claudia was smiling at me and she seemed absolutely genuine. Maybe it even was. I had been thinking of myself and how hurt I had been for so long that I hadn't even given a second thought for how she might be feeling. This might be awkward for her too. I'd hated her for so long from afar that I'd forgotten that she'd actually been my best friend once. Someone that I really liked. Maybe the evening wouldn't be so bad after all.

35

A commotion at the door made everyone swing round. I knew before I looked over that Melissa had arrived. Ever since she was a little girl, she had certainly known how to make an entrance. And ever since she could be, she was also always late. Her excuse was that she had to be on time at work so she didn't see why in her leisure time she should have to watch the clock. Over the years, we'd tried to explain that her tardiness impacted other people, but she literally didn't care. How I'd managed to bring up two daughters who were so inconsiderate to others, I honestly didn't know. Maybe when I lived closer to them, I hadn't really noticed it, but now I was feeling a little more distance from them, both emotionally and geographically, I realised that it had actually been staring me in the face all along.

She flung herself in the vacant chair next to Lucy and when Lucy pointed out that it belonged to Rebecca, one of her best friends, the response was typically Melissa.

'Oh, well, she'll have to find herself somewhere else to sit, won't she?'

When I glanced over at Mum, she was shaking her head in disbelief.

Melissa spotted me across the table and waved very nonchalantly. 'Hi, Mumsy.'

She turned to her sister and they whispered to each other, thick as thieves as always. Maybe I should just be grateful that they had each other, I thought to myself, and despite the fact that they fought like cat and dog as children, they were the best of friends now. I vowed not to get stressed and knew that we had lots of time over the next day or so to catch up. I was looking forward to some time with my girls.

The waiter, who'd appeared at my shoulder, coughed lightly to get my attention as he took my napkin and laid it out on my lap.

The meal was absolutely lovely. I had baked camembert with pink onion marmalade and focaccia for a starter, which was delicious – I always seemed to overcook this particular dish. My main was pan-fried salmon on a bed of vegetable rice, its earthy spices tickling my taste buds, leaving a delicious aftertaste. Even though I said I was too stuffed to eat dessert, or pudding as we always called it in our family, I managed to put away a small portion of lemon panna cotta drizzled with a raspberry jus. However, it was divine. When you live alone it's amazing not to have to think about and cook your own dinner and it really had been a splendid meal.

Feeling totally sated with the glorious food, I was so relaxed that I even managed to find the strength to make small talk with Claudia. It was, after all, Lucy's special time and I wasn't going to spoil anything by being a total bitch to the woman who in essence had stolen and then run off with my husband. Mum had once said to me that she wouldn't have been able to steal him if he wasn't, in her words, 'proper up for it'. She'd always said that she never trusted him entirely and felt that he'd always had a roving eye. Something I'd clearly been too busy to notice.

I popped to the ladies' before the main event started – none of us had any idea of what was to come as Lucy was keeping it a total surprise.

While I was reapplying my lipstick in the large ornate mirror, Mum wandered in.

She kissed my cheek and stood beside me.

'Well done, darling. I'm so proud of you.'

Puzzled by her words, I turned to face her.

'Me? I haven't done anything, Mum.'

'Oh, but darling, you absolutely have. You are the epitome of class and sophistication. You look fabulous and you are carrying yourself with poise and grace. Not everyone would have been able to do that in these circumstances. As much as I love my darling granddaughter, she hasn't once thought about how this would affect her mother. As long as Lucy is OK, then all is well in her world. It's about time she started to consider others.'

'But she does, Mum. In her job she has so much to contend with. I just don't think she has the capacity to think about much else.'

'You can say that. I can say that she's a selfish little madam who only ever thinks about herself.'

I went to interrupt her but she held her hand up.

'She might be your daughter but she's also my granddaughter and I am allowed to speak the truth. I still love her, of course. They are both amazing young women but, to be honest, with you as a mother and me as their Glamma' (she had always refused to be called Grandma or Nan as she claimed these names made her feel older than she was) 'how could they not be fabulous!' She grinned and her eyes shone bright with mischief. She was wonderful and never ceased to make me smile. 'Anyway,

I'm busting for the loo. Wait for me and I'll walk back out with you.'

The orangery had changed format when we returned and Becky guided us to our new seats, around a circular table, Mum on my left and both of us opposite Lucy. My heart sank as Lucy clapped her hands together and announced that we were going to play 'Couples Truth or Dare'. I looked over to Mum in horror and could see her eyes blazing and nostrils flaring. Lucy glanced between the two of us and I saw a look of doubt cross her face. I knew everything about that face; I had been looking into it for many years and in that moment the penny finally dropped.

'Oh, gosh! I'd totally forgotten that there would be single people here. Don't worry. There are questions that will be suitable for you too, Mum. Although I'm sure now you have your new boyfriend, you'll have lots to share about him.'

I couldn't believe that my daughter had been this insensitive. Maybe Mum was right after all and I needed to acknowledge this quality in my daughter instead of constantly defending her actions, which I felt like I'd been doing for her all my life.

Mum leant towards me and whispered in my ear.

'Hold your head up high, darling. I'm right here and won't let anything awful happen to you.' I turned towards her and she winked at me. 'Stay classy!'

These two words were words she'd said to me throughout many circumstances since I was a young girl. 'If you can be nothing else in life,' she had told me, 'you should be classy.' By all means fall apart when a particular moment is over and you are alone, but in front of people, stay classy. Over the years, it felt like her mantra had been engraved on my brain and had got me through many tricky situations.

Nodding my agreement at her, I smiled at Lucy and saw her shoulders relax. The wedding planner handed her a silver box which she unwrapped the bow from and then reached for the Prosecco bottle and spun it. There were ten of us sitting waiting apprehensively. As it approached my side of the table, it slowed right down. It was hovering on me. I looked up and said a silent prayer. Dear God, please do not be this cruel to me. Not today. Thank goodness, it wobbled a bit more then landed on Mum. I let out the breath I'd been hanging on to.

Lucy picked out a card from the box and read the first question out loud.

'How did you meet the love of your life?'

Now Mum loved an audience and everyone relaxed as she started to unravel her story, holding everyone captive. She was a wonderful storyteller and the girls had always preferred her at bedtime. They were totally mesmerised by her because she'd conjure up the most amazing tales.

'Well, when I met Ron, the *first* love of my life, I was at the local institute which was like a community hall which held functions. I used to work behind the bar and one evening, I found myself staring into the eyes of the most handsome man I'd ever seen. I fell well and truly under his spell, and we were married six months later. Discovering very quickly that he couldn't have children, at first we were devastated but then we looked into other options and twelve months later,' she turned to me, 'our darling Jo came to live with us. We were a perfect and incredibly happy little family. We had a wonderful life for five years, until he had a heart attack one day and we were robbed of his wonderfulness.' I looked down at the table, willing the tears not to fall. 'I spent my life bringing up Jo the best I could, in the way I hoped he would have approved of. I threw myself into my family and,' she reached out for my hand, 'Jo was and is my everything.'

The room fell silent, spellbound by her story.

'But don't we all love a story with a happy ending, ladies?'

Nods all around showed everyone's agreement. 'Fast forward to many years later when a friend of mine asked me to go to her crib club with her. To be honest, I'd got to the stage where I didn't feel that Jo or her girls needed me any more. They had families of their own and I finally admitted to myself that I was incredibly lonely.'

A gasp escaped my lips. I hoped it wasn't too loud but I did notice a few glances flicker my way. I hadn't ever considered, even in the recent years of feeling this way myself, that my own mother had felt the same way. Honestly, I felt awful for never picking up on this.

'I'm so sorry, Mum. I didn't know that.'

'I know, darling. I didn't want you to know. It was my job to find what made me happy; it was not your responsibility to do it for me.'

'But...'

'But nothing.' She winked at me again and smiled. Then, turning back to her attentive audience, she continued her tale. 'At the crib club I was introduced to a man called Barry who I thought was the shyest man I'd ever met. But then, as time went on and we played crib together, I realised that he was actually the kindest, most loving, incredible, wonderful man I'd ever met. At first, I felt that I didn't deserve someone in my life like him. That what Ron and I had could never be replaced. I kept my distance for a while but a friend of mine pulled me to one side and said that I should give him a chance. Then, when I allowed myself to do just that, I fell in love all over again. I never replaced Ron. I just found Baz and he's amazing.' There were oohs and aahs all around. 'So this goes to show, ladies, that second chances do come along and when they do you have to grab them with both hands. Life is short and you have to live it to the full to do justice to the people who aren't here any more to do that for themselves.

We owe it to them.' She looked over to me at that point and held my gaze before raising her glass to Lucy. 'And of course, Lucy, my darling, your love and marriage will last forever so you won't have to worry about anything like this.'

Lucy got up and walked around the table and gave Mum the biggest hug I'd seen her give her for years.

'Thanks so much for sharing that with us, Glamma. And I'm no fantasist. I know not all marriages last forever but I can only hope that we'll be happy together for as long as we can be.'

'That's right, darling. Always the optimist!'

We all laughed and it took away the tension.

'Right!' exclaimed Lucy. 'Next question.'

When I groaned, I hoped that it wasn't too loud.

36

Considering I hadn't seen either of my daughters for a good few months and was really looking forward to seeing them both, I was feeling disappointed that we hadn't had much time together to catch up. My handbag vibrated on my foot and I reached down to pick it up. As I reached for my phone, my hand brushed against the organza bag and my heart lifted. Perhaps Lucy would feel differently when I gave her the surprise gift that I'd brought.

When Michael and I got married, Mum had given me the most beautiful horseshoe on a ribbon. As she gave it to me the morning of my wedding, she told me that she loved me more than she ever dreamed it was possible to love a child and when she walked me down the aisle and gave me away to Michael, there were tears in her eyes. At the time, I hadn't realised what an emotional moment that must have been for her, doing the job that a bride's father would normally do. I had saved the horseshoe for the first of my girls to get married. I just needed to find the right moment to give it to Lucy.

However, it was as if Mum knew, as the next words she spoke gave me the perfect opportunity.

'Lucy, darling. Have you got your something old, something new, something borrowed, something blue?'

Lucy laughed. 'Well, you know I don't normally go in for all that bollocks but I did think that maybe it wouldn't hurt.' Everyone laughed and leaned in as she continued. 'My something new is my dress, something borrowed is Melissa's necklace, something blue is the garter that Luke bought me. Cheeky bugger. Just need something old now.'

Clearing my throat and reaching into my bag, I went to speak.

However, the very last person I wanted to hear from right then beat me to it.

'Lucy, your dad and I were talking and we'd like to give you something which is the perfect thing for that old category.' Claudia beamed at my daughter as she handed her a parcel across the table. God! She'd already taken my husband and my house in Spain. Was she going to get my daughters too? I felt like my heart could break into two at any moment.

Mum saw me put the organza bag back in my bag and smiled narrowly at me. She mouthed 'Stay classy!' and I blinked away the tears that were starting to form.

Lucy carefully unwrapped the parcel and squealed when she saw the gift.

'Oh my God. This is Granny's veil. Melissa, you big sneak! Is this why you wouldn't let me get a veil?'

My two daughters grinned at each other. Lucy stood and moved towards Claudia, embracing her in a tight hug.

I thought that when Michael left me, I felt awful, but this seemed even worse. Melissa, Michael and Claudia had clearly been in cahoots about their little plan and Lucy was beside herself with emotion. Michael's mother had died when the girls had just become teenagers and they had adored her, devastated that she had been taken far too young for their liking.

'Claudia, no one has ever have done anything more thoughtful for me. Thank you so much. You've made me so happy.'

Melissa joined their hug and I had never felt so excluded from something in my life. Quietly, and hoping that no one would notice, I removed myself from the table and headed for the ladies', locking myself in one of the cubicles and trying to pull myself together as quietly as I could because I could hear that there was someone in the cubicle next door.

As I was wiping the tears from my eyes, I heard the main door go and someone walk in. There was no way in the world that I was going to go out there. I didn't want anyone to see me right now and certainly not before I had put some more make-up on. I ferreted around in my bag, pulling out a compact, and used the mirror to wipe the mascara from my cheeks, then applied some bronzer to hopefully cover up the streaks and finished off with some lipstick. Not sure why, but lipstick always made me feel better. I think from my youth, when whenever I was feeling down, my own nan used to take me shopping and treated me to a new one, insisting that a new lippy always lifted your mood.

I heard a few doors banging open and closed again and was pretty sure that I was alone. But when I entered the main bathroom area, I realised that I had company. Familiar blue eyes stared back at me from the mirror.

'Jo, how are you? You look lovely, by the way.'

'Claudia.'

I nodded, not knowing what on earth to say to her now we were alone. What did you actually chat about to the woman who used to be your friend and behind your back shagged and then stole your husband? She turned so that she was standing with her backside resting against the basins with what looked like a martini in her hand. All I could focus on was the olive floating around on the top of her glass. Then the cocktail stick she was nervously twizzling between her fingers came to my attention and I thought about how much I'd quite like to ram it in her eye at that very moment.

'I hope you didn't mind me giving Lucy the veil. I probably should have asked you first. Michael said I didn't need to but I did look at your face when I handed the parcel to her and you looked a little uncomfortable. I hope it was OK with you.'

All I could think of was what Mum would say now if she was next to me. I channelled my inner Jacqui and took a deep breath just as Claudia speared the olive and put it into her mouth.

'It was really nice of you, Claudia. Thank you.'

As I turned, I heard a choking sound. She clearly wasn't expecting me to thank her and it would appear from the retching sound that was now coming from her that the olive had got stuck in her throat.

My head went into a frenzy. What should I do? What would I do? Two very different things. Claudia struggled to catch her breath, now going quite a strange shade of purple, and went from grasping her throat to grabbing hold of the wash basin as she slid to the floor. Her eyes locked onto mine as the most horrendous noise gurgled from her throat and I could just about make out the words that she'd spoken.

'Help me, Jo. *Please.*' I turned on my heel and slammed the door behind me.

37

'Quick, I need some help in here. My friend is choking.'

I ran back into the corridor and, thank goodness, the wedding planner just happened to be walking past the toilet door. I practically screamed at her. She followed me back into the ladies' room and we both went over to Claudia. I put my hands on her shoulders and tried to calm her down.

'Don't worry, Claudia, we're going to get you sorted out. Just try not to panic.'

Becky went up behind her and performed the Heimlich manoeuvre. I wasn't aware that you could do it from a seated position but it clearly worked as the olive shot out of Claudia's mouth and splatted on the far wall. We all watched the squished debris sliding downwards and Claudia and I slumped against the sink unit. Becky took a deep breath, smoothed her hair back into place and promptly left as quickly as she had arrived, totally underwhelmed and not at all affected by the fact that she may have just saved someone's life.

The intense silence that followed was palpable.

Claudia reached out for my hand and squeezed. I knew that I should probably withdraw it, but didn't.

'Oh my God, Jo, thank you! I honestly thought you were going to leave me to die.'

I smiled sweetly.

'Oh. As if.' I overexaggerated my words, pretty sure that she would know that I didn't mean it.

'I think if the roles were reversed, I probably would have done, you know.' She had the good grace to look quite ashamed at what she was saying.

'Well, it's a good job it was this way round then, wasn't it?'

Groaning loudly, I stood.

I reached down to her and offered her my hand and after only a slight hesitation she reached out and pulled herself up.

'Jo, I have something to tell you.'

'Can it wait? I think we both need a stiff drink.'

'Yeah, maybe you are right? But maybe without the olives this time, eh?'

We grinned at each other and left the bathroom. Funny how things turn out.

38

When I met up with Seamus later in the bar, it sounded like he'd had a particularly testing evening too.

'Shall we just go to bed?' he asked. Much as I thought it might be awkward once we got up to our room, I just wanted to see the back of tonight. He ordered a bottle of red wine and the waiter handed him two large glasses, which he carried upstairs, while in my hands I held my shoes, my dignity leaving at the same time that my feet started to ache like hell. My head too.

'Honestly, Jo. I thought I was being interviewed for a job. In fact, I don't think anyone has asked me that many questions, *ever*.'

'I'm so sorry you had to go through that, Seamus. It must have been awful for you. I should never have asked you to come.'

He smiled. 'I'm glad you did.' He kicked off his own shoes at that point and it felt strangely intimate. 'And it certainly sounds like I came off better out of the two of us.'

'It was horrendous. I couldn't believe it when Lucy asked Claudia what was the most romantic thing that Michael had ever done for her. When she repeated the exact same thing that he did for our twentieth wedding anniversary, I didn't know whether to laugh or cry.'

'Of all the people in the world, I would never have put you and Michael together, you know.'

'Really?'

'Yeah, he's loud and brash and proper in your face. And you're... well... lovely.'

'He wasn't always like that. And thank you.'

'When did he change?'

'We had nothing, you know, to start with. When we first got together, we both worked really hard to build the business from scratch. He worked all hours and then the first few weeks after I'd had Lucy, I worked around her. The same when Melissa came too. My mum was great and would have the girls while we both worked. Then when he landed a massive contract, and the money started rolling in, he changed dramatically and insisted I gave up and became a stay-at-home mum.'

'And what about Claudia? Where does she fit into everything?'

I sighed loudly and sat in one of the large armchairs in our suite, tucking my feet under me, while he went into the bathroom, returning with a glass of water which he handed to me. I gulped it down, suddenly very thirsty. I put the glass down on the table next to the chair and then Seamus poured us both a glass of wine. Already, it felt like the pressure from my head was starting to lift. Maybe it was because I was finally feeling relaxed for the first time in hours, despite knowing that we were going to have to deal with the sleeping arrangements. We sat and chatted, and I finally started to feel the tension release in my shoulders. The first time I'd really relaxed all day.

'We took Claudia on about ten years later. I'd known her for years as she used to work at our doctor's surgery and I'd always thought she was lovely. Always bright, smiley and eager to help and she just seemed to want the company to succeed as much as we did. We all got on like a house on fire. She was married to Simon at the time and the four of us used to get together a lot outside of work. We became what I thought of as really good friends. The girls loved her. They clearly still do. But obviously Michael loved her the most.'

I felt a huge sigh leave my body.

'How long had they been seeing each other? Do you know?'

'I know when things changed. I presume it was around then.'

'But you don't know for sure.'

'I didn't want to know exactly when it was, to be honest. I couldn't bear to think about the two of them laughing about me behind my back. When I found out, she tried to tell me it wasn't her fault but, hey, she started seeing a married man. She was hardly innocent in it all, was she? I was gutted. Not only did I lose my husband, I also lost a really good friend. She was the person I turned to when Michael started to change. She told me I was imagining it; that he'd never do anything to break up our happy home. How silly of me to confide in the person who was shagging him behind my back.'

'It's easily done, Jo. We never really know the people who are closest to us, do we? But it was his responsibility to say no. He was the one who was married to you.'

I could feel my eyelids starting to droop. It had been a big day and it was starting to take its toll on me.

'Shall I sleep in the chair?' Seamus asked.

'Look, we're two grown adults. I'm sure we can share a bed, can't we? We're friends, right?' The slightest raise of an eyebrow caught my eye. 'And to be honest, even if Bradley Cooper was next to me in bed tonight, I'm too bloody knackered to do anything about it anyway. I don't mind if you don't?'

'OK, I'll let you use the bathroom first.'

When I came back, I quickly slid under the covers as we swapped and he went in to brush his teeth and wash up. It did feel kind of intimate but nice at the same time. I'd been alone for a couple of years now, and I really missed company. Just having someone to do nothing with. Just knowing that even if you weren't talking to each other every minute, that there was someone else in your space. It was... nice.

I turned off the light and when he came out I pretended to be asleep. It just seemed the easiest thing to do in the circumstances and would save any awkward good-nighting. Although I did hear him whisper, 'Good night, Jo Jenkins,' just before I heard his gentle snores.

39

Luckily, when we headed down to the dining room the following morning for breakfast, which was being served in the stunning orangery, apparently the rest of the bridal party had yet to show up, so it was much more relaxed than I originally thought it might be. I'd left Lucy's gift, still wrapped in the organza bag, with the receptionist, asking her to get it to the bride. The sun was shining, casting a golden glow over the stunning landscaped gardens and it was warm enough to have the French doors open. The forecast for the day ahead was to be bright and around 18 degrees, so hopefully perfect for the occasion. Nothing worse than a bride who was sweating her boobs off in a fancy dress on what was supposed to be the best day of her life.

The wedding was at 4 p.m. so there was still a whole day to get through, although apparently Michael had booked Melissa, Lucy, Claudia and myself in for some spa treatments. I couldn't work out if this was a really nice thing to do or a really bloody stupid one. Did he really think that Claudia and I were going to be the best of friends again? I was trying to be calm about it because Melissa and Lucy kept saying how fabulous it was. When I was handed a glass of Prosecco by the spa receptionist, I practically downed it in one but just stopped at the last half, realising that everyone's eyes were on me, so I put my glass on the side, determined to sip the rest. Couldn't really turn up at the wedding being smashed before the main event had even started.

It was so lovely to see Michelle and Emma arrive just after lunch. They were only staying for one day and had booked a nearby hotel as this one was full by the time that I'd decided that I'd like to invite them. Lucy did say that adding another two people to the guest list was a 'proper nuisance', but as mother of the bride, and someone who'd put a small fortune into the wedding, I thought that I had some right to have a couple of friends with me. Despite Michael flashing his cash around and telling everyone he'd managed to upgrade our room suite, I was paying for most of it anyway. But then again, I'd been lucky enough to have been able to not work full time for many of our years together, so I should be grateful for that. Some people work full time for years without having a break, so again I considered myself to be reasonably fortunate in this way.

'God, am I glad to see you.' I enveloped them both in my arms and squeezed tight.

'That bad?' Michelle stepped back and held me at arm's length. 'You're looking great though, my friend. Glowing, in fact.'

'That's the spa treatments. I'm hoping that the "glow" dies down a bit before this afternoon or the make-up artist will have an awful lot of work to do. It won't be the bride being a pain in the rear, it'll be me being Mother of the Bridezilla.'

'Well, we're not stopping. We just wanted to come and see you and say hello before we go and get changed out of our scruffs, but more than that, to come and give you a bit of moral support.' Emma always managed to look glamorous even in casual wear. She was one of those women who exuded elegance. Michelle was just naturally beautiful, she'd toned down a lot of her make-up recently, preferring a more natural look, and it suited her very much. I couldn't wait for Mum to meet them. I knew that she would love them both.

The wedding itself was really rather lovely. When Lucy walked towards her groom, I noticed that along with her flowers, she was holding the horseshoe and it warmed my heart. She subtly raised it as she walked past me and mouthed thank you and smiled. A tear pooled in the corner of my eye. I had never seen her look more beautiful.

Once Michael had passed Lucy over to Luke, he joined Claudia, Seamus and me in the front row. Seamus held my hand tightly all the way through the ceremony and smiled at me, handing me a tissue when I teared up again as the bride and groom kissed for the first time. When we had photographs taken, the photographer was sensitive to the situation and took several shots involving many combinations and I relaxed when that was over and done with. Mum kept telling me how well I was doing and when we sat down to the meal, I felt a little calmer. The speeches went well. Michael, for once, was quite respectful of our split family in his speech; still said 'Jo and I' when he talked about the girls when they were younger and at one point our eyes connected and we smiled, our joint memories being shared in front of everyone. It actually wasn't as bad as I thought it would be and I felt more relaxed as each stage of the wedding was completed. Maybe I had built it up to be something much more than I'd needed to.

Breathing a sigh of relief that the meal was over, I stood from the table, just as the DJ's dulcet tones filled the room. There was just one more 'family' thing that we would have to do now.

'Ladies and gentlemen. Please give a round of applause to the bride and groom who will be taking to the dance floor for their first dance together as a married couple. They will be very shortly joined by the mother and father of both parties.'

This was the bit I'd been dreading probably more than any other. Let's hope that the music would be so loud, that we wouldn't have to speak, I thought to myself. Sadly that wasn't the case, as Michael came over and took my hand and led me to the dance floor.

'It's been a lovely day. We've done a great job.'

The cheek of him. He'd done hardly anything towards the wedding at all. Apart from the finances, to which he'd hardly contributed, from what I'd gathered the very few times that my daughter did call me, panicking because something wasn't going her way and she'd had a disagreement with the wedding planner, he'd also hardly had anything to do with the planning.

Trying not to bite and let him wind me up, I smiled through gritted teeth. I could feel my body stiff and defensive as he held me. A song only lasted around three minutes so that would be all that I had to endure in this weird intimate close proximity. It was strange how you could love someone so powerfully, so intimately, so unconditionally, and then within a short space of time be so irritated by them, wondering how you ever spent all that time together.

'So Claudia and I have some news,' he said to me, leaning his head closer to my ear.

I could feel myself roll my eyes. What now? She had stolen my husband. My daughters clearly thought the world of her. She lived in the house of my dreams, literally that we built to our spec. Maybe they'd finally sold the business.

'Have you?' I knew that my voice was resigned to whatever he had to say deflating my current state of mood but I never, for one moment, expected what he said next.

40

'You're what?' I knew that I was raising my voice but I couldn't help myself.

'I said, we're having a baby.'

'At your age? At her age? You can't be serious.' I could feel my nostrils flaring and my pulse beginning to pound, heat soaring through my body, this time nothing to do with my age. 'She's drinking too. I saw her earlier.'

'She's not drinking alcohol, Jo. Have you not heard of mocktails and alcohol-free drinks?'

'Bloody hell, Michael. What on earth are you two thinking? You can't possibly think this is a good idea.'

'Calm down, Jo. You're making a scene.' He held me by the shoulders.

There was nothing worse when you were mightily shocked or pissed off than someone telling you to calm down.

'You were a terrible father, Michael. You were never around for our girls when they were babies or toddlers, come to think of it.'

'Yeah, maybe I wasn't. I never found them very entertaining

and to be honest you kind of took over anyway. I felt like an outsider in our family.'

'That was because you were barely there. The business was more important to you than they, or *we*, your family, were. I don't think you've ever changed a nappy in your life.' I wasn't sure why this thought jumped into my mind at that moment.

The dance floor had filled and there were more people dancing now; laughing; having fun all around us. It was bizarre. Their world was continuing like nothing had happened, yet in mine it felt like a massive bomb had detonated and I was now having to deal with the aftermath.

'Well, maybe I've got a chance to do it the way I should have done now. Maybe with Claudia, things will be different. She's ten years younger than you and even though she's classed as an older mum, this feels right. I will be marrying her obviously. As soon as we can. I didn't want to take the shine off Lucy's wedding by announcing ours just yet.'

Marrying her. The ink was hardly dry on our divorce papers and he was getting married again. This man was incorrigible.

'What about the girls? What on earth do you think they're going to say?'

I looked over at Lucy and Melissa, who were watching us from the side of the dance floor. Melissa was biting her nails and Lucy was twiddling her hair. They both looked really shifty and it then dawned on me that I was the last to know. Could this day get any worse? Apparently it could.

'While we're chatting, and you're already pissed off with me, I may as well let you know that you'll also be hearing from my solicitor, Jo. I'm contesting Aunty June's will. She was my aunty and not yours and with us having a baby on the way, we're going to need all the money we can get. That house is rightfully mine. She wasn't even related to you.'

My jaw dropped open. I was honestly staggered by what he was saying.

I looked over to the table where Mum was sitting and caught her eye. She looked completely flummoxed, clearly she hadn't been in on the family gossip. Michelle and Emma were beside her and I noticed Emma mouth something at me which I couldn't make out. I shrugged my shoulders. She held up three fingers and then made a T shape with her pointed hands. I nodded and smiled, remembering Aggie's three t's rule of tummy, tits, teeth, and slowly pushed out my chest and held in my tummy. I raised my head and looked him straight in the eye.

'In that case, Michael, I wish you all the best. I hope it all works out well for you.'

I turned on my heel and walked away, my head held high as a tear trickled down my left cheek, followed swiftly by another on the right.

41

Seamus followed me out and he caught me when I wobbled and thought I was going to fall. Rubbing my back, he held me tightly as we reached the top of the stairs and then he held me round the shoulders as he guided me over to the bed. Michelle and Emma were close behind.

'What the hell is going on?' they both asked in unison. When I explained, all three of them were totally and utterly flabbergasted.

'Fancy choosing tonight to tell you all of this. I'm going to go and...'

'You'll do no such thing, Seamus. But if I can ask you for one favour it would be that you take me home. I can't stay here now. I knew I shouldn't have come. I should have listened to my instincts.'

'But it's your daughter's wedding. You can't go.'

'They probably won't even notice that I've gone. I'll leave a message at reception. Tell them that I had a huge migraine and have gone home.'

'Why don't you try to get some sleep and see how you feel when you wake up?'

'I just want to go home. Please.'

'Right, let's go and pack, Michelle, and we'll follow you back.'

'You don't have to do that. Stay.'

'We only came for you. If you're going home, we're coming with you. We're The Lonely Hearts Club. We stick together.'

I smiled through my tears and despite having one of the most awful nights of my life, I managed to doze nearly all the way back to Cornwall, apologising for being awful company when Seamus dropped me off, and for spoiling his weekend.

'Don't worry. Fancy hotels aren't really my thing. I'm sure Theo will be glad I'm home. He hates staying with Dad. He won't give him any treats and doesn't let him on the sofa. It's just after 1 a.m. now and Dad's a bit of a night owl so they might still be up. Are you sure you'll be OK? I can stay if you want me to?'

'No, honestly, Michelle has just texted to say they're five minutes away, so I'll be fine. Thank you for everything, Seamus. Even if it hasn't quite worked out the way we planned.'

He leaned across and kissed my cheek. 'I'd probably do anything for you, Jo Jenkins. You are one very special lady.'

And then he was gone.

Michelle and Emma came crashing through the door just a few minutes later. Emma ran up to her rooms and came back with a bottle of vintage brandy which she said she'd been looking for an excuse to drink for months. She also suggested we do something really naughty and out of character to make ourselves feel better.

'Oh, I know what we could do.' Michelle had a glint in her eye. 'Go and get that old suitcase that the dame told you not to open, Jo. Let's have a mooch.'

'I couldn't do that. I promised her I wouldn't.'

'Yeah and Michael promised you that he'd be by your side till death do you part but he broke that one in a big way, didn't he? She'll never know, Jo. Go on. I've been dying to look inside it since you told us about her visit.'

I shook my head. 'No, it's not fair to her. She was so upset when I told her I'd found it.'

'All the more reason to look, I reckon. Go on, Jo. It can just stay between us. We don't have to tell a soul.'

I wavered. 'Well, it would satisfy my curiosity. I've not been able to stop thinking about it.'

That was the only approval Michelle needed as she bounded off to the cloakroom to drag it down from the top shelf and placed it on the floor between the three of us.

'Right, Dame Tessa Wylie. What have you got to hide?'

42

Most of the photos were of what we presumed were Tessa and June from their younger days. I'd never known Aunty June with her husband. He apparently died many years ago, but I didn't know much about him or how he died. Apparently, she never discussed it. But it was clear from these photos that if this were him, then they were very much in love.

At the bottom of the case was a baby blanket, which meant we'd got to the end of the photos. However, there was a slight bulge underneath. When I delved further, I found a padded envelope at the bottom of the case. I looked at the girls and shrugged, before taking it out and opening the flap. Very carefully I looked inside.

In a small see-through packet, there was a lock of hair. I shuddered. I'd always thought it was a bit of a strange thing for people to keep. Michael commented once that he'd read a book where a serial killer kept a lock of hair from each of his victims so it always gave me the creeps. I was a bit apprehensive to go further but when I looked at Michelle and Emma for approval, they both nodded.

Inside there was a pair of the tiniest baby booties I'd ever seen, along with a tiny medical wrist tag, the name hardly visible. I gasped when I saw that the larger medical wrist tag was marked with the name Tessa Wylie. I don't think I'll ever forget the looks of astonishment from the other two when I passed it over.

'Someone's a dark horse!' Michelle exclaimed.

I got a really strange feeling low down in my belly and I felt uncomfortable as I took a smaller envelope with Aunty June's name on the front. This was a total invasion of privacy and while I knew that it was wrong and incredibly personal, I was compelled to look further. I unfolded the letter and out fell another photograph. This time it was a picture of one of the women, holding a baby within her arms. But instead of looking joyful, she looked haunted. Sadder than I've ever seen anyone look. This was someone who was in an enormous amount of pain. And when those staring eyes bored into my soul, there was no doubt in my mind that this was Tessa Wylie.

With trembling hands, I smoothed the letter onto my lap and began to read out loud.

My darling Juney.

I'm sending this to you for safe-keeping. Please guard it with your life. Not being able to share my biggest secret with you has brought me such great sadness. My best friend, since we met as four-year-olds. My closest and dearest friend in the whole world. I'm sorry I've been unable to tell you this until now but I was sworn to secrecy.

This is my darling daughter.

Whatever had happened to her daughter? Aunty June had never said anything about her having a goddaughter, which I would have thought, if they'd been such good friends, she would have mentioned. Maybe she died. It must be that. How terribly sad. It might have explained why she was a bit of a recluse. Something like that would affect you for years. Then I reread the words I'd read first, 'when I joined the services'.

What the hell, Tessa? A dark horse indeed.

Enthralled to continue, I read on.

By the time you read this, my beautiful little girl with the most perfect button nose, and the tiniest little fingers that are constantly gripping mine, will have been taken from me. They tried to do it yesterday, but I screamed the place down and told them that they owed me just one day with my baby. My beautiful little girl was prised from my arms this afternoon. I don't know how I'm going to survive this, Juney. My heart is breaking so much I'm not sure I can breathe. I'm not sure I have the strength to go on without her.

After an already emotional day, tears were streaming down my cheeks and sadness swept through my whole body at the thought of Tessa, just a girl herself, being put in this position. I could focus my eyes on the letter to continue. I took a huge swig of brandy and had to have a moment or two before I could go on.

Juney, when they originally said that I would have to give up my daughter, I never thought it would be this painful. When my parents died, I thought I'd never recover. Then when I met William, he mended my broken heart and as you know, he was the best thing that ever happened to me. When he was killed in action, I thought that his dying would be the worst thing I'd ever have to face and that's why I wanted to sign up to help.

But that was before I met my little girl. I never thought that it would hurt this much or that I would love her this much. But as my captain says, if I truly love her, the right thing to do is to give her up. I'm sure he's right but at this moment in time, it does not feel good and I'm not sure I'll ever recover from this. Please say you don't hate me for what I've done. I truly think that I have to do as they say and give her the best chance in life I can and this seems to be the only way. My captain says that I will make her proud by serving my country, so I have to trust that he has my best interests at heart.

I feel so very lonely now, Juney, and you are now the only person I have left in the world and I hope you don't hate me for asking you to keep this a secret. I'll write again as soon as I can, but I have to rush this off now as one of the nurses has said she'll take this and post it on her way home. I only hope that I can trust her to do that.

Love always
Tessa x

When I looked up, all three of us were crying. Poor Tessa and poor June having to keep this a secret. I wondered whether anyone else ever did find out over the years or whether Aunty June took it with her to the grave. It made me so sad to think of the deep friendship that these women had over the years. The trouble now that we had this information was what we did with it. We could never unread what we'd read. How could I ever look Tessa in the eye again?

I realised now why this felt so deeply personal to me and that was because it made me think of my birth mother. I had always known that I was adopted. It had never been kept from me but I loved my mum dearly and vowed never to try to find out more about my birth parents. I felt like there was nothing that they could give me that my own mum couldn't and I just never felt the need to look any further. But reading this letter now brought it all to the surface and I wondered how my birth mother felt when she gave me up.

The tears that I hadn't realised I'd been holding inside me for years and years racked my body and my friends wrapped me in their arms and let the sobs come. They hadn't a clue why I was crying. They knew nothing about my past but they let me cry it out and in the short time I'd known them, I realised that the one thing that connected all the women in my Sandpiper Shore life was loneliness. And if it brought us together, so that we could all help and heal each other, then what a wonderful thing it was.

43

'I don't care if you don't want to go. We're taking you. End of. Now get in the car.'

'Honestly, Michelle, I'm fine. I feel a bit better now.'

'You think that clutching your chest and telling us you think you're having a heart attack and then saying you are fine fifteen minutes later is going to make us say, "Oh, that's OK then. We're off now"? Now, I'm not saying it again, Jo, *get in the car.*'

Reluctantly I climbed into the passenger side of Emma's car. I felt like such a fool, but honestly, I really thought that I was having a heart attack. The letter I received this morning in the post had, as my mum used to say, put the willies up me. After everything that had happened recently with Michael, I didn't think that he could stoop any lower. How wrong I was.

Just thinking about it made the pains come back again and I felt incredibly short of breath. Maybe it was good that they had insisted on taking me. They do say that stress can cause a heart attack and I was annoyed with the fact that it was Michael that had brought it all on.

I felt like my life was flashing before me. I had tried so hard not to dwell on the past. Mum's positivity over the years had taught me that it had no purpose and that you had to acknowledge the past but keep moving forward. And I tried so hard to do that. But as the pains were getting worse and worse, I thought about the girls and whether they'd be OK without me. I knew they would in fairness. They had their dad, Claudia, a new half-sister on the way and their own busy lives ahead of them. Yeah, they'd be sad without me, but they'd cope. The saddest part of feeling like this was that apart from Mum, I didn't think anyone else would really care about whether I was here or not.

One of the worst parts for me since I'd split up with Michael was the feeling of not belonging, to a marriage, a partnership, a family even. The utter emptiness that the feeling brought for me; the not feeling part of something. Some days before I moved I could go for days without speaking to or seeing a soul. I would watch the clock for hours on end, waiting for the hands to move, waiting until it was a reasonable time for me to go to bed to relieve the sheer loneliness I felt. That was until I moved here and met these two wonderful ladies who were ferrying me to the nearest A&E department because they cared about me. It had been a long time since someone cared and I was so glad that I'd moved here and started over. And now I could have it snatched away. The palpitations started again just thinking about it.

'So tell us again what the letter said, if it's not too painful.' I could see a look pass between Michelle and Emma and knew that they were just trying to keep me chatting to take my mind off what was going on.

'The sneaky bastard's solicitor said that they were going to appeal Michael's Aunty June leaving the house to me because I wasn't even family and that in hindsight, he should never have agreed to the divorce settlement that he did and that they should have contested it at the time. They will be letting me know about their findings in due course.'

The huge tear which had been welling in my left eye plopped onto my lap. I had always loved that house, but now, even more so. I felt like we'd really got to know each other. At first, I was wary of staying there. Lying awake at night listening to the creaks and groans of a different house freaked me out a little, especially being on my own. But, daft as it probably sounded to everyone, I felt like we'd come to an understanding. That the house knew that I was going to restore it and bring it back to its former glory. I already loved it more than the modern characterless family house that we'd moved to once the business had started to thrive. I'd done what I could to make it home, but it had been hard. I'd preferred the two up, two down terraced house we'd bought when we were first married personally. But Michael wanted to show his friends that we'd 'made it'.

Emma and Michelle kept me talking all the way to the hospital. Every time I closed my eyes, Michelle shouted at me not to go to sleep.

'Should I slap her round the face?' she asked Emma. 'I saw on *Grey's Anatomy* that you shouldn't let a patient sleep if they're unwell.'

'Only if you want a punch in the face back,' I replied and they both laughed.

'You're clearly not that bad if you are joking about things,' Emma said. 'At least you haven't lost your sense of humour.'

'Not yet I haven't but I can assure you that if anyone slaps me, I will.'

'Okey dokey. We get the message. No slappers in this car.' We all tittered, despite the circumstances.

When we arrived and checked in at the reception desk, I did indeed feel calmer and the receptionist looked at me like I was a complete fraud when I explained the symptoms that I'd had earlier. She over-emphasised some of her words.

'So, you *were* feeling pains in your chest? But you're not *any more*?'

'That's right.' I nodded.

'So, can you describe what symptoms you are feeling *right now*?'

'Well, actually I feel OK right now,' I told her. She rolled her eyes. The bitch.

'Do you feel excessively hot at all?'

Emma appeared from nowhere and stuck her face up against the glass barrier.

'She's a bloody fifty-year-old woman. Of course she feels excessively hot.' She peered at the receptionist's name badge. 'Welcome to our lives, Jade. It's all right for you youngsters. You have your whole exciting life ahead of you, while we don't. It's nearly all over for us. Especially us...' she fake sniffed back a fake sob, 'widows.'

Michelle appeared on my other side.

'I do apologise for my friend Emma. She has apparently officially entered the peri-menopause stage of her life and thinks it's the end of life as she knows it. And she has this constant rage. Although that might be something to do with the fact that she's a... well... you know...'

'Widow?' I volunteered.

'Bitchbag, I was going to say.'

A slight smirk did appear on Jade's face. I do have to say that even in my current circumstances, the three of us had a witty repartee which fed off each other and we thought we were highly amusing.

'Please take a seat in the waiting room, ladies. There is quite a delay at the moment.' She pointed to the clock on the wall, which showed the waiting time.

'Two and a half hours. Are you kidding me?'

'We're very busy, I'll have you know.'

I thought Emma would be the next one to need checking out. Her blood pressure must be sky high.

'Oh, fuck off, Duck Lips,' she muttered.

'Emma!' both Michelle and I reprimanded her. Duck Lips smiled at us. And the clock changed to say three hours.

'Both of you please just sit down. You're stressing me out.'

Subdued, they sat either side of me.

'Anyone fancy a game of I Spy?'

'Me first,' yelled Michelle. 'I Spy something that starts with HFD.' She had an extremely smug look on her face as she crossed her arms and we looked around the room.

'Hormonal Fat Divas,' Emma yelled. We all guffawed. Loudly. Duck Lips glared.

'Sorry!' I sheepishly shouted over.

'Hot Fricking Dames,' was my guess.

'Nope!' Michelle's face was getting smugger by the second.

'Hairy Faced Damsels,' Emma yelled out and I snorted which set us all off again.

'Speak for yourself.'

I laughed at these two people who three months ago I had never even met, but who were now some of my best friends. It made me think about friendships. Life is ever-changing. And friendships were the same. Sometimes friends that we've had for years fade into the background of your life. Sometimes that's because life takes over and people have their own priorities. A busy friend isn't a crap friend, they're just a busy one and probably doing their very best to keep juggling all their balls in the air.

And that's OK. Newer friends come into your life and at that particular time, because your worlds align, they become your closest confidantes and that's OK too. And we should appreciate and celebrate them all. And right now, these were the two ladies who had my back. They'd been by my side at one of the most difficult times of my life and I would be eternally grateful to them.

'Do you give up?' Michelle asked. 'You'd drifted off a bit there, Jo.'

'We give up!' Emma and I said in unison.

'Hot! Fucking! Doctor! Look at him!'

44

'Do you believe in love at first sight, ladies? I never thought I did but for the first time in my life, I think I'm head over heels in love.' Michelle clutched both her hands to her chest and visibly swooned when the doctor she was referring to walked through the accident and emergency department. She was literally all of a dither.

'I thought you'd sworn off all men forever, Michelle. And anyway, I thought you liked Seamus?' I questioned. Bearing in mind that Emma and Michelle had recently nicknamed Seamus 'the best fake-dater' when he had accompanied her to a work function. Even though there was nothing in it apparently, she'd come back swooning over how wonderful he was. At the time, I thought that she was just clearly braver than me in being more accepting of his possible bisexual status.

'He was just helping me out by coming along to the do at work. If he hadn't, I'd have been the only one without a partner. It was really nice of him, but I got a bit fed up of all the Jo this, Jo that. Seriously, Jo. You cannot see what's in front of you, can you?' Michelle said.

Puzzled, I could feel myself frowning at her.

'She's right, Jo. He was the same when I went out with him recently to that awards ceremony. All he talked about was you. There was me thinking this widow might be going to get her leg over for the first time in ages, and there wasn't even a sniff of a kiss, let alone any sexy time.' Emma sniggered. 'And I literally offered it to him on a plate.' She lowered her head and sniffed her armpit. 'Unless it's just me he wasn't interested in. Ridiculous as that might be.' She winked at me.

'Well... I even slept in the same bed as him and he didn't so much lay a finger on me. Maybe he's just not interested in having a partner at all. Of any sex.' I remembered waking up in the hotel room and he'd already got up, dressed and had gone out for a walk.

'It's as clear as day, Jo. He literally never stops talking about you or following you around like a lost lamb. How can you not see what we can see? I'm sorry but I think somewhere down the line you've got something very wrong.'

Gulping, I couldn't bear to believe what they were telling me. I'd told myself that when he offered to take out Emma and then Michelle that he was probably just a serial shagger and that he loved having lots of women fighting over him. What if I was wrong? What if I'd totally misunderstood his intentions towards me? In a bit of a daydream, I heard someone saying my name and looked up to see a nurse rolling her eyes at the fact she'd had to repeat it because no one had responded to her. I stood and she led me through to a cubicle with Michelle and Emma by my side. She took a lot of information from me, despite my friends trying to answer all the questions on my behalf, and then left, telling us that a doctor would be with us as soon as they were free.

'Anyway, let's get back to talking about me.' Michelle was quite excitable considering our location. We were all cramped up in a small cubicle. 'Imagine if it was Doctor Hottie. Could we ever be that lucky?'

'It's actually nice to see you getting excited about someone for a change,' Emma said. 'It's about time you let someone into your life. Not everyone will let you down and you'll never know if you don't try. I had so many happy years with my man before he died and there must have been times when Jo and Michael were deeply in love, even though she hates him now.'

'I don't hate him, it just makes me sad.'

'It makes you sad that he's now trying to screw you over for your inheritance? I'd be fucking livid.'

'Yes, actually, that's a very good point and I am fucking livid. I can't believe he'd do that.' I could feel the heat rising up my neck.

The nurse who had been in previously popped her head around the curtain.

'OK, ladies, please calm down and remember why we're all here, please.' Michelle pulled a face and Emma flicked her fingers up as she closed the curtain again. Honestly, these pair were like kids sometimes.

'Why don't you two go and grab a drink or something?' I suggested. 'There was a vending machine in the foyer. I'm fine, honestly. The pains seem to have subsided now.'

Reluctantly, Michelle left but only on the condition that I allowed Emma to stay so I wasn't alone. Then she flounced off, dramatically closing the curtain behind her.

Predictably, Doctor Hottie appeared the moment she must have turned the corner and Emma and I exchanged a grin as he approached me. Softly spoken, he introduced himself as Dimitri and he had the hint of a soft Greek accent. He was very thorough in his questions and said he'd like to run a few tests just to be sure that all was OK, but also said that he was pretty confident that it might have been a panic attack given the circumstances.

He must have thought me ridiculous, bothering a busy accident and emergency department with something so silly, but he was very kind and said that we absolutely did the right thing by getting me checked out. His big brown eyes bored into me as he talked and even I felt like I could get lost in them. He raised a hand and ran it through his messy, curly dark brown hair and stood to leave.

The next scene unfolded as if in slow motion. Footsteps approached the cubicle and Michelle very loudly said, 'I've looked everywhere for Doctor Hottie but I think he must have gone off shift. Just my bloody luck. The first gorgeous man I've seen in months and he's disappeared.'

The curtains were flung open and she and Dimitri just stood and looked at each other. It was almost as if time stood still. They both flushed the colour of beetroot and continued to stare at each other. Even Emma and I exchanged a glance. Michelle then suddenly turned on her feet and left as quickly as she had arrived.

'I'm so sorry about our friend. She doesn't get out much.'

He laughed. 'Well, if she was talking about me, then I'm flattered.'

'She was definitely talking about you. She spotted you ages ago and hasn't shut up about you since.' I think once the words left Emma's mouth she regretted it because she immediately closed up, not wanting to betray her friend.

'I'm honoured. She is a very beautiful lady.' With that, he closed the curtain behind him and Emma and I giggled.

'What the hell happened then? Did we just see Cupid at work?'

We chatted and laughed about how funny it would be to tell the story of how they met, in our little fantasy world. When Michelle returned around ten minutes later, she had a smile as wide as the ocean. She plonked herself down in a chair and crossed her arms.

'You will *never* believe what's just happened to me.'

'Oh, I love a guessing game,' Emma replied. 'Let me see. You just bumped into David Beckham in the corridor.'

'Ha! I wish. I wouldn't be sitting here now if I did. I'd have dragged him into a side room and shagged him senseless. That's what they all do on *Grey's Anatomy*.'

'What? Shag David Beckham? I didn't know he was in *Grey's*.' Emma laughed. These two, honestly.

'No, the doctors and nurses in *Grey's* all shag in a side room or cupboard.'

A little voice came from the other side of the curtain and a head popped through. It was the nurse who initially brought me in.

'Hello, my name is Chelsea and I can honestly tell you that none of the doctors and nurses in this hospital, in the twenty years I've worked here, have been shagging in a store cupboard. We don't have the time and if we did, we certainly wouldn't have the energy.'

We laughed at her. This was the first time she'd cracked her face since we'd met her and I realised that, rather than my assumption that she just had a resting bitch face, she was probably absolutely knackered.

'On *Grey's*, they diagnose everything with iPads too. It's very clever and I wish we had them but it's good old-fashioned healthcare here, I'm afraid. The only doctor worth a raised eyebrow is the one you've just seen and he's absolutely not interested in any of us lot. We all thought he was gay to start with but we don't think he is. He just keeps himself to himself. Shame but it's nice to have someone to drool over while we're at work.'

I looked over at Michelle, who was still grinning like a

Cheshire Cat, and I knew her well enough now to know that she was bursting to tell us something.

The nurse took some bloods from me and left us alone again.

'Come on then. You've clearly got something to tell us.' I grinned at her behaving like a schoolgirl.

'Oh. My. God. I went to the coffee machine after I'd totally and utterly embarrassed myself and who came up and stood right beside me but Doctor Hottie.'

My hands flew to my mouth.

'I wanted to crawl up my own arse and disappear but unfortunately there was nowhere to hide.'

'So what happened next?' Emma moved to the edge of her seat.

'He nudged my shoulder and said hey.'

'He did not!' Emma practically yelled.

'Did too! And then guess what?'

We waited with bated breath. She was so enjoying the drama of the situation. She should definitely be on the stage.

'He only asked me for my number.'

'He did not!' Emma yelled again.

'Can you please not piss on my bonfire? He bloody did. He asked me for my number and asked me if he could call me.'

'What did you say?' I asked.

'Well, obviously, I said I'd rather he didn't and that I wasn't the type of woman who picked up random men in hospitals.'

'You did not!' It was me who yelled this time.

'Of course I bloody didn't. At first, I said that I didn't date. He asked me why and I said that if you don't date, you don't end up falling in love, falling out of love and then having to nurse your broken heart.'

'Michelle, you muppet! What did you say that for?'

'Because it's bloody true. But guess what happened next?'

We both looked at her, eagerly waiting for the next line.

'He said that maybe you date, you fall in love and you stay in love. He also said that if you don't try, you'll never know the outcome and surely that once in a lifetime, you should take a gamble and maybe things could work out better than ever before. Maybe soulmates were a real thing.'

'Oh! My! God!' I was proper excited for her and really hoped that she would take notice.

Emma raised her eyebrows. 'So?'

'He said he was going to ask me again and hoped that this time I might have changed my mind. And then he asked me if I was ready to be asked.'

'He's a keeper! I love him already.' We both laughed at Emma's enthusiasm. 'What happened next? God! This is like trying to get blood from a stone. Did he ask you again?'

She nodded. 'I tried to say OK and act really cool, but I couldn't stop smiling at him. He took my phone from me and put his number in. He said he's working for the next few days but wondered if I might like to grab lunch when he's next free.'

'Oh, Michelle. How exciting.' Emma reached across and squeezed her hand.

'I know. Who'd have thought it? After all this time of not looking for someone, I found them when I least expected it. Thanks, Jo, for having a heart attack. I really appreciate it.'

'Well, Doctor Hottie said that he thinks it was just a panic attack. Classic symptoms apparently.'

'But just imagine, if you'd never felt ill, we'd never have come here and I'd never have met my future husband Doctor Hottie.'

We laughed at her getting carried away with herself. It was lovely to see her excited about a man. Maybe this would make her realise that there are some nice men and that you just had to put yourself out there. Make the most of opportunities. And yes, I was totally aware that this was quite ironic coming from me. However, I think I was still processing what they'd said earlier about Seamus really liking me. Just when I had resigned myself to the fact that I'd probably be on my own forever and never have another big love in my life, they threw that at me. Now what did I do with that?

45

'So what about you, Emma? Now Michelle's all loved up with Doctor Hottie, what's your plan going forward? Got your eye on anyone?' I wanted to be clear that she hadn't got designs on Seamus before I thought any more about him and the possibility of there being an us.

'Do you know what, Jo? I think living here with you two has given me complete and utter clarity on my life.' Emma held her cup with two hands and sipped at her coffee, while we sat staring out to sea.

'Go on...' I was intrigued.

'I feel at peace, Jo. I think that's what it is. I was so lost and lonely when my husband died. I thought my heart would never heal, and while I know life will never be the same again, I feel like I can finally start to work out who I am. Our Lonely Hearts Club has done more for me than you'll ever know.'

'How so?'

'It's not just about the company, is it? It's great, of course, and just not having that deathly silence around you. It's about the support, the companionship, the learning from each other. There are other widows that have said they'd love to come along to the meet-ups and some of them are still in that lost pit of despair, whereas others are forging forward in life, working out what they want to be and do and even have and give to others. I know that you and Michelle have been amazing, but no one knows what it's like to be a widow unless they've experienced it themselves. It's not just the grief for the here and now, but the grief for the future you'll never have. Your hopes and dreams, the things that you've worked towards for a whole lifetime, suddenly snatched away. And you can either continue to do them, or you can find things to fill your life. You can sit and wallow and be sad, or you can live your life to the best of your ability to honour the person you loved, who isn't able to do that any more. Does that sound daft?'

I honestly thought that Emma was one of the bravest people I knew. She'd been through so much, and she tried so hard to be upbeat, but I knew that there were times when she felt desperately sad. I'd seen her stop in the middle of doing something and her eyes would fill with tears and she'd make an excuse and leave the room. I know I'd lost my husband and best friend, but in a very different way. They were still there, in the background. She'd never see her loved one again. And that must be so hard to cope with.

'So, I'm done wallowing, Jo. It's time that I picked myself up, dusted myself down and learnt to love myself again. I've put so much of my energy over the last couple of years into grieving that I'm exhausted. It's time now to start to look at the life I've got left and make the most out of every minute. I've decided to organise The Lonely Hearts Club's first solo holiday.'

'Gosh, that's a big thing to do. Are you sure you'll be OK on your own? Do you need someone to keep you company?'

'Well, there'll be other Lonely Hearts Club people there too, all being well, even though this will be the first time in my life that I've been away on my own. I'm actually really looking forward to doing some research over the next few days and then I'm going to make it happen. I just hope I don't lose my confidence. I'm going to make sure we can do what we like when we like, not have to worry about pleasing anyone else. We can go to bed when we like, get up when we like. I'll be fine, Jo. I need to do this for me. So that I can get to know who I am without him. You've inspired me so much.'

'*Me*? I'm not sure I've ever inspired anyone.'

'You are kidding. You're amazing. You've come to a new part of the world to live, you've created The Lonely Hearts Club, with our help, of course.'

'Of course.' We both laughed.

'You've raised two clever, bright, confident girls.'

'Who've near on abandoned me.'

'Ah, Jo. Don't see it like that. Kids are only yours for a short time. It's your job as their mother to raise them with enough about them to go and take on the world. And look at them. They certainly do that. In time, they'll realise how much you've done for them and I'm sure they'll come to see you more often. They're torn between their father and their mother and that's hard no matter what age a family splits up.'

'I suppose so.'

'And you've helped so many people. The club is a huge success. You've connected people and taken some who hardly ever left their house, for fear of being lonely, and turned them into go-getters like you.'

'Me, a go-getter. Again, not a word I would use for myself.' I laughed.

'Well, you should take a minute and look at what you've done. This house, for instance, you had a dream to bring it back to life and you have. You've gone from being lonely and sad to being confident and in charge. You organise the events for that group like an army leader. You've made friends in a brand-new part of the world and everyone loves and trusts you. Honestly, Jo, you're amazing.'

'Well, thank you, I suppose.'

'Yeah, just take a compliment when you're given one, will you?' She laughed at me.

'Thank you, Emma.'

'There you go. Not so hard, was it? Oh, God, I forgot to tell you. I've just come from the shop and Mary said I'd just missed Seamus and Al. She was gobsmacked as Al had just disappeared off the face of the earth a couple of years ago and Seamus hadn't been the same since. Said they were as thick as thieves, mind, like they'd never been apart.'

My heart sank. It just showed me not to build my hopes up. There was me thinking that maybe Seamus and I did have a chance to be together after all and now he'd got back with his ex. It just showed me that I shouldn't be depending on anyone else in my life. That maybe I needed to take a leaf out of Emma's book and be comfortable with being alone.

'I couldn't have done it without you. And Michelle. And most definitely couldn't have done the house without Seamus. I don't know how I can ever thank him.'

She winked.

'I'm sure you'll find a way.'

My heart sank at the thought that he and Al were probably now back together and that after my hopes had been raised, they'd been dashed all over again.

However, there was one other thing that I really wanted to do. After reading the emotional letter, I felt that I could offer someone else who might be feeling lonely the gift of friendship.

46

I knocked on the door of the house on the hill. I'd not been here before and I took a moment while I was waiting to take in my surroundings. Chickens were clucking in the small fenced-off area next door and I could hear goats bleating in the next paddock over. It was slightly whiffy so I presumed that the pigs, or even pegs, were not too far away.

'What you doing here?'

'That's a fine way to greet someone who's just baked you a lemon drizzle cake, Tessa.'

'Ah, you should have said.' She grinned. 'You gonna stand there gawping all day or you coming in?'

I stepped into the house, over muddy wellies with jackets and dog leads hanging up in the entrance porch, expecting it to be a typical old lady house, but was pleasantly surprised. It was decorated beautifully and was way cleaner than I imagined. I smiled as I noticed a jigsaw on the large coffee table in front of the window.

'What an amazing view, Tessa. Is that...?'

'Yes, that's your lane you can see there. Juney always used to say that she felt like I was watching over her at all times.'

'How lovely.'

Tessa folded her arms together and sighed.

'So what have I done to deserve a visit and a cake today?'

'Two things really, firstly I wanted to invite you along to The Lonely Hearts Club.'

'Mmmm. I've been hearing about that on the village grapevine. Someone is talking about it every time I go in Mary's shop, but it sounds like one of these modern dating clubs. Not for me, thank you.'

'It's far from it. It's for people who have felt lonely at some stage in their life and are trying to find like-minded people to spend time with. People like me who are divorced, like Emma who is widowed, like Michelle who is, or should I say was, determined to be a loner for the rest of her life to protect her heart from hurt. Some may have lost friends or even children along the way.'

I watched her reaction closely. Her left eye started to twitch, she took a deep breath and those staring eyes bored into mine once more.

'You know, don't you?' Her voice was croaky with emotion.

'I'm so sorry, Tessa. I owe you the hugest of apologies. I did look in the suitcase despite promising you that I wouldn't.'

Tessa stood and went to the sideboard behind her and opened the drawer. She passed me an envelope. It was the same type as the one that I'd discovered in the suitcase.

I carefully unfolded the flap and slid out an aged photograph.

'This is my daughter.'

I touched the baby's face on the image in front of me and looked up at Tessa, noticing a lone tear sliding down her papery-thin wrinkled cheek.

I sighed out loud and looked back at the photograph. My heart felt so sad for this woman and the loss that she had experienced, still clearly so very painful for her so many years on.

'She was beautiful, Tessa.'

I looked back at Tessa as a loud sigh escaped her body and her jaw clenched.

Through trembling lips, she whispered, 'She still is.'

I caught my breath as I turned the photograph over and read the words on the back, as clear as day.

Joanna Riddle Wylie.
18 August 1972.

47

As I dropped the photograph on the floor, I couldn't even bring myself to look at Tessa. Pushing myself up from the chair, I fumbled my way to the hallway and struggled to undo the front door. I could hear my name being called but there was no way I was staying there. I ran all the way home, not sure how I'd made it there through the tears. When I got inside, I slammed the door behind me and fell to the floor. My chest tingled, I felt light-headed and I was struggling to breathe. Thank God Doctor Hottie had diagnosed me with panic attacks or I really would have thought I was having a heart attack this time. I knew I just had to try to calm myself and get through this. It was just a moment in time and it would pass.

So much was going through my head, my thoughts totally scrambled, and I was trying to make sense of everything, trying to find a logical reason for what I'd just seen. Tessa must be lying, but why would she do that to me? It couldn't possibly be true. Could it?

Annoyed that this was a day when neither Emma nor Michelle were home, I urged myself to breathe slowly. Only I could make myself feel better. Deep breaths, like Doctor Hottie talked me through, finally made me feel a little less panicky.

When there was a thumping on the door that I was leaning against, I jumped a mile. But when I regained my composure and slowly felt well enough to stand, I pulled myself up onto my feet, though my legs still felt wobbly.

As I opened the door, I hoped and prayed that it might be Seamus. He was the exact person I needed to help me right now.

It wasn't.

'I know I'm probably the last person you want to see right now, Joanna, but I really think we need to talk.'

'You've got a nerve showing up here.'

'I know I have but please, hear me out.'

She reached out and touched my arm, but I flinched and pulled away. On my run home, I'd built her up to being a nasty, cruel monster who'd lied to hurt me for some reason that I couldn't fathom. But in front of me now stood a scared little old lady and I realised that the staring eyes that had spooked me so many times since I'd met her were exactly the same as mine. But was I ready to hear what she'd got to say?

48

I stood aside to let her past. I needed some time to think, so asked if she wanted tea and then my brain went off on a tangent, wondering why we British think that a sweet cup of tea is good for shock. This time, she didn't get china cups and a tea tray. Two mugs was all I could muster up under the circumstances.

In the kitchen, I was glad I'd removed myself from the situation, for a few minutes at least. Some deep breathing would hopefully allow me to calm down enough that I could listen to what she had to say to me.

'I'm sorry you had to find out that way, Joanna,' she said when I'd returned to the lounge where she sat on the sofa. 'Juney always said that I should reach out to you but I was too much of a coward. How do you find the words to tell your daughter that you gave her up? I tried once many years ago but was told that you didn't want to be contacted. Then, when we found out – by pure coincidence – that you'd married Juney's nephew, it was almost like it was meant to be. But because you'd said you didn't want to know me, I never came forward.'

I just couldn't find any words that were appropriate. I sat with my arms folded across my chest.

'Does my mum know?'

I couldn't bear the thought that my mum had known all along and hadn't said anything. Had everyone been lying to me for the whole of my life?

Tessa shook her head.

'No, she knows nothing.'

'Well, I suppose that's something. I feel like she should be here for this.' I knew I was glaring at Tessa, but I couldn't seem to help myself.

'I don't really know where to start, Joanna.'

'Why don't you try at the very beginning? And then you can tell me why you gave me up.'

49

It was hard not to feel sorry for the woman who sat in front of me. As she was talking, tears streamed down her cheek. Normally, if anyone I knew was in this type of distress, I would go to them. Try to comfort them in any way I could but I just couldn't do it. My heart had immediately put up barriers and I needed to hear what she had to say.

'I was just a young girl when I met your father. We were so in love, Joanna. He was my everything.' She paused before taking a deep breath and continuing. 'I met him at a party in the late summer of 1971 and asked him boldly, which I absolutely wasn't, to take me out to supper. He was in the navy and so handsome in his uniform. I knew there was a risk involved in what he did, but he reassured me that he would always be OK. After a whirlwind romance, we'd saved up and were due to marry in early 1972 and in the times that he was home, our life was amazing. When he was away, I pined for him and missed him so much.'

Another pause kept me gripped to the edge of my seat. I had so many questions and was having to try hard not to interrupt.

'To keep myself occupied, I joined MI5.'

I felt my eyes widen. I was *not* expecting that.

'Yes, I am aware of how far-fetched that probably sounds but it's true. I was approached one day by a woman in the street, who said she'd been observing me for a while. It was strange because I'd only told William the week before that I'd felt a little bit uncomfortable walking home from the cinema with Juney and thought that someone had been following us. I'd been on my guard since then. But anyway, sorry, I digress. This woman approached me and said that MI5 had been watching me for a while and they felt that I could be a huge benefit to them. At the time, I was lost and lonely without my man and I thought that I had nothing to lose so I asked to find out more. She arranged for me to be picked up in a car and taken to a hotel and it was then that I realised the seriousness of what I was doing. But with William being in the navy, I thought it might keep me occupied. They said at first that I would just be doing an administration role. I was told that I had to sign the Official Secrets Act and that I was only allowed to tell one person. As he was in the navy, I chose William, knowing that he would understand. I felt so guilty and alone that I couldn't share this with Juney though. She was my best friend in the whole wide world and the person who was with me when William was away at sea.'

It suddenly occurred to me that maybe the fact that my father was in the navy was the reason why I felt an innate need to be by the sea. That thought felt like another tiny chip at my heart.

'Go on.' Compelled to find out how on earth this story led to the situation we were in today, I wasn't going to make it easy for her, even though her tears were still flowing, although they had slowed down somewhat.

'After a while, I was put onto covert surveillance.'

'What did that involve?'

'I'd rather not say. I'm sorry but I took a pledge and never told anyone what I did. Not even William. He knew how religiously I abided by the pledge I'd made to my country and I knew he'd understand.'

The biggest intake of breath came from her body, which up close made her look even more small and frail than before.

'One day I got a call at work telling me that William had been swept overboard in a storm out in the middle of the sea around the Gulf of Mexico. They'd been searching for him all night before they called me but needed to let me know that I had to prepare myself for the worst. His body washed up on shore a week later.'

A sob escaped her body and she closed her eyes, I was sure, living the nightmare all over again.

'When they did their investigations, it was discovered that someone on board the ship had pushed him over in a fight. They'd found a letter I'd written to him and totally misinterpreted something in it, presuming that I was working for Russia, of all countries. I have blamed myself from that day. That man's father had been killed in the war by a Russian soldier and something flipped inside him when he read my letter and he took it out on William. That man served fifteen years in prison before he died of a heart attack. When I was given that news, I fainted. And that's when we found out that I was three months pregnant.'

I blew out air from my mouth, not quite believing how something so good could go so wrong.

'At that point, I told Juney everything and she was by my side. However, the people I worked for told me that an unmarried mother would bring shame on my family and I was told that it was my fault that he died. If I hadn't written him that letter, then he would still have been alive. I knew that I shouldn't have allowed it but they persuaded me that the best thing I could do for my unborn child was to give birth and then hand them straight over to the adoption agency. I was thick with grief and guilt and shame and I allowed it to happen.'

Her eyes reflected mine as they connected and I could see the deep sorrow they held.

'If I could change the past, I would,' she whispered.

'Did you not want me at all, Tessa?'

'Oh, darling. While you were still growing in my belly, I tried so hard not to think about you. But the minute you were born, I wanted you more than I could ever imagine possible. But by then I was told you were already promised to a wonderful couple who couldn't have children of their own. Apparently they promised they would allow your middle name to be the same as mine. I was allowed one more day with you and for those twenty-four hours, I held you constantly in my arms and while you fed from my breasts, something else that I had promised them I wouldn't do, I sang you lullabies and told you all about your wonderful daddy and how much he would have adored you. I stayed up all night because I didn't want to waste one minute of the very precious time I had with you. The following day they prised you from my arms and my already broken heart was smashed into smithereens. I remember curling up into a little ball and crying myself to sleep. I honestly thought I would die. If it wasn't for Juney, I was pretty sure I would have given up on life.'

Tears were now streaming down both of our cheeks and I did go to her and sit beside her, taking her hand. This poor woman had been through so much. She smiled at me through her tears and reached out and took my face in her palm.

'I never thought I'd ever see you again, my angel. It's beyond my wildest dreams. When you and Michael got married and we realised who you were, it was like a miracle, that you'd come back into my life. This house...' she raised her hand, 'belongs to you. When I left MI5, I'd saved up enough money to buy this and I'd already been left the house on the hill by my own parents. So Juney lived here, but it was always going to be yours.'

'So that's why she left it to me and not Michael?' This time it was my turn to smile through my tears. I knew he'd be gutted to know that he didn't have a claim on it after all.

'My only hope is that one day you can forgive me for what I did.'

'I can't promise you anything right now, Tessa. This is such a lot to process.'

'I understand, my dear. I'm going to go home and leave you to your thoughts.'

'Will you be OK, Tessa? Shall I call Seamus and ask him to walk you back?'

She raised her hand back to my face.

'I feel lighter than I have in years, Joanna. A walk along the beach and back up the hill will do me the world of good. I'll be fine, honestly.'

As I watched the little old woman, who I now knew as my birth mother, step through the French doors and walk through the dunes away from my home, I had no idea what my emotions were doing. They were completely in turmoil. I sat and wept for the woman who'd lost everyone she'd ever loved, as well as for the woman who had just discovered the story of how she came to exist.

50

'What on earth was so important that I needed to come all the way to Sandpiper Shore?' Mum blurted out as soon as she walked through my front door. 'You know I have bowls on a Monday afternoon and I've had to cancel it to make the five-and-a-half-hour journey to Cornwall. This had better be good, lady. I'm using the train next time. At least there's a lav. I've sat in umpteen roadworks and there's nothing worse than sitting in a traffic jam after you've just gone past a services to make your bladder feel immediately full. Twenty-five miles until the next one too. Can you imagine how mortified I was when I was so desperate I had to empty a whole tin of Quality Street out into the passenger seat and use the tin to have a wee in? The lorry driver in the cab next to me got a right old display. Thank goodness for his sake that I was wearing a skirt.'

Despite knowing that I was about to drop a bomb into her world, I laughed at her being such a drama queen the minute she flounced through my door. I loved this woman more than she would ever know.

'Hello, Mum.'

'Hello, darling. Present for you.'

She handed me the tub and I mock heaved.

'I did say that one day you'd be cleaning up after me when I was incontinent.'

'You did, Mum, but I wasn't expecting it to be quite so soon.'

'Bloody hell, Jo. This place is absolutely gorgeous. I knew from the before and after photos that you'd worked wonders. But the photos do not do it justice. Let's have a cuppa and then you can tell me all about why I'm here. The grand tour of the house can wait till later. I don't think I can wait any longer.'

I took a deep breath and everything came tumbling out.

After sharing the news about Tessa to my confusion about my feelings towards Seamus, Mum was silent and I couldn't gauge at all what she was thinking as she gazed out at the sea. Leaving her with her thoughts, I went to make yet another pot of tea, not because I wanted one, but because I needed to do something.

When I returned to the lounge, she turned to me, took the tray from my hands and placed it on the table. She held both of my hands in hers.

'Darling, I'd like to meet Tessa. Could you arrange that, do you think? I think we need to talk.'

Mum and I walked up the hill to her smallholding, no words needed along the way, both of us lost in our thoughts.

Tessa opened the door before we had chance to knock and we all went through to the lounge where, despite being invited to take a seat, Mum remained standing and turned to face the woman we now both knew to be my birth mother.

As I looked between these two women, I realised that both in looks and personality, they were as different as chalk and cheese, but that between them, they were united by me. They were both responsible for my existence here today. One gave me up and one took me on. One gave me life and one taught me about life.

Mum walked over to Tessa and I wondered if she was going to slap her face. But her face broke into a smile and she launched herself at Tessa, flinging her arms around her and whispering, 'Thank you, thank you, thank you.'

Tessa hung on to her, the exact same words leaving her mouth. Tears fell freely from all three of us and suddenly my heart felt like it was too big for my body. But I knew that one way or another, everything was going to be OK and for the first time in my life, I felt something that I never knew I needed. To feel complete.

51

Mum stayed for the next few days. We sat up talking till the early hours. Sometimes Tessa joined us and sometimes she didn't. There were times when we visited the house on the hill and my mothers chatted together, Mum filling Tessa in on my childhood years. I wasn't sure if it was helping Tessa or making her feel worse. All I knew is that she'd aged noticeably since that discovery visit. It was nice to learn that my middle name, Riddle, was a family name that had been passed down the generations. Tessa told me about her parents and grandparents and I learned things about my blood family.

'Are you sure you're not staying for the carnival?' I asked my mother.

'It's a lovely idea, darling, but I won't. I've missed Barry more than I thought I would. I'm going to go back and be with him and let you do what you need to do.'

As I waved her off, she finished her hug with the wisest of words.

'Don't dwell on what happened in the past. It serves no purpose. Look forward to what's in front of you now. You've now met the woman who gave her most precious gift to me. I can never be sad about that. If she hadn't done that, we wouldn't have had what we have.' She smiled and her eyes were brimming with tears. 'I will always be grateful to Tessa Riddle Wylie. And you too have now been given a gift. You can either choose to be kind and try to understand why she did what she did. You can spend time with this incredible lady and be the shining star in the final chapter of her life. Or you can shut her out and be bitter for the rest of yours. You can introduce the girls to a new member of the family that they might love. Only you can choose what to do.'

'But it seems like I'm being disloyal to you, Mum.'

'That's nonsense and I would never feel like that. You've been mine for over fifty years, Jo. And you will always be mine. But once, many moons ago, for a very short time, you belonged to Tessa and I think you owe it to both of you to form a relationship. It's not as if you are losing this mother. There's not a cat in hell's chance of that. Look on it as you gaining another one. A new member of your family. You can't change the past but you can move forward now and make some wonderful new memories. You've been sad and lonely since you and Michael parted and that's made me sad too. But you had to find yourself. I can see that you are happy here and now you have a chance to start a new chapter. Grasp it with both hands, darling. You only get one chance at life. So make it count. I'm not going anywhere. I'll always be here for you. But it's Tessa's turn now to be your mother.'

This woman who stood before me might not have given me life, but she had given me everything else. She had opened her heart to me and claimed me as hers and I couldn't love her more. She had always made me feel like I was enough. She taught me everything I knew about how to be a mum. And even in my darkest moments, she had been my beacon of light. I had her to thank for *everything*.

She pulled me to her chest. I knew now that this was exactly what I wanted to do. I would do what I could to be in Tessa's life as much as she wanted me to.

'I love you, Mum.'

'To the moon and back, my darling. Always.'

52

A sharp rap on the door made me wonder what she'd forgotten and I was grinning as I opened it to find Seamus staring back at me.

'Oh, it's you.'

'Hey, Jo, delighted to see you too.'

I stood back to let him in. He stood leaning on the doorframe and I tried not to look at him while waiting for the kettle to boil. I'd never been so sick of drinking tea, but it still seemed to be the solution to keep myself busy.

I could feel his eyes watching me but was determined not to turn and meet his eyes. It was too painful. I was trying to push away all those rollercoaster feelings of did he like me? Yes, he did. But was it just as friends? I didn't think I had the capacity to deal with this on top of everything else I'd discovered lately. He needed to just say the words and then I could move on from him.

'Are you going to the carnival later?' I asked, trying to make small talk.

'Yeah, I'm hoping to. I thought I'd come and chat to you now in case we bump into each other later. There's something I wanted to tell you. I've been spending a bit of time with Al recently. Al, my ex.'

'Yeah. So I heard.' I could hear my own voice deflating.

'Ah, yes. I thought that the Sandpiper Shore gossip line must be quite warm at the moment.'

'Red hot, I'd say.' I glanced out the window, focusing on one particular seagull sitting on the edge of the decking.

'She's going to live in Dubai.'

My head snapped back.

'Who is?'

'Al.' He looked puzzled.

'Al?' My brows furrowed.

'Yes, Al.'

'Al is a she?'

'What are you talking about, Jo? Of course Al is a she.'

'Oh, right.' My head was starting to spin.

'What the hell is happening here, Jo? What did you think Al was?'

'A man?'

'A *man*?'

'Are you going to just keep repeating everything I say, Jo?'

Realisation was very slowly starting to sink into my brain.

'Is Al short for something, Seamus?'

'Of course it is. It's short for Alice. Why?'

'Ha!' The half-laugh sound left my mouth before I had time to think about it.

'What the hell is happening here, Jo?'

'I thought Al was a man. You said he was a Sky engineer.'

'Al... she... is a Sky engineer.'

'But Sky engineers are men.'

'I didn't have you down as a misogynist.'

'I didn't think I was. I just assumed...'

Shock registered on his face.

'So you thought I was gay? Seriously?' He started to smirk. He was so beautifully handsome when he smiled. It dawned on me then that it was OK to think this. That I could admit to myself once more that I did have feelings for this wonderful man who had come into my life. I laughed again.

'Well... I... actually, yes. Or maybe bi?'

'So you didn't think that all the time we spent together was because I fancied the pants off you then?'

'You fancied the pants off me?'

'Jo, you're doing that repeating thing again.'

Seamus took a step forward towards me, and reached out to tuck a stray hair behind my ear. As he touched me, it was like a spark ignited in my body.

'You are an idiot, Jo Jenkins.'

'It appears that I actually might be an idiot, Seamus Shaffernakker. So, just for the record then, you're not gay? Or bisexual?'

'I am not. If it helps, I could tell you how hard it was for me to sleep in the same bed as you the night before the wedding. How I had to get up early and escape the room, because I was scared that you might wake up and find me staring at you, thinking about how wonderful you were and how much I wanted to wake you up and make love to you.'

He cupped my face in his hands. I shivered at his touch.

'Or I could tell you, when I saw you walk into the pub that night after you'd had your makeover, how utterly stunning you looked and how much I wanted to kiss you in front of everyone.' He edged even closer to me and lowered his head to mine, and I could feel his warm breath as I pulled him closer still.

'You did?'

'Or I could tell you how, when we drove back from the hotel the night of the wedding, I wanted to pull over and take you in my arms, showering you with kisses and wanting to protect you from the world forever.'

'Oh!'

'Yes. Oh.' He pressed his lips to mine and I heard a loud sigh escape my body. His lips were soft and gentle at first and then I could feel the intensity increase. I pulled away slightly.

'Why didn't you make a move on me, Seamus?'

'Why? Because you couldn't have made it plainer that you just wanted to be friends. You even said that you didn't fancy me at one point and loved me being your friend. So I backed right off and settled for friendship.'

'That's because I was trying to convince myself. I didn't think you felt that way about me. But you've been spending time with Al. Alice. What's that all about?'

'Alice and I had always been good friends. We should have stayed that way. She wanted to apologise for treating me the way she did and make everything right before heading off to Dubai. She's finally found someone that she wants to settle down with and she needed my help with a couple of practical things. She actually wants to propose to him. That's all. We're just friends now. I also told her about this incredible new woman that I'd met and she said that she'd already known it because when I spoke about you, I lit up inside.'

'Oh.'

'There's nothing between me and Al. Or me and anyone else for that matter. I wasn't looking for anyone, Jo. And then you came along and exploded into my life.'

I sighed, everything suddenly feeling quite overwhelming.

'I'm scared, Seamus.'

He tilted his head. 'Of what?'

I scoffed.

'Of everything. Of letting you down. Of not having the body of a twenty-year-old. Or the mind, come to think of it. I'm scared of a new relationship. Of trusting someone again. Relying on someone. Becoming dependent upon someone. I'm scared that you'll find someone better, younger, nicer, thinner, smarter, blonder, more beautiful. Of having something wonderful and somehow buggering it all up. I can be a bit of a mess, Seamus. But most of all, I'm absolutely petrified of giving my heart away again.'

'Now you listen to me, Jo Jenkins. I can't promise you what the future holds, and there might be times when we don't agree on things, mess things up, and we might even fall out, but I can promise you that we can work it all out. Together. Through the good times and the bad. And through it all, I promise that I'll be careful with your heart. Don't think about it as giving your heart away. Think of it as sharing it with me. And I'll share my heart with you. And you only.' A little bark outside the front door alerted us to the fact that maybe there was someone else that held a very special place in his heart too. Seamus rested his forehead against mine before we heard another little bark and I broke away to open the door. Theo ran in, went to his blanket, turned round a few times and settled down, his head on his paws. Seamus shrugged.

'Well, maybe my heart belongs to my dog too. Talk about killing the moment.' We both laughed and moved together again like magnets. We fitted together perfectly. 'Now, where were we, Jo Jenkins?'

His hands slid into my hair as he gently teased my face up towards his and as he looked into my eyes, I melted. He made me feel safe and secure and I knew that I could trust him with my heart. I felt like I already knew every part of him. As I wrapped my arms around his back, there was literally no space between us and then we were lips on lips. One hand moved downwards from my hair and a soft moan escaped from somewhere within me as his hand brushed against my ribcage.

53

A loud ringtone burst into life and reluctantly we broke apart. I retrieved my phone from my rear pocket, looked at the name, rolled my eyes and pressed accept, mouthing that I had to take the call. Seamus nodded and took a seat. I knew that whatever we had could wait and that we had our whole lives ahead of us. In that moment, my heart felt totally and utterly full.

'Jo, it's Michael.'

'Yes, I know it's you, Michael. Your name comes up on the phone. Remember?'

'Ah yes, I forgot that. I wanted to talk to you about contesting the will. The solicitor said...'

'I'm going to stop you there, Michael.' I looked up at Seamus and he winked at me. My tummy flipped and I realised how very much in love with him I was and had been for a while. I smiled at the thought. 'I've got a story to tell you,' I said to Michael, 'but not right now. I have a carnival to go to. With Seamus.'

Seamus and I spent a wonderful afternoon at the carnival, where we proudly held hands all afternoon and were very much at ease with our public displays of affection. We bumped into Bill outside the lifeboat station who said that it was about time we got together. And that he'd known that very first day he'd met me that his son and I would be perfect for each other.

While the carnival was still in full swing, and the locals were enjoying the late-afternoon sun, we snuck away and came back to my cottage and proved exactly how much we meant to each other. Despite me being totally petrified at being naked in front of someone new, making love with Seamus was mind-blowing. We gelled together as we did in every other way and it felt like the most natural thing in the world. Afterwards, we dressed and sat on the terrace wrapped up in blankets, watching the stars shimmering in the inky-blue crystal-clear night sky.

'Look!' Seamus pointed up. 'A shooting star. It must be our lucky night.'

'It might be yours again later, sunshine, if you're up to the task.' I wasn't quite sure where this brazen, husky voice had come from but it made me smile.

'Try me!'

Just as he kissed me once more and I melted against him, Emma and Michelle came round the corner arm in arm, giggling, slightly tipsy. As Seamus nipped inside and brought out a bottle of brandy and four glasses, I thought back on my life over the last six months and how much things had changed since I'd moved to Sandpiper Shore. The future was bright.

Emma was glowing, full of passion for her new friendship group project. Michelle was excitable for the possibilities with the hot doctor. Who knew whether things would work out or not for any of us but I knew now that it was about the journey along the way. That was the exciting part. If the past hadn't happened then none of us would be where we were today. Life was not about looking back on what was in the past but full of the here and now, and what the future *might* hold.

As I looked up at Tessa's house on the hill, I realised how much I was looking forward to spending time getting to know the woman who gave birth to me as well as learning more about my father. And in the final chapter of her life, I would be someone that she could rely on and learn to love too. As the myriad-coloured fireworks exploded over the sea, my bursting heart had never felt more grateful.

As I looked across at the man by my side and reached for his hand, I realised this was my present, and that my future would have this wonderful man and I had to be thankful for all that would be.

'A toast,' I declared. 'To us!'

The four of us clinked glasses and sipped at our drinks, each in our own private thoughts.

Maybe we were all lonely in some way and looking for something to make us feel whole. However, loneliness isn't about how many friends you have or don't have or how many people are in the room or not. It's about learning to be alone and still be content. It's about making peace with yourself and not relying on another person to complete you. When you dig deep, there is only one person who can stop the loneliness and that's you. It's about taking back your power and saving yourself.

And if in the end you do find someone extra special whom you get to go on adventures with, or someone who will just do nothing with you, someone who will support you in anything you choose to do, who will kiss you when you are least expecting it, hold your hand for no reason, make you laugh like never before, and make your heart skip a beat from time to time, then that's just a big, beautiful bonus.

* * *

MORE FROM KIM NASH

Another book from Kim Nash, *The Bookshop at the Cornish Cove*, is available to order now here:

www.mybook.to/BookshopCornishCove

ACKNOWLEDGEMENTS

As always, thank you hugely to the incredible support from the book blogging and reader community. I am honestly blown away by the love I've been shown. There are so many books to choose from and I truly appreciate it when you pick one of mine. And to the readers who reach out to me to tell me how much you've enjoyed one of my books, you'll never know what a difference that makes on a day when I might be tearing my hair out because I can't make sense of my own words when I'm writing one book, editing another, and just want to go and write about the next shiny idea that's calling out to me. Special thanks to Sarah Price and Sue Baker who are both amazing.

To those author friends who have supported me over the years, I really do value your love and support. It's a mad world and it's hard to keep up with your own books and dates and writing, let alone your friends'. But thank you to everyone who has found the time to message, comment, share posts etc. Truly appreciated.

To the Boldwood team. Thank you for all that you do both behind the scenes and up front to get your authors' books into a fabulous product and then market it to readers. I know that this does not happen by magic and I really do acknowledge and appreciate all your hard work and commitment.

Special thanks as always to Emily Yau who made my dream of being a Boldwood author come true and for helping me to shape the books and make them even better.

Thanks and love always to the friends who support me on this mad journey of being an author.

An enormous thank you goes to the amazing staff on Ward 403 at The Royal Derby Hospital. You'll never know how amazing you are and how much your kindness meant to our family at a very difficult time.

To the Jenkins family – Lisa, Peter and Marcus. You're all incredible and have shown what family is all about over the last year and a half. You all deserve a medal.

And finally thanks to my son Ollie. My biggest supporter and my favourite person in the whole world. Love you always.

ABOUT THE AUTHOR

Kim Nash is the author of uplifting, romantic fiction and an energetic blogger alongside her day job as Digital Publicity Director at Bookouture.

Sign up to Kim Nash's mailing list for news, competitions and updates on future books.

Visit Kim's website: www.kimthebookworm.co.uk

Follow Kim on social media here:

- facebook.com/KimTheBookWorm
- x.com/KimTheBookworm
- instagram.com/kim_the_bookworm
- bookbub.com/authors/kim-nash

ALSO BY KIM NASH

The Cornish Cove Series

Hopeful Hearts at the Cornish Cove

Finding Family at the Cornish Cove

Making Memories at the Cornish Cove

The Bookshop at the Cornish Cove

Standalone Novels

Amazing Grace

Escape to the Country

The Cornish Cottage by the Sea

BECOME A MEMBER OF

THE SHELF CARE CLUB

The home of Boldwood's book club reads.

Find uplifting reads, sunny escapes, cosy romances, family dramas and more!

Sign up to the newsletter
https://bit.ly/theshelfcareclub

Boldwood

Boldwood Books is an award-winning fiction publishing company seeking out the best stories from around the world.

Find out more at www.boldwoodbooks.com

Join our reader community for brilliant books, competitions and offers!

Follow us
@BoldwoodBooks
@TheBoldBookClub

Sign up to our weekly deals newsletter

https://bit.ly/BoldwoodBNewsletter